THE TEA ROOM INHERITANCE

HANNAH LANGDON

Storm

Ebook ISBN: 978-1-80508-716-8
Paperback ISBN: 978-1-80508-724-3

Cover design: Rose Cooper
Cover images: Shutterstock

Published by Storm Publishing.
For further information, visit:
www.stormpublishing.co

ALSO BY HANNAH LANGDON

The Feywood Sisters

Escape to the Country Kitchen

Escape to the Country Garden

A Manor House Christmas

Christmas with the Lords

Christmas with the Knights

Christmas with the Princes

PROLOGUE

'But it's nine days until the wedding!'

I was dizzy and dissociated, my head full of mushy cotton and hot tears as I tried to take in what Matt had said. Now, he was looking at me with the puppy dog expression he used when he knew he was in the wrong but wasn't going to apologise or back-track. I had seen it enough times over the past four years to know it well. He blinked his big blue eyes at me slowly.

'I know, Belle, but isn't it better to do it now? Cleaner?'

I shook my head, as much to try to clear it as to disagree with him.

'No! I mean, are you serious, you want to call the wedding off?'

He inclined his head, tinging his sorrowful look with a touch of sincerity, like he'd seen that guy who read the evening news do to such great effect. You know – the one who was currently serving a seven-month prison term for romance fraud.

'I'm afraid so, Belle. It's not your fault.'

'Well, I know *that*,' I spat, fury at being patronised momen-tarily cutting through the shock. 'But *why*?'

He sighed.

'Look, getting upset isn't going to help anything.'

Upset? I'm not five years old.

But I held my tongue, conditioned from childhood not to express myself in any way that might aggravate someone else. He continued.

'I've been having second thoughts for a while, and now the wedding is so close I've realised I can't go through with it, I'm sorry. My parents agree.'

Of course they do. They never wanted their golden boy to marry me in the first place.

'But why didn't you say something sooner? We might have been able to fix it.'

Now, the tears were coming to my eyes, and I let them spill over, hoping they might soften him.

'I was hoping my feelings would change, that it was a temporary thing, wedding nerves.'

'But it's not?'

'No.'

A horrible thought came into my head.

'Is it– is it only the wedding, or everything? Us?'

He nodded gravely.

'I'm afraid so, Belle. I don't feel that way about you anymore.'

I stared wildly at him as thoughts spun around my head in a terrifying whirlwind. My entire world – everything I knew, everything I had hoped for – came crashing down, like a china-smashing stall at a fairground.

Bang! There went the wedding and my happy ever after.

Smash! Hopes of having Matt's babies lay in smithereens.

Boom! Gone was the house we had planned to buy together.

As my mind's eye surveyed the wreckage, Matt went on.

'Because the invitations were all digital, it shouldn't be too hard to cancel everything. I'm sure that one click will do it, and you're so good at that sort of thing.'

'Sorry, *what?* You want *me* to do it?'

'You're so efficient, Belle – it would be better.'

Anger was beginning to rise now – not just anger but real, grown-up rage – and I tried to keep my voice steady. I knew from experience that any show of emotion would provoke comments about my supposedly fragile mental health and inability to deal with things like an adult.

'Matt, I am not going to be the one to cancel this wedding. You're the one calling it off, so you can do it. All of it. I'm going to go and stay with my parents for a few days; we can talk about the house and everything later.'

He inclined his head in a sort of bow.

'Very well, although you should take the responsibility for some of it. It's a lot of work.'

A peevish tone had crept into his voice, but I didn't feel like appeasing him the way I had always done. Instead, I shrugged.

'It was a lot of work to organise, and I did most of it. I'll deal with the bridesmaids and flowers, but the rest is up to you. We're going to lose a lot of money.'

'Well, my parents are,' said Matt. 'They were so generous, but they agree that cutting our losses is the best thing to do.'

It wouldn't have improved anything to point out that his parents had only funded so much of the wedding because they wanted power of veto over everything and had insisted on what they thought best for the venue, the food and a good third of the guest list. But I nodded. Now the shock was wearing off and reality was setting in, I didn't think I could sit there in the living room of our rented home with Matt for one more second. I was scared that, if I did, I would either completely break down or throw myself at him and beg him to change his mind. Neither of which would have done any good. I loved him, loved him so much, but I knew him well enough to know that nothing was going to change. I stood up.

'I'll go and pack.'

'Of course,' said Matt. Then, as I reached the door, he said, 'And Belle?'

I turned. What was there left to say right now? Maybe he *had* changed his mind, was going to offer something else, temper the horror? A tiny flame of hope ignited in my chest.

'Yes?'

'My parents think it's probably for the best if you look for a new job. It might be uncomfortable, us all working together.'

ONE

Just over a week later I was driving down to Dorset, on the south-west coast. My father had been his usual dismissive, critical self after Matt's calm destruction of my entire life, sighing whenever he saw me, as if to say, "Are you *still* here?" But Mum had been brilliant, and her best move had been to encourage me to go and stay with my godmother, Diana, for a while. I had told Diana the news almost as soon as it had happened, straight after I had told Mum, as I did with so many things. I didn't have the chance to see her in person as much these days, but she had been special to me since the day I was born. She wasn't just a godmother in name, some distant friend or relative that your parents chose and you barely ever met. Instead, she was more like another parent to me, albeit with a very different style. She had never married, or had children herself, and this made her advice less cluttered, somehow.

'Belle, I'm so very sorry to hear that,' she said in her deep, clipped voice. 'And telling you to deal with all the admin? Well, that's worse, I think, than calling off the wedding. He has shown you who he is: believe him.'

I nodded and sniffed.

'Yes, thank you.'

'I know you don't believe me, but it's true. And you will feel better, I promise, even though that seems impossible right now. So! The next thing you need to do is decide what's next.'

'Maybe. I feel so exhausted, and sort of... *limp*.'

That lethargy was what annoyed my father so much, but I didn't seem to be able to pull myself out of it. I was sleeping late, picking at then bingeing on food and checking my phone a million times a day. That usually only yielded fresh messages from confused wedding guests, but I lived in hope of something from Matt, explaining that he had made a huge mistake and begging for my forgiveness, which – despite everything – I would have given, instantly.

'Of course you do, it's the shock. Look, come down here to Spindrift Bay for a while. I've got plenty of room and can always do with more help in the tearooms, when you're ready. I'd love to see you – and it would help, you know, to get away.'

As soon as she said it, I knew it was going to happen, but I prevaricated, too confused and sad to make any decisions. I did tell Mum, however.

'I can't believe we didn't think of it before!' she had said excitedly. 'It's a great idea! The change of scene would do you a power of good, not to mention Diana's company. In three days, she'll have you asking: *Matt who?*'

I'd looked at Mum and frowned as my bewildered brain tried to make sense of the suggestion. Diana lived in a small village in Dorset, very near the sea, and ran a successful tearoom, The Coastal Kettle. My mother had met her many years ago, when they both lived in France, and they had been close ever since. I had been to visit her both in France and when she returned to England and moved to Spindrift Bay. She was kind and practical, with a wisdom and insight I had benefitted from in the past. I answered before my tired brain could put up any more of its feeble resistance.

'All right, I'll go. Thanks, Mum.'

For the first time since Matt had dropped his bombshell, I had felt a spark of hope that wasn't connected to the possibility of him coming back to me. I pulled out my phone and tapped on Diana's name. After a couple of rings, she picked up.

'Belle, my dear girl.'

I heard my voice catch as I answered her warm tones.

'Hello again.'

'I hope this phone call means you're going to come down?'

'Yes, it does. Sorry, I should have said "yes" right away – I'd love to see you.'

'It will be my absolute pleasure to have you. You don't mind helping at The Kettle?'

'Of course not, I'd like to.'

'Wonderful. I've been a little tired lately, so I'm sure Tessa will appreciate your youth and vigour.'

Tessa was Diana's only employee, who I had met once or twice, and liked.

'Good. Although I don't feel very vigorous at the moment.'

'Of course you don't, you've had the stuffing knocked right out of you. But we'll get you back on your feet. Life doesn't always work out the way you hoped, I know that well enough myself. But there's still plenty of joy to be found, I promise.'

We spoke for a few more minutes, agreeing that I would head down the next day. When we hung up, I felt so much better. The heavy knot of sorrow still weighed heavily in my stomach, but a tiny chink of light now came in, through a window opened by Diana's kindness and empathy. For the first time in a week, I could entertain the idea that being back to square one in life might mean not only despair but also opportunity.

I had driven away from home just before two, waving to Mum until I turned a corner. Dad, of course, was nowhere to be seen, doubtless glad that I was out of the house and he could once again command Mum's full attention. My little car was full, not only of the things I would need in Spindrift Bay, but of all the things I had collected from mine and Matt's house when I had moved out. I had taken only what belonged to me, leaving behind everything we had bought together. I wanted no reminders of that life with me – the memories in my heart were painful enough. The only thing that I hesitated over, and eventually stuffed in a bag, was a photo of the two of us, taken on holiday a year or so previously, looking as loved up and happy as was possible. We had printed and framed it proudly. I still didn't know what had gone so wrong between us, and was struggling to accept that I might never understand. If I understood, I could fix it, surely?

I was glad of an easy drive down, and it was just before half past four when I pulled up to Diana's pretty stone house with its thatched roof. It adjoined the tearooms, which at some point in their history must also have been a house. I took my phone out of its holder to turn off the GPS and ran my eye down a couple of emails about the wedding. I had been inundated, thanks to Matt forwarding every possible wedding email to me, and I was still receiving them daily. Some were kind and sympathetic, and I read and replied to these with as much grace as I could muster. Others, however – mostly from Matt's invitees – were not so understanding. The girlfriend of an old university friend of his had taken it upon herself not only to hold me entirely responsible, no matter how many times I referred her back to Matt and his parents, but was hellbent on some kind of compensation. Her previous email had listed the expenses they had already incurred:

"I bought a new dress (£250) and shoes (£195) as well as a matching handbag (£319). I would not have purchased any of these items had I not been coming to your wedding and am now significantly out of pocket."

It was all I could do not to reply to her saying that my wedding dress had cost less than hers, and I was the bride, and couldn't she return the items, but instinct told me to stay well out of it. I saw now that another message had arrived from her, this one headed, 'Deposit expectations'. Pulling a face, my desire to appease people at an all-time low, I forwarded it to Matt and his parents. I wasn't going to do their dirty work for them.

Turning off the screen and throwing the phone onto the passenger seat, I stepped out of the car and went round to the tearooms. To my surprise, they were locked and shuttered. Maybe Diana had shut up shop early as she knew I was coming? I couldn't see her in the house, though. Maybe she was in the garden? I wandered over to the front door and knocked, but it stayed resolutely shut, the house beyond silent. I returned to the car for my phone and tapped Diana's name. A shaky-sounding voice, not hers, answered.

'Hello, Belle?'

'Yes. I'm trying to get hold of Diana. Who is this?'

'It's Tessa. Are you here?'

'Yes, I'm outside the house. What's going on, is Diana all right?'

She emitted a huge sob, then took a ragged breath before speaking again.

'No. I'm in the tearooms, I'm coming now.'

The call cut off abruptly and I was left staring at my phone, hardly daring to wonder what was going on. I didn't have to wait long. Tessa came hurrying around the corner, still holding Diana's phone, her face tear-streaked. I stepped towards her and she fell into my arms.

'Belle. I've been waiting for you, I knew you were coming, of course. Oh, Belle, Diana's dead.'

Patting her on the back, I tried to make sense of her words.

'*What?* I don't understand, I was talking to her yesterday...'

She pulled back and stared at me with hollow eyes.

'I—' she gulped. 'I found her, this morning, at the bottom of the stairs. Diana had epilepsy, you know?'

'Yes, I know, but wasn't she in remission?'

'She had been, for several years, but it had relapsed recently. Didn't she tell you?' I shook my head. 'They – the doctors who came – think that she had a seizure and fell down the stairs. Oh, poor Diana, she was too young.'

She started crying again, and I put my arm around her and held her as she sobbed, muttering soothing words even as my own tears fell for my dear godmother and thoughts about what to do next tumbled around my head.

'Did you say you were in the tearooms before?' I asked gently.

She nodded.

'Yes, I was trying to get things straight. They won't open today, of course. I don't know when they will again.'

Her voice rose to a wail, and I tucked my arm through hers.

'Let's go in there, have a cup of tea.'

That inevitable English reaction to bad news.

We walked inside and soon we had taken a couple of chairs down and were sitting with a hot cup of tea each. I didn't open the curtains, and we peered at each other in the gloom.

'Do you want to tell me what happened?' I asked, my voice hoarse with shock.

Tessa's sobs had diminished, but I could feel mine building as the truth sank in.

'I came to work as normal, but everything was shut up, which I couldn't understand. There's a door from the kitchen here into the house, so I found the key and went in, calling. I thought she'd over-slept or something, even though she never does... did.' Tears threatened to overwhelm her again, but she breathed deeply and carried on. 'I didn't hear anything, so I went further into the house and then I saw her, lying there. I ran to her, and realised she was still alive. I called the ambulance, but by the time they got here...' She stared at me, her eyes dry now but wide and her face pale as she relived the experience.

'You poor thing,' I said, my mind simultaneously trying to picture the scene and rejecting the terrible image.

'Then the police came and were here for ages until they said she could be taken away. They're doing some sort of inquest – it's horrible.'

'You haven't been here on your own all this time?'

'No, no, my husband was here, too, but he looks after our little boy when I'm working. It wasn't the right place for a child. My mum could have taken him, I suppose, but I've been all right. I wanted to make sure the tearooms were packed up just as Diana would have wanted, and to see you.'

'I really appreciate it,' I said. 'Do go home now, though, you must be exhausted.'

'What about you?' *What about me? I had barely taken in the news yet.* 'Where are you going to stay? I'd ask you to come and stay with us, but we don't have any room.'

'Don't worry,' I said automatically, although I was over-whelmed with worry myself. 'There must be a B&B or something near here?'

'Yes, yes, there's a place called Seaspray Lodge run by a lovely woman called Gloria. I've got her number here somewhere...'

'Tessa, please,' I said, putting my hand over hers as it fluttered to find her phone. 'I'll look it up, don't worry. Get home to your husband and your little boy and I'll be in touch.'

She smiled at me with gratitude.

'Thank you. Here.' She pulled a napkin out of the dispenser on the table and wrote on it. 'This is my number. Call any time. I want to help.'

'You've already been amazing.'

It was true. I was in awe of her courage. I don't know how I would have coped if I'd found someone dying in such shocking circumstances. I had a feeling that Tessa was going to be a staunch friend to me in Spindrift Bay.

'I hope so. Oh, and the police looked up Diana's next of kin – it's your mother. I would have called her, but I knew you were coming down, and I thought maybe you'd like to speak to her yourself?'

Her voice rose questioningly, and I hurried to reassure her.

'Of course. Don't worry, I'll call her now.'

. . .

Moments later, I was making a video call to Mum. I felt desperate to see her and hoped against hope that she would be able to come down to Dorset quickly. I smiled wryly as I waited for her to answer; I had been about to get married, all grown up, but it appeared that I still needed my mum. Relief flooded me when her face appeared.

'Hello, darling.' She stopped short, instantly seeing that something was wrong. 'Are you okay? Is it Matt?'

With a monumental effort, I held back my tears as I explained what had happened and watched the shock and grief suffuse her face. Then my father appeared in the frame behind her.

'What's going on?' he demanded. 'Not still crying over that wedding, are you?'

Mum pushed her chair back slightly from the table and I saw my father grab at his cup of tea as it wobbled in its saucer.

'Careful,' he said, in that voice that chilled my spine, even two hundred miles away.

'It's not the wedding,' said Mum, her voice calm. In the years of being married to that man, she had trained herself to stay calm in all situations, to avoid provoking him any further than possible. 'There's been an accident. Diana's dead.' He grunted sourly, and she continued. 'I'm listed as her next of kin. I'll have to go down there, organise the funeral.'

'Nonsense,' barked Dad, and I saw Mum wince. 'Belle's already down there – it doesn't need two of you.' He thrust his face at the screen. 'You'll have to represent the family there; we can't all go.' He turned to Mum. 'What did the woman think she was doing, making you her next of kin when you're not even related? It's an absolute nuisance. You can help organise the funeral from here without too much trouble, although I hope some financial provision has been made. I'm not footing the bill.'

My father earns six figures and has never allowed my mother to work. Since being old enough to recognise an abusive relationship, I have never been able to comprehend why my mother stays with him, but she refuses to talk about it. I made the decision many years ago to be there for her in every way I could, short of living in the house, and to support her, no matter how little I understood.

'I'd like to go to the funeral...' she now whispered.

His face filled with scorn.

'Well, of course you can't. I can't go, I have far too much work to do, and I need you to be here, not wasting time and money on Diana. I'm going out now, I'll be back by eight.'

And with that, he left. I wished I could reach through the screen and hug Mum. I heard the front door slam.

'Don't say anything, Belle,' she said. 'I know. I *know*. Don't worry about me. I have my memories of Diana, and I don't want you to miss out on your opportunity for a fresh start. You must stay. You will be a huge help to me, sorting things out from that end.'

'All right. I'm here for you, though, always.' That was true, although I was still reeling from Matt, and now this. I kept talking, to stave off the desolation. 'I wonder why Diana did list you as her next of kin? Doesn't she have any family? She never talked about it.'

'No, she didn't. Even when I first knew her in France, she would never go into any detail. She mentioned a brother once, but I didn't even know his name, and I don't think she was in touch with him. When she asked if it was all right to list me as her next of kin, I didn't hesitate to say yes – but I also didn't tell your father. I got the feeling that there had been some sort of rift with her family, but, as I said, she made it clear she didn't want to talk about it and of course I respected that. Maybe you'll learn more now you're there.'

I wondered if I would. I didn't want to pry, but I had always been curious to know what more there was to Diana's life beyond a long stint in France and a seaside tearoom. Maybe something to do with the things in life that didn't work out as she'd hoped, which she had hinted at in our last conversation?

'Where are you going to stay?' asked Mum. 'I suppose you can't stay at Diana's now.'

'Tessa gave me the details for a B&B,' I said. 'Hang on, I'll look it up. Yes, here it is, Seaspray Lodge.'

From the photos it looked clean, if a little cluttered and quirky, but it was my only option unless I wanted to stay outside the village, and the nightly rate was reasonable.

'I remember that place,' said Mum, who was looking at the same website on her end. Watching her drop her glasses onto her nose to read the tiny screen, her face screwed up, clearly forgetting that I could see her, squeezed at my heart. 'Yes, it's run by a woman called Gloria, that's it. She's a real character.'

'Does that mean I'll love or hate staying with her?' I asked, raising an eyebrow.

'I couldn't say, but you'll not be bored!'

TWO

Part of me wanted to stay on the phone to Mum all day; it felt too painful to say goodbye and be left with a blank screen. But it was getting late, and if Seaspray Lodge didn't have a room for me, I would need to find somewhere else. I decided to drive over. It was close enough to walk, but I didn't want to carry my bags. I shut up the tearooms, using the spare key Tessa had given me, and got back into the car to drive the short distance. I pulled up outside a pebble-dashed building, painted white, its name displayed in flamboyant gold lettering on a huge, purple board outside. I took out my phone to check a text I had heard ping when I was driving, then jumped a foot off my seat when there was a loud rapping on my window.

Shoving my phone in my bag, I turned to see a woman's face there, her nose practically pressed against the glass. She had dyed blonde hair arranged into an enormous, fluffy bouffant, secured with diamanté clips. Her lipstick was crimson, and she wore long, thick, false eyelashes. She was wearing a deep purple velvet dress, with silver embroidery on the sleeves and neckline, and a little cape. I wound down my window cautiously.

'Sorry, am I not allowed to park here?'

She gave a gravelly laugh and spoke in a deep, mellifluous voice.

'Oh *no*, darling girl, you absolutely *are*! You're so very welcome. You are Belle, are you not?'

'Er, yes.'

How on earth did she know who I was?

'How marvellous! I'm Gloria, and I am delighted to host you at my modest establishment. Come along inside, you must be famished. We'll have high tea and then worry about your luggage; it will be perfectly safe here.'

If there had been room, I had been expecting to go straight to my room and have some time to myself – something I was looking forward to – but I could hardly refuse my host, who had now opened the car door and was ushering me out in a cloud of heavy, floral perfume.

'Tessa mentioned you might be coming by,' she said, and I marvelled at how quickly news gets round in a small village. 'We were all so very shocked and sorry to hear about Diana,' she continued as we went into a large, square hallway with a dark, wooden polished floor, dramatic red-flocked wallpaper and a couple of gigantic ferns in enormous painted jardinieres on stands. A wide oak stairway stood to the left and there were three doorways leading off the hall. I felt as though I had stepped onto the set of *My Fair Lady*; maybe Rex Harrison would appear at any moment and tell me off for not pronouncing my h's clearly enough. My ex-mother-in-law-to-be, Celia, had clearly been dying to. 'She was your godmother, wasn't she?'

I tore my eyes away from a large ginger cat I had spotted, curled up on a leather armchair in a corner, and turned to Gloria in surprise.

'Yes, she was, but...'

'How did I know?' she asked, smiling. 'Spindrift Bay is a tiny place; I'm afraid news travels very fast here. We already knew you were coming down.' I followed her through one of the doorways into the kitchen. 'Sit down, I'll put the kettle on. And I'm so sorry to hear about the wedding – what a lot you've had to cope with. It probably doesn't feel like it now, but it'll be for the best. Better to know now that he's feckless than two years down the line with a baby and a mortgage. Coffee or tea?'

'Er, coffee please,' I managed to say, taken aback by Gloria's casual acquaintanceship with my news, news that I considered private, and that I had been hoping to leave behind me when I came to Dorset. I certainly didn't feel much like talking about it now, while I had barely come to terms with Diana's death.

'Sorry,' she said, sounding completely unapologetic and putting a plate of delicious-looking cakes in front of me. 'I know I can be too straight. I've always found it easier; everyone knows everything about me. I'm not nosey, or a gossip, believe it or not. We've got Beverly for that. But now you know that you can be honest with me, and that I'll be honest with you. I know it's nearly dinner time, but have a cake, freshly made – not by me, though, obviously.'

I didn't know why that was obvious, who Beverly was or why this woman would think that I wanted any kind of relationship with her, honest or otherwise. But as I sank my teeth into a divine lemon cupcake, sipped some coffee and glanced around the cluttered but homely kitchen, the tart words I had been tempted to reply with subsided. There was something comforting about the whole set-up, and I could see how easy it would be to spill everything out to Gloria.

'Thank you,' I said. 'Did you know Diana well?'

'I did and I didn't,' replied Gloria, selecting a slice of chocolate gateaux with a cherry on top. 'We moved here at about the same time, not so long ago, so we bonded over that, navigating the village, who to avoid and so on. She was great company but wouldn't talk about herself or her past at all. She told me that straight, and I respected it, although she loved to hear about all my shenanigans.'

'What were they?' I said, grasping at the opportunity for a diversion. 'If you don't mind me asking?'

'Oh, of course not, my darling! Have a look around you – most of it's on the walls.'

I stood up, taking my coffee with me, and looked more closely at the framed newspaper cuttings dotted around.

'Is this you?' I asked, pointing to a slightly blurry colour photo of a young woman wearing a red and white striped bikini and white high heels.

'That's right,' she said, pride in her voice. 'That was the beauty contest on *Seaside Special* in 1977. All completely unacceptable to a young thing like you these days, but we had a high old time parading around inside the Big Top, meeting the stars of the day and visiting all the seaside resorts, even France once. It was like one long summer holiday, although we had to work pretty hard.'

'Who did you meet?' I asked, looking at some of the other, simi-lar, pictures. 'Isn't that Cilla Black?'

'Oh yes, darling Cilla, wonderful lady. And Vera Lynn, Stu Francis, David Hamilton...'

I shook my head.

'I've heard of Vera Lynn, of course, but not the others.'

'No, well, it was a long time ago. Happy memories for me, and it led to a career in showbiz. Not the kind of thing people dream of now – number one hits and tours and influencing and so on – but a career, nonetheless.'

'What did you do?'

'Look at that one there,' she said, pointing to another framed picture, this one signed to her in a flourishing script. In it, she was standing with a suited man on a glittering gold set with a huge pound sign and the words 'The Price is Right' emblazoned across it. 'That's darling Leslie Crowther,' she went on. 'Such a kind man. I was a hostess on that show for three years.'

'TV?' I asked.

'Yes, primetime, loved by millions. And there were other things: pantomimes, of course, end of the pier shows, even Sunday Night at the Palladium once.'

I looked at each of the photos in wonder, knowing nothing about the world they showed, but entranced by the glamour and fun that radiated from each one.

'So, how did you end up here?' I asked. 'Isn't it boring after all that?'

'Oh no, you do get weary of it in the end, and I was ready for a change once my daughter left home. Besides, London wasn't the same without my husband, Georgie. Great fun he was, but he had to leave in a hurry.'

Despite my initial reservations, I was being pulled further into Gloria's orbit. I went to sit down.

'Why was that?'

'Well, darling,' she said, pushing the plate of cakes towards me again. I took a slice of Bakewell tart this time. 'When I married him, I didn't know him that well. He showed me a good time, took me out, made me laugh, bought me presents and was kind. Then he produced this.' She held out her left hand to display a gigantic sapphire engagement ring. 'Very Lady Di. I was impressed and couldn't marry him fast enough. Of course, he turned out to be a gangster.' She sighed. 'Surprisingly common then, or it seemed to be amongst my crowd, anyway.'

'A gangster?' I said, horrified. 'What did you do?'

'Well, I had my daughter, Tiffany, by then, and the work had dried up, so I turned a blind eye. We all did. It was fine for a long time, but then a few years ago the police got too close for comfort. Georgie did a flit to Spain, but I didn't much feel like the Costas, so I stayed home for a few years, then bought this place. Georgie's made sure I never had to worry about money, but I wanted to keep busy.'

'Wow,' I said, staring at her. 'And I thought *my* life had too much going on at the moment.'

She gave her husky laugh again.

'At least Georgie was loyal to me, still is. We're still married. It seems to suit us, living in different countries.'

'Don't you miss him?'

'Sometimes, but I visit a couple of times a year and we're always in touch. It'd be nice to have him here sometimes, but too much of a risk. Ah well, life is life.'

I stared into my mug as a lump came to my throat. Gloria's perceptive eyes missed nothing.

'Darling girl,' she said, laying an immaculately manicured hand on my arm. 'You're going through a tough time, but things will pick up. Do you want to talk about the man?'

I swallowed. I hadn't wanted to talk about Matt at all, but Gloria's strange mix of comfort and confidence loosened my tongue.

'It was such a *shock*,' I whispered. 'One minute we were perfectly happy and about to get married, and the next he had ended everything. His parents sided with him in a way that made me feel like I had done something terrible, but I *hadn't*.'

I looked up at her in despair, hoping she wouldn't think I was hiding something awful I had done. That was how Matt's mother and father had treated me, and I needed to prove to people that I was innocent.

'Well, of *course* you hadn't,' said Gloria, taking a third cake. 'That's one of the oldest tricks in the book that men use: make you think it's all your fault.'

'Really? Matt was the only serious boyfriend I've ever had, so I don't know much.'

'Well, take it from me as someone who does. No one thinks it's your fault, even him. He's trying to make himself look – and feel – better.'

'And then he thought that *I* would cancel everything,' I said, sniffling and accepting a piece of shortbread. The memory of this unfair cruelty rallied me slightly. 'I told him he should do it, but then I went into my email and found one hundred and eighteen unread messages. They were all asking what was going on, and it turned out that Matt had just gone onto the paperless site we had used for all our wedding admin and sent out a generic cancellation email, no details, nothing, with my email address as the point of contact.'

'Naughty boy,' said Gloria, going to the fridge and getting out a bottle of rosé. She poured two large glasses and put one in front of me. Given the day I'd had, wine was either a brilliant or a terrible idea. I decided to risk it and sipped while she continued talking. 'He put you in an impossible position: he'd done what you asked, but so poorly that you would have to manage everything, after all. The guests probably thought that was a computer error or something.'

'Exactly! I tried calling him, but his phone went straight to voicemail.'

'Of course. Coward.'

'So, I rang his horrible mother.'

My mind drifted back to that conversation, my phone on speaker so that Mum could hear everything, as I rang his parents' landline, which still sat on a special telephone table in their gracious hallway.

'Rotherton 4125?' came the memory of his mother's cut-glass tones. At least their reluctance to leave the twentieth century meant no call screening; I was sure she wouldn't have chosen to talk to me.

'Celia? It's Belle.'

'Oh. How can I help you?'

'Is Matt there?'

'I'm afraid not. Matthew has gone away for a few days.'

'Well, can I have his contact details? His phone's off and there's a ton of wedding cancellation stuff he's dumped at my doorstep.'

'I'm afraid I'm not going to put you in touch. Matthew needs time to heal after all the stress he has been through, especially after you refused to do your share of the work in dealing with the wedding.'

'Ex-*cuse* me? I don't know what he's told you, but I am going to have to do far more than press 'send' on an email. He's completely dropped me in it, and none of this was my doing in the first place.'

'I think it's always true – don't you? – that in adult relation-ships blame can rarely be laid at only one person's feet.'

I was gaping, unable to compose a reply to this. Celia, of course, took my silence as agreement.

'So, do your bit, please, Isabelle. Chin up. And we'll be sure to pay you a month's salary in lieu of notice; that will be more comfortable for everyone. Was there anything else? No? Then I wish you well.'

The phone was put down briskly at her end and I was left staring at my screen. I looked up at Mum, who squeezed my hand.

'I know it's raw at the moment, and awful, but I promise you that people like that are best forgotten. They're like parking tickets: do what needs to be done and move on. No dwelling, no impotent rage. You have much to look forward to in life, darling. Start now.'

'Your mother sounds like a wise woman,' said Gloria, topping up our glasses.

'She is,' I said. 'Except for staying with Dad. I wish she was here now; I hate thinking of her on her own at home. She'll be devastated about Diana.'

Gloria, with unexpected sensitivity, didn't ask about my parents' relationship. Instead, she said soothingly, 'You've both been through a very tough time. When was the wedding going to be?'

'Tomorrow,' I said, huge tears for Mum, Diana and myself now rolling down my face and neck and soaking into my collar.

'Well then, tomorrow we need to be doing something to take your mind off it.' She paused. 'I suppose funeral arrangements aren't the most cheerful of activities, but it'll be a good distraction. Flowers or coffins?'

Despite my misery and the subject matter, I couldn't help but smile.

'That's more like it,' said Gloria. 'Nothing for it but to keep going.'

'Thank you. My mum's organising most of it from home, so I'll call her and see what we can do to help.'

'Attagirl. Now, I've got a manicure booked in for the morning, and I'm sure they'll squeeze you in if I ask. What do you think?'

THREE

Gloria kept me busy not only for the rest of that day with dinner and stories of her dazzling youth, and the following day, when we had an unexpectedly enjoyable trip to choose flowers for Diana's funeral, but for the whole week. I still found myself pausing outside wedding dress shops, staring hungrily at the gowns and headpieces, but Gloria steered me firmly away. We visited the church and spoke to the vicar, with my mum on Zoom, we had an appointment with the undertaker, and we tasted and chose what seemed to me like a huge buffet and bar table.

'The whole village will turn out,' said Gloria. 'And people expect a good spread after a funeral. Everyone's sad and shocked, but also euphoric that they're still here to enjoy it all. Both conditions make them ravenously hungry, so you can't skimp.'

Our final outing, the day before the funeral, was to buy something to wear. Although I had all my belongings with me – mostly still crammed into the back of my car – I didn't have any suitable clothes, other than a work suit, which Gloria deemed 'all wrong'. I suspect that the outfit was fine, but that she was finding ways to keep me occupied, and I was grateful for her generosity with her time as much as for the distraction. I wished Mum could have been there too, and I pictured her at home, running around after my father, everything she did having holes picked in it for not being good enough. It felt wrong to talk about my parents in detail, but the evening before the funeral, after a couple of glasses of Gloria's favourite Dubonnet and gin – 'the Queen Mum's favourite tipple, you know' – which I was fast developing a taste for, I opened up a little and told her about his controlling behaviour.

'When I was staying with them, Mum was amazing, but he didn't try to comfort me at all, or give me any encouragement. There was one morning, when I had managed to make a cup of tea, which felt like an achievement in itself. I couldn't drink it, because my throat felt so tight, and I was crying into it in the kitchen, too drained to put any clothes on, so still in my pyjamas with tangled hair. I suppose I did look a mess, but it was too early days to "pull myself together".'

'Of course it was – it still is,' said Gloria, patting my hand. 'For what it's worth, I think you're bearing up like a trooper.'

'Thank you. Well, his only comment was: "Can't say I blame Matt. Men these days do want a woman who can be a real partner, not fall apart at the slightest thing. You should have got yourself some proper skills, not just allowed yourself to be looked after."'

'Oh, charming. Did you tell him that having your entire life pulled out from underneath you was hardly "the slightest thing"?'

'I didn't dare. I also wanted to point out that if I do sometimes lack initiative, it was largely down to thirty-three years of his bullying, controlling behaviour. I was more inclined to agree with him, as I had been rigorously trained to do. I felt then' – *still do now* – 'that it was in some way my fault Matt had left.'

'Well, we'll have to stop you thinking like that,' said Gloria robustly. 'Might not be easy, though, particularly if you still love him.' *How did she know?* She smiled at my unspoken question, which must have been written all over my face. 'I've been around a long time,' she said. 'You'll get over him, darling, I promise.'

I remembered Diana saying the same thing and a wave of grief crashed over me. Gloria waited, without fussing, until the tears had subsided and I had managed to get my breath back.

'I miss him so much.' I hiccupped and blew my nose, hard. 'I feel so stupid. I check my phone constantly in case he's been in touch. I can't sleep. I just lie there, torturing myself by remembering the good times. I'm always imagining him taking me back.'

'It's not stupid, lovey, it's all so *normal*.'

'Mum saved my life in that first week after he cancelled everything. She made me eat, shower, dress and got me out of the house on gentle little missions to buy milk or stamps. I wish she'd leave my father,' I concluded, draining my glass.

'Nothing you can do about that,' said Gloria, shaking her head. 'Other than make sure she knows you're there to support her, always. My first husband used to knock me black and blue, but it was surprisingly hard to walk away. Seems crazy now, but you don't have to understand. That becomes like criticism and makes the person feel worse about themselves than they already do after years of being belittled.'

I stared at her, and she frowned.

'Sorry, darling, have I overstepped?'

'God, no,' I said, leaning my glass forward for the refill she was offering. 'I hope I'm as wise as you one day.'

She gave her throaty laugh.

'Well, I hope you don't have to go through the mill as I have to learn some of these lessons. It's not that hard; all you have to do is ask yourself, "What is the kindest thing to do?" and that will usually get you through okay. And never forget that you have to be equally as kind to yourself.'

That night was the best night's sleep I had experienced since Matt left me, and I woke in the morning calm and refreshed. After breakfast I dressed in my new clothes – a simple dark grey dress with a flowing, pleated skirt, and an embroidered shawl – and Gloria and I walked to the church. It did seem as if the whole village had come out for Diana, and I was incredibly touched as I saw more and more people heading in the same direction. I recognised one or two of them to smile 'hello' to. Some I had met with Gloria over the past few days, and I knew Tessa, of course. She came over now and we hugged.

'Are you all right?' I asked. 'It must have been so awful – being the one to find her.'

Her eyes were full of tears.

'It was good she wasn't alone when— when the end came,' she said, and I was glad that she found comfort in that.

She went back to her husband and soon we were all in the church for a ceremony that was serious but truly heartfelt and painted a picture of a woman who, although she had not lived in the village that long, was well-loved and respected. Several people stood up to share their memories, and I discreetly recorded these on my phone, knowing that Mum would appreciate hearing them.

Afterwards, we went into the church hall, where the caterers had done us proud. Three trestle tables groaned with food and drink, and I felt the lightening of people's moods all around me as they walked in.

'You were right,' I said to Gloria. 'People needed this.'

I found myself very hungry, too, and was soon balancing a laden plate and full glass, trying to eat but also make polite conversation as people came over to offer their condolences. Tessa stopped to chat for a while, along with her husband, Caleb. We were soon joined by an older woman with grey hair in a neat bob and her thin lips set in a disapproving line.

'This is my mother, Beverly,' said Tessa, and we shook hands. Gloria gave a tight 'hello', which was most unlike her. I remembered her mentioning the name previously, and that she had insinuated the woman was a gossip. She was quickly proved right.

'Hello, Belle,' she said, gazing at me in an unsettling way. 'So sorry about Diana. I understood that she and your mother were very close – couldn't Vivienne make it today?'

'No,' I said, in as neutral a tone as I could muster, unwilling to give her any material. 'Sadly not. Did you know Diana well?'

'As well as anyone in the village, I suppose,' she replied. 'Kept her cards close to her chest, did Diana. I have wondered if there was more of a story there than simply "retiring to open a tea shop".'

She stared at me intently, as if expecting me to spill out some litany of secrets about Diana's past. I was about to answer rather more sharply than would be appropriate, given the circumstances, when Tessa stepped in.

'I'm sure there isn't, Mum. And it doesn't matter, anyway.'

'Mmm.' Her eyes flicked between the three of us and as we clearly weren't going to be any more forthcoming, she changed the subject. 'Did you see Sir Henry and Lady Talbot in the church with Luke and Sam? I was most surprised they had attended.'

Not knowing who she was talking about, I glanced at Gloria.

'Henry is the baronet. They live at the manor house – you remember we passed it the other day?'

'Why shouldn't they come to Diana's funeral?' I asked Beverly.

'Oh, well, no *reason*,' she said. 'Only I didn't realise they were... so close.'

'She knew Luke well,' said Tessa. 'They did all that beach cleaning stuff together. His parents and brother were probably being supportive.'

'I suppose so,' said Beverly, reluctant to let go of a potentially interesting piece of gossip. 'But I'm still surprised. The nobility doesn't turn out for just anybody.'

'I'm sure they'll make a special effort when it's your turn,' said Gloria, in an unusually tart tone of voice.

Beverly might have come back at her, had Tessa not frowned and said, 'Oh dear, do you think Edward's all right?'

I glanced in the direction she was looking, to see an older man standing alone, holding a cup of tea and visibly upset.

'He looks distraught,' said Beverly. 'Another one I wouldn't have thought was so *close* to Diana.'

Gloria shot a look of disgust at the other woman.

'He was a good friend to Diana, and she to him. Come and meet him, Belle.'

I hurried after her as she swept away, temporarily starving Beverly of the gossip oxygen she seemed to thrive on.

'Edward,' said Gloria, laying a gentle hand on his shoulder. 'How are you bearing up?' She carried on so that he didn't have to answer and had time to gather himself. 'This is Belle, Diana's goddaughter.'

I offered my hand and he shook it gently.

'What a pleasure to meet you,' he said, in a voice that surprised me with its strength and depth. 'Our paths never crossed on your previous visits, but Diana mentioned you and told me you were coming down. She was so looking forward to it.'

'Oh, gosh, we only arranged it the day before she...'

'The day before she died,' he said. 'Yes. Diana and I chatted now and then. We shared an interest in the sea and conservation. Do get in touch if you'd like me to share some of my memories of her.'

'I'd love that,' I said. I was glad that Diana had been good friends with him; she seemed to me to have had a lonely life, never having married or had children and, according to Mum, sticking to one or two friends, rather than having a busy social whirl of engagements.

'Well, I think I'll head off now,' he said, finishing his tea. 'My dog, Doris, will be wondering where I am. You and your mother have done Diana proud today, Belle, thank you.'

We shook hands warmly and then, with another muttered 'thank you', he hurried from the room.

'What a pleasant man,' I said to Gloria. 'And he was obviously close to Diana.'

'Indeed,' she replied. 'He's going to miss her badly.'

I had the feeling that she was going to say more, but we were interrupted by a man with thick, dark, wavy hair and the friendliest brown eyes I had ever seen outside a Labrador. He was around the same age as me, a little taller, and wearing a smart suit with a burgundy silk tie.

'Luke!' said Gloria, her face lighting up. They embraced briefly, and she turned to me.

'Belle, this is Luke, our wonderful village vet. Luke, this is Belle, Diana's goddaughter.'

We shook hands.

'I'm so pleased to meet you,' he said. 'Diana talked about you a lot.'

This was the second time I had been told this in the space of a few minutes and, despite the warmth of Luke's smile, all my sorrow of the past week came rushing to the surface.

'I'm so sorry,' I said, dabbing at my eyes with a napkin. 'I wish I had seen more of her and now it's too late.'

Luke was unembarrassed by my tears, merely taking another napkin from a nearby pile and exchanging it for mine, now sodden with tears and streaked with mascara.

'You were in touch a lot, she felt very close to you and understood that it wasn't easy to spend time together. She loved your texts and photos, though, and was looking forward to the wedding.'

This, of course, set off another torrent of tears and, as Luke got me yet another napkin, Gloria quickly explained.

'Unfortunately, the wedding was called off. Belle was coming down to visit Diana when we lost her.'

'Oh god, I'm so sorry,' said Luke. 'I had no idea.'

'It's okay,' I said, glancing up at him and, despite my misery, hoping that I didn't have eyes that were red from crying and black from smeared make-up. He was decidedly good-looking as well as kind and still apparently unfazed by the handful of soggy napkins. 'It's all come at once. How did you know Diana?'

'We were both interested in ocean conservation,' he said. 'We clear up garbage on the beach, write to our local council, things like that. Diana once got me to travel to London for a protest, but it turned out to be too hardcore for us. Neither of us wanted a night in a police cell, let alone a criminal record, so we donated some money to the Marine Conservation Society instead, then went for a long lunch.'

'I wish I'd been there, it sounds fun.'

'It was. I'm going to miss Diana. Do you know what will happen to the tearooms?'

'No,' I replied. 'I hadn't thought about it, to be honest...'

'All in good time,' he said. 'It's a lot to take in.'

The room was beginning to thin out now, and the caterers were discreetly tidying up.

'I think we should go home,' said Gloria. 'After a long day like this what we need is a film and some dinner. Would you like to join us, Luke?'

'That sounds perfect,' he said. 'But I've got some paperwork that won't do itself, and a couple of house calls I promised I'd make. Lovely to meet you, Belle.'

The early evening was mild, and I enjoyed the sound of the sea as Gloria and I walked back to Seaspray Lodge.

'Is Luke the one Beverly mentioned – the baronet's son?' I asked, as we entered the welcoming hallway.

'That's right,' said Gloria. 'The eldest. Doesn't live up at Spindrift House, though, and has his own career as a vet, so I don't know what will happen when he inherits. Not that it's any of my business, but one can't help feeling curious.'

I could easily feel very curious about lots of things concerning Luke Talbot, but I pushed him from my mind and turned my attention to the takeaway leaflets Gloria was spreading out on the kitchen table. Deciding between a chicken curry or a *quattro formaggi* pizza was enough for me right now.

FOUR

When the knock on the door came, Gloria and I both assumed it was our dinner.

'That was quick,' she said. 'I haven't even had a chance to open a bottle.'

'I'll go,' I said, 'and you can grab the corkscrew.'

But when I opened the front door, I knew immediately that the smartly dressed man on the step was no pizza delivery boy.

'Miss Walker?' he said. 'Isabelle Walker?'

'Yes, that's me.'

'My name is Peter Masterson, I'm your late aunt's lawyer, and the executor of her will. I'm sorry for calling on you at such a late hour, but I was in the area, so I thought I'd come by rather than call.'

'I see,' I said. 'Would you like to come in?'

'No, there's no need. I wanted to introduce myself and ask you to come to my office at your earliest convenience, so that I can share the details of her will with you.'

I took the card he was offering as Gloria came up behind me.

'Peter!' she said. 'I don't suppose you've brought a pizza, have you?'

He looked confused for a moment and then, as a bright red

moped buzzed to a stop on the road, he gave an unexpectedly warm smile.

'Oh, I see! No, I'm afraid all I came bearing was a business card. I have some availability over the next few days, Miss Walker, so please do get in touch.'

He left, with a nod to the person delivering our pizza, and soon Gloria and I were sitting in her cosy kitchen with our food and wine. I put the lawyer's card on the table.

'I wonder why he wants to see me,' I said.

'Diana must have left you something in her will,' replied Gloria. 'Something big would be my guess, if he's calling you in. If it was five hundred pounds, he'd send you a cheque.'

'What about her family? Mum said she thought there was a brother, and that they were estranged, but Diana never talked about him or anyone else.'

Gloria shook her head.

'No idea, my love, but I'm sure it will all become clear in the fullness of time. Now, shall we top up our wine and go and watch some glamorous real estate reality show?'

It was the perfect end to a difficult day. I decided not to think about Peter Masterson, wills, or anything else more taxing than whether I might choose Carrera marble or concrete for the floors in my fantasy LA mansion.

The following morning, I rang up Peter Masterson's office and was given an appointment for that very afternoon. Until then, I sat down with Gloria's accounts at her request, which she'd managed to get into a muddle, and I barely noticed three hours passing. It was only when she called me for lunch that I checked my watch.

'Oh goodness, I'd better have something quick, I need to be there in an hour.'

'How are my books looking?' she asked, putting a fat cheese sandwich, oozing homemade onion chutney, in front of me.

'A bit... topsy turvy,' I said, trying to be tactful. 'But nothing I can't untangle. You've been paying too much tax, if anything.'

'I must pay you for your time,' she said. 'I've agonised over those numbers, and it looks like you're on top of them in a single morning.'

'It's fine,' I said. 'It's good for me to keep busy, and maybe you'll be able to give me a reference or something when I start looking for a job.'

'Of course. Where are you going to look? Around here?'

'Here?' It hadn't occurred to me for a second. 'No, I was thinking of going back to be near my parents. I suppose I could stay in this area, though – I love being so near the sea.'

'I could put the word out, if you want? I'm sure there are plenty of opportunities for a bright girl like you.'

I bit into my sandwich so that I didn't have to reply. I was touched at her kindness, but not used to my intelligence being complimented – other than by Mum, anyway, but that's her job, isn't it? Matt's parents had treated me as if I was dim, even when I kept their books in perfect order, and my father, of course, never had anything kind to say. I had generally assumed that good accounting was more a matter of being organised than being clever, but maybe I should have a rethink.

As I drove into the market town about fifteen miles away, where Peter Masterson had his offices, I wondered if there would be anyone else at the meeting. Presumably not, seeing as it was me who had suggested the time, but an image of a movie-style gathering of long-lost relatives came into my mind, nevertheless. Maybe I would find out something about this mysterious brother, or any other relatives Diana had been keeping quiet about.

Of course, when I arrived, my fantasies of a gathering of secret family members snarling over a contentious will were quickly put out to pasture. I climbed four stone steps to a glossy black doorway and pressed on a well-polished brass bell button. The door was opened by a woman of around my mother's age, wearing a smart charcoal skirt and neat olive-green twinset.

'Miss Walker?'

'Yes, I have an appointment.'

'Of course. Please follow me.'

I recognised her soft tones as those of the woman I had spoken to yesterday on the phone. I followed her along a navy-blue carpeted hallway and through into a large office, where I was ushered to sit down in a leather armchair. I felt almost naughty, taking my phone out to pass the time, as if I should have produced a novel to read instead, or made notes in a pocket diary. The lawyer's premises were timeless more than old-fashioned, but seemed somehow sullied by my flicking through Facebook. Despite this, I was soon engrossed in a friend's photos of her recent trip to Italy and jumped guiltily when the receptionist materialised in front of me and murmured, 'Mr Masterson will see you now.'

She opened a heavy oak door opposite, and I passed through into exactly the room I had been expecting. The thick carpet and sense of hush continued, along with the smell of wood polish and old paper. Two of the walls were lined with shelves of leather-bound books and against a third stood several tall, black filing cabinets. Peter Masterson was sitting behind a vast antique desk and thankfully tapping away at a sleek computer, rather than scratching out his notes with a quill and ink, which wouldn't have come as any big surprise to me. He rose when I came in and held out his hand.

'Good afternoon, Miss Walker.' He turned to the woman. 'Thank you, Petra. Please can you bring some tea?' He turned to me. 'Or coffee, if you prefer?'

'Tea would be perfect, thank you,' I replied, and sat down in the chair opposite him. He smiled at me and picked up a long, white envelope.

'My condolences on the death of your godmother,' he said, and I inclined my head in acknowledgement. 'I have here her will – ah, thank you, Petra.'

I hadn't even noticed her open the door and glide in with tea for both of us and a plate of shortbread fingers. When she had left, Masterson took a thoughtful sip.

'As I was saying, I have Diana Dalton's will here. You are the only beneficiary, hence my needing to call you in.'

My cup hovered halfway between my mouth and its saucer.

'I'm sorry, the *only* beneficiary?'

'Yes, that's right. There is one clause, which I will explain, but essentially Miss Dalton left everything to you.'

I stared at him, not knowing what to say. He gave me a kind smile, then continued.

'I understand that this is probably something of a surprise to you. Miss Dalton spoke to me at length about her wishes, and her reasons for taking the choices she did. In addition to the will, she wrote this letter, which explains things in her own words.'

He handed me the white envelope and a silver letter opener and stood up.

'I'll leave you for a few minutes so that you can read it in private.'

I slit the envelope open and pulled out the single sheet of paper it held, covered with Diana's flowing handwriting. A lump came to my throat as I started to read, her voice resonating in my head.

Dearest Belle,

Peter will have told you by now that I have left you everything in my will – the house, the tearooms and some money, most of which can be used to sort out any expenses relating to my estate and funeral. Of course, I don't know where you will be in your life when you read this – hopefully happily married with a beautiful child or two.

I broke off from reading and stared at the opposite wall for a moment, blinking away tears as the future Matt had smashed to pieces, and that I had tried so hard to forget about over the past couple of weeks, returned to my head in vivid technicolour. I took a deep, shaky breath and read on.

If this is the case, then please sell everything and use the proceeds as you see fit, for your family. If, however, things have not worked out as you planned, then I want you to use my legacy for a fresh start, whatever that looks like to you. I understand, dear Belle, what it means to be a small boat tossed in the rough seas of others' decisions about your life, and also how difficult it is to move away from that, but I urge you to do so. You are a woman with so much to offer, so many skills, such kindness, good brains. Could it be your time, finally, to shine? I would love to think I had made this possible.

She knew. I don't know how she knew, but she did. About Dad, about Matt, about it all. And she wanted to help. I wondered what 'rough seas' she had encountered and if I could find out more about her life.

I have also put an unusual clause in the will, regarding Vivienne, your mother. Peter tells me that it is not legally binding and that you can decide whether to honour it or not, but I trust you to do so, should the occasion arise. I want to help her, but no one can do that unless she decides to help herself. Peter will write to her separately with details of my offer, if you agree. I'm sorry not to be more explicit about this, but I hope you trust me.

Vivienne and you have been my family all these years, and I hope you receive my gifts in the spirit with which I submit them: with love, with gratitude and with optimism.

All my love,

Diana

Tears blurred my eyes as I finished reading. I put down the

letter and fumbled in my bag for a tissue. I knew that Mum had loved Diana, but that it was hard for her to see her as much as she wanted to, because of Dad. I had always adored her, but the truth was, I had not known her as well as I might, only seeing her once a year at most. To read that she considered us her family brought a wave of emotions: sorrow, guilt and regret were at the fore, but there was also gratitude – not only for her bequests but for the care she showed us. I wished I had understood sooner and been able to reciprocate in some way. Then, drawing in a breath to steady myself, I reread the letter, and one part stood out to me in that moment, as clearly as if she had highlighted it in neon yellow: *Could it be your time, finally, to shine? I would love to think I had made this possible.* Was this the way I could honour Diana's love for Mum and me? By taking her legacy and making the very most of it? I had spent two weeks, since Matt's bombshell and Diana's death, cycling through grief, anger, despair, numbness and bravado, but now, for the first time, something else flickered inside me. Was it hope? Excitement? Determination? Whatever it was, it finally felt *good*, and I resolved then to nurture that feeling and help it grow. That – along with signing off on the clause Diana had included about Mum, which was never in doubt – would be my salute to Diana.

I was tucking the tissue, no longer needed, back into my bag, when the door opened with a delicate, deliberate rattle, and Peter Masterson re-entered the room.

'Have you had sufficient time to read the letter?' he enquired.

'Yes,' I said. 'Thank you.'

He took his seat behind the desk.

'Miss Dalton's bequest to you is significant. First of all, I have to ask you if you accept it?'

I frowned.

'Well, of course I do. Don't I have to?'

'No, it is possible to refuse, and people do. The next question is one of a clause Miss Dalton included. I don't know if she mentioned it in the letter?'

'A clause regarding my mother? Yes, she did.'

'Again, it is your choice as to whether you wish me to follow through with this. If you agree, the exact details will remain secret although, of course, your mother may share them with you. It could ultimately mean that she might receive a portion of Diana's money – around fifteen thousand pounds, once taxes have been paid. There are certain conditions attached to her receiving this money, and thus it would be held in trust for her until such time as she met these conditions, which have no time limit. If she chooses not to, the money would eventually come to you on your mother's death.' He smiled awkwardly. 'It is, I'm afraid, complicated and *highly* unusual.'

I gently blew the flickering flame within, and it flared.

'It's fine,' I said confidently. 'Please fulfil Diana's wishes as she laid them out.'

He inclined his head.

'Very well. The next step, then, is to examine some of the paperwork regarding Miss Dalton's house and business. She specified in her will that, if you would like to live there, you should be able to do so right away, rather than waiting for probate. As her executor, I agree that this would be the best course of action. Is that what you would like to do?'

'Yes.'

It was a huge question, one that should have required time spent soul searching, planning, considering practical implications, but the word slipped out of my mouth before my brain had time to engage. The slight shock I felt as I heard myself utter it only fanned the flame further.

'Yes,' I repeated. 'I'd like to move in.'

'Good. In that case, for now, I need you to sign some paperwork and I can give you the key. You won't own anything until probate is complete, and until then any major decisions must be passed through me, but I don't anticipate it taking long, hopefully no more than a few months. There is also the question of inheritance tax, which I can help you manage.'

'Thank you. I do have a good understanding of tax and accounts, so I will make it a priority to look closely at everything. Do you know where Diana kept her records?'

'They are all accessible via her personal computer, kept at the house.'

He produced another sealed envelope from the folder.

'This contains her passwords and various account details. She updated it every six months, but help is available if you have any difficulties accessing the information you need.'

I took the envelope and slipped it into my bag.

'It leaves it to me to hand you these,' he said and, with a smile, gave me a bunch of keys. 'I hope you will be as happy in Spindrift Bay as Miss Dalton hoped.'

As my hand closed around the keys, the little flame burst into a blaze, and I grinned at Peter Masterson.

'I have every intention of being the happiest I possibly can,' I said.

Rather than driving straight back to the village, I went instead to a cliff walk I remembered enjoying a few years ago when I had visited Diana in Dorset. I parked up and strode out along the path, enjoying the wind which buffeted me even on a fine day like today, finding it refreshing and invigorating. As I walked, I put my hand in my pocket and fingered the keys there. For the first time since being in the lawyer's office, my resolve wavered. *What have you said yes to? Moving your entire life down here, taking on a house and a business you know nothing about? Ridiculous. You should sell, you know you should, and use the money for something more sensible.* The energy drained from my body, and I sank down onto the grass, where I could stare out to the calm yet ever-moving, ever-changing sea. If only Diana was here to advise me! Although, of course, her advice had come across clearly in her letter, as if she had known the circumstances in which it would find me: *make a fresh start.*

As I sat there, gazing at the horizon, a memory floated into my head from many years ago. I had only been young – nine, perhaps – and Mum and I had made one of our rare visits to France to see Diana one Easter holiday when Dad had gone skiing. At that age, I had felt both very shy and devotedly admiring of her. She had such vitality, and warmth, and although her no-nonsense approach could feel intimidating, she was not unkind or critical, and I wasn't scared of her. It was more that she urged you to search your own soul for answers, rather than seek them from others, and I didn't always want to do that. I was having problems at school, and felt very anxious about seeing the girl involved again when term started. I hadn't mentioned it to Mum, not wanting to add to the stress I could see that Dad put her under, but I was quieter than usual, and she had asked me several times if anything was bothering me. I had said "nothing" and tried to perk up, which she had appeared to accept. Diana, however, wasn't having any of it and had spoken to me in her little garden, when my mother was resting upstairs.

We were picking gooseberries when she suddenly said, 'You'd better get it off your chest, whatever's troubling you. Keeping it secret isn't doing you any good, and your mother's worried.'

'I'm fine.'

'What nonsense. Anyone with half a brain can see that you aren't. Don't insult my intelligence. Talk about it to me. I probably won't be able to help much, but you'll feel better for airing it.'

I had looked at her in astonishment. So many adults professed to have all the answers, yet here was she asserting that she probably *couldn't* help. It was strangely comforting, maybe because it confirmed the severity of the situation, as I saw it, or because it meant that she wasn't going to tell me to talk to my friend, the idea of which terrified me.

'There's a girl at school. She's called Sophie. I think we're friends, she says we are, but she's quite mean.' I paused, but Diana said nothing, just carried on picking gooseberries. 'She said I had to give her my panda pencil, if I wanted to be friends. It's my favourite one and I said I didn't want to. Then she said I wasn't a real friend. She told some of the other girls that I was a bad friend, and now they're not talking to me, either. Melody said I just have to give her the pencil and it will be all right again, but I don't want to. And she had a party at the end of term and didn't invite me. And' – I gulped, shame rising inside me, my voice a whisper as I said the worst of it out loud – 'she said I smell and need to wear deodorant. It's so embarrassing.'

Diana put down her basket and looked at me.

'Thank you for telling me, Belle,' she said, her voice serious. 'I know it's hard to share these things. I hope you feel better?' I nodded, swallowing away tears. 'I think I can offer some advice, if you would like it?' Again, I nodded, desperate now to be helped. 'All right. First things first, this Sophie is a bully, not a friend. It's important that you get this clear. You mustn't think of her as "my friend, Sophie" but as "that bully, Sophie". You have done exactly the right thing by refusing to give her your pencil. Why should you? You don't want to, which is reason enough. And poor Sophie doesn't seem to realise that friendship can't be bought.' She must have seen surprise flash across my face, because she continued, 'Yes, poor Sophie. She has her group around her right now, but they're only there out of fear, or because they're dazzled by her. Not because they love her for who she is. You have two choices: completely ignore them, or speak to a teacher. I won't tell you which to take, but if it gets any worse, then you *must* tell someone other than me, okay? And as for the deodorant, we can throw one in the shopping this afternoon, if you like?' I stared at her as if she was a goddess. How long had I agonised over this, the humiliation eating away at me and making the simple process of telling Mum, who I knew would help, seem impossible? And here was Diana, solving it in one swoop, with no awkwardness at all. I was passionately grateful.

I invoked her now, trying to hear her voice reply to my wavering thoughts. *What would that 'more sensible' thing be?* I asked myself sternly. *A return to the home counties where you have no home of your own, no job, no discernible future?* The blunt honesty of this internal voice shocked me, and, for a moment, I wanted to hide from it, to offer up my vulnerability, ignorance and aloneness as evidence of why running back to the familiar would be the best thing to do. But then I remembered Diana, and what she had written in her letter, how she had intimated that her choices had been taken from her in life and that she hoped to offer me other options, a fresh start. I didn't know what her past had held, but I thought about the woman I had known, taking a nine-year-old girl seriously as she picked gooseberries. Whatever had happened to her hadn't stopped her making a life for herself, at first in France and then in Spindrift Bay. Maybe those things hadn't been her first choices, but she had made the most of them. Diana understood, and had offered me a lifeline. I could have returned home without her legacy; to take it up seemed nothing short of foolish. But there was one person I worried about being so far away from. I took out my phone.

'Mum?'

'Hello, darling. How's it all going down there? Thank you for the videos of the service, it looked beautiful.'

'It was. I wish you could have been there.'

I went on to explain my visit to the lawyer, who had already contacted her about the clause in the will.

'That was quick,' I said. 'I only left his office an hour ago.'

'I suppose he wants to get everything in place. I hope you don't mind, Belle, but I'm not going to share the details of Diana's wishes with you yet. I have a lot to think about.'

'I do too,' I said.

'I disagree,' replied Mum. 'Don't change your mind, Belle, please.'

'But what about you? I don't like being so far away.'

'You're two hours away,' she said, with a smile in her voice. 'And I am a grown woman, not your responsibility. I love you, and I am so grateful that you want to be near me, but I mustn't – I *mustn't*,' she said fiercely, 'figure in your decision making. *I'm* the one who has thinking to do, not you – unless it's how to run the tearooms, which will be plenty enough to be going on with.'

'I can barely make a fairy cake,' I said, a nervous giggle bubbling up inside me. 'How am I going to manage?'

'You'll find a way,' said Mum. 'Start small, but *start*. Okay?'

'Okay,' I said, although I was still far from sure, after my earlier confidence, that I had made the right decision.

I walked for another hour, alternating between letting the meeting with the lawyer rattle around in my head and pushing it away, trying to think of other things. The 'yes' had come so easily in Peter Masterson's office, as if my heart had said it before my head could get a look in, but now that I had more time to think, my head was determined to make itself heard.

You haven't worked in hospitality since your shifts behind a student union bar!

You don't know how to bake!

You've never lived alone!

All these things were true and should have been enough to make me pick up the phone at once and confess my ridiculous mistake. But still the brave little flame flickered, fanned now by Mum's words of encouragement.

When I got back to the boarding house, I was exhausted from both the mental wrangling and the physical exercise, which had been much more strenuous and lengthy than I was used to. But I knew that Gloria would be dying for the lowdown on what had been said and, truth be told, I was hoping for her advice.

'I'm back,' I called out as I entered, for all the world as if I'd arrived home rather than at an establishment I was paying for.

'In the kitchen!' came the reply and I hurried through to find the kettle already boiling and the customary pile of cakes and other goodies on a plate on the table.

'So, how was it?' asked Gloria as she made the tea. 'Have something to eat and tell me. You were gone for ages!'

I selected a custard slice and told her everything that Peter Masterson had said, other than the clause about Mum which, even though I didn't know the details, wasn't anybody else's business.

'So you're moving to Spindrift Bay!' said Gloria, knocking her tea mug against mine in celebration. 'Welcome!'

'Well, I don't know about that,' I said awkwardly. 'I was an eager beaver when he first told me, but now it's had time to sink in, I'm not so sure.'

Gloria frowned at me.

Uh oh. Here comes the advice I thought I wanted.

'But darling, what are your options? The money may take ages to come through if you decide to sell, and what are you going to do in the meantime? Go back and live with your parents?'

My stomach dropped.

'I suppose so. I haven't had much time to think about what I want to do with my life now I'm not marrying Matt. Wouldn't it be sensible to give myself some time?'

'Well, that's a very noble ideal, but you can do that equally well – better – here. You've been given the keys, so I can see no reason at all why you wouldn't at least go and have a look around the place, give it a chance. This is a door opening, my girl, you have to run through it. If it turns out that you hate it' – she grinned at me and winked – 'you can sell up and join Georgie on the Costa del Sol!'

I returned her grin.

'Keep my options open?'

'Always. You've got plenty of life ahead of you to make plans and mistakes and more of both. I won't be staying here forever myself.'

I was surprised. Gloria seemed so happy and settled in Spindrift Bay, and the boarding house the perfect retirement option.

'You'll move again?'

'For sure. I've got a few more adventures left in me – and so have you. Think of this as your first one, but not your last.'

'I shall. And if I get fed up with living here, or inadvertently poison the teahouse customers with my very amateur baking skills, there's always Spain!'

Once I had made my mind up, I knew I had to act immediately. I only had to pack a few things into my suitcase, and just before five o'clock that afternoon I arrived at Diana's property. The tearooms were firmly locked and shuttered, and I left them that way, putting the key in the lock of the heavy front door of the house and stepping inside, pushing away some post and leaflets that had collected on the doormat. I closed the door and stood for a few moments. It felt intrusive letting myself into somebody else's house, although I had to think of it as my house now. How long would that take? At first, it was silent, but as I waited quietly, several gentle, comforting sounds came to my ears. There was, of course, the regular plashing of the sea, which you could hear everywhere in Spindrift Bay. There were the unusual keow and mew calls of the seagulls. And there was an almost imperceptible hum, which every house had in its own way and was produced by heating, pipes or electrics; the pulse of a house that beat steadily, even when its previous owner's did not.

The noises reassured me. I scooped up the papers from the mat and walked through to the large kitchen, with its wide windows that made the most of the view into the pretty cottage garden and the sea beyond. There was a door on one side which, I knew, led directly into the tearooms, where there was a second, more utilitarian kitchen. Everything was spotlessly clean, albeit dusty from a week's build-up. I put down the post and ran the tap for a few moments while I found teabags and mug, then filled the kettle and set it to boil. In the meantime, I wandered around the rest of the ground floor, remembering each room from my previous visits. It was a large house – too large for one person – and a couple of the rooms were shut up. These had their curtains drawn and were home to a few sticks of spare furniture and some boxes.

But it was the sitting room at the front of the house that brought the memories of Diana flooding back on a wave of grief. It was both immaculate and very cosy; I had never felt awkward taking off my slippers to tuck my feet up on the sofa, but, at the same time, I would never have dreamed of going up to bed in the evening without first plumping and smoothing the place where I had sat. I had cried very little for Diana, spent from the weeping I had done over my cancelled wedding, my cancelled life, but now I dropped down into a soft armchair, upholstered in wide pink and white stripes, and the tears flowed freely. Being here, in her space, brought sharply to mind her kindness, her tendency to be personally reserved, whilst allowing one to spill forth stories and emotions, which she absorbed with steady compassion. After a while, my sobs ebbed and I was so much lighter, if still sad.

'Better out than in,' I said aloud, my voice shaky. 'Maybe they're right.'

I returned to the kitchen and was soon sitting at the table with a steaming mug of black tea – there was no way the milk in the fridge would be fresh – and a packet of chocolate chip cookies I had found in a cupboard. I raised the mug in a toast and spoke into the quiet house.

'Thank you, Diana,' I said. 'Thank you for your wisdom and for your gift. I hope that I can do it justice.'

FIVE

That evening, with a burst of optimism and energy, I brought in all my belongings from the car. It wasn't only the suitcase I had been using during my stay at Gloria's, but all the things I had stuffed into the back seats when I moved out of mine and Matt's house. Heaving the boxes and bags into the house now, and glancing into them, I half wondered why I had bothered taking most of it. At the time it had felt precious, and comforting, and the prospect of letting go of a flattened cushion or half-burnt candle had been unbearable. Now, it all looked like a melancholic collection of disparate odds and ends. Rather than letting this pull me into a spiral of sadness, as it threatened to, my life with Matt reduced to this meaningless bric-a-brac, I glanced around Diana's – now my – space and squared my shoulders.

'Let's see what the charity shop could benefit from,' I said out loud, and stacked everything on to the hall floor, leaving my clothes, laptop and books aside. First, I separated out practical items and compared them against duplicates in Diana's drawers and cupboards, keeping whichever was best. In half an hour I had a box full of mostly kitchen utensils and household linens; these had been easy to tackle, as even I couldn't work up much sentiment over a tin opener. Next was 'not good enough for charity – or for me', and this bag received the old cushion, a couple of squeezed-out hand cream tubes, a pair of slippers from Matt's mother that I hated and a severely grazed handbag I had carried on our first date, when it was brand new. The candle I lit, seeing as it was a favourite scent of mine. Now came the difficult part, and the energy drained from me as I surveyed the remaining items: a handful of picture frames; a lamp I had spotted in a vintage shop and fallen in love with, but Matt had dismissed as kitsch; a dressing table mirror on a wooden stand he had given me; a small fine china Wedgewood tray in which we had kept our watches, my earrings and his cufflinks overnight. This last piece was the final straw, and I slumped against the wall, surveying the mess in front of me. I didn't feel brave and pioneering anymore, but tired and lonely. Slowly, I pulled myself up and packed everything into an empty box; this, I pushed into one of the unused rooms, where it joined the other abandoned things that, it seemed, Diana had not known what to do with. Clicking the door shut, I wondered how long they would sit there, and decided it didn't matter. If I wanted to get rid of them one day, I could; if I couldn't face them for years, then maybe I wouldn't have to. With my last scraps of strength, I took my suitcase and a couple of bags upstairs and looked at the bedrooms. Here was Diana's, at the front of the house. The bed was neatly made, the few personal effects on her dressing table waiting in forlorn expectation. I pulled the door shut; it didn't feel right to sleep there. A little passage led off to three more bedrooms, above the teahouse, which I knew from my previous visits were unfurnished, so I went into the room where I had stayed and found it as calm and beautifully ready for a guest as it had ever been. The double bed bore a fat duvet in a smooth, pale blue cover, the pillows were plump and inviting in their white cases with blue piping. There was a wardrobe, empty save for an array of hangers, and a chest of five deep drawers. A small dressing table stood next to this, and there was a door in the corner that led into a tiny bathroom. This would be my room, and I would tackle Diana's as and when I needed to. I went to draw the curtains, standing for a moment to take in the lavender dusk and the sound of the sea that would lull me to sleep tonight. Sleep now was all I wanted, so I pulled my pyjamas out of my suitcase, brushed my teeth and, after a quick check downstairs that everything was secure, I slipped into the cosy bed and read my book until I dropped off.

Having gone to sleep so early the night before, I woke early as well. I was still tired, but less low than I had been. I probably needed some breakfast to perk me up. I dressed quickly and went downstairs to the kitchen, where the morning light flooding in through the windows lifted my spirits immediately. I made some instant coffee – black again, of course, and then checked the freezer, where I discovered half a loaf of bread. I managed to prise off a couple of slices, which I put in the toaster, and after eating these liberally spread with butter and jam, felt significantly better. After washing up and clearing anything out of the fridge that had gone mouldy or rancid – thankfully there wasn't much in there – I spent twenty minutes on a shopping app arranging for a delivery of food that afternoon. I knew I should walk down to the village and use the shop there, but I wasn't ready yet to go out into the world; the need to get my immediate circumstances sorted out overwhelmed everything. I had to prove to myself I was coping before I went and tried to prove it to anyone else.

Next, I went to look at the rest of my inheritance, the tearooms. I had only been in briefly on previous visits, when Diana had left it in someone else's charge while we spent time together. I entered it now through the door in the house's kitchen, finding myself in near darkness, the daylight spilling through the doorway not reaching far. I had left my phone upstairs, switched off, not wanting to hear from anyone, so I had no torch and blinked for a minute or two to accustom my eyes to the gloom. When I was more comfortable, I stepped inside and groped around the walls for a switch. A few minutes later, I had turned on the lights and the small, clean kitchen stood quietly before me.

'I'll have to check this fridge too,' I said. My voice sounded loud and awkward, but it also normalised things and made me feel less like I was in some creepy, apocalyptic film. 'Probably also full of yucky milk,' I said boldly. 'But I'll sort that out later.'

I walked through to the door that led to the main part of the building and let myself in. Light seeped around the edges of the drawn blinds, and I could see well enough to get to the windows and raise them all although, of course, I left the sign on the door saying 'closed'. The white painted chairs were all upside down on the tables and I took one down and sat on it, gazing around at my new empire. It was as sweet and charming a seaside tearoom as anyone could imagine with its old, dark wood beams, shabby chic painted chairs and tables, uneven quarry-tiled floor and white-washed walls. Vintage crockery and painted sea scenes hung from the walls and on the counter stood baskets and cake stands – empty now, of course. Everything was, as in the house, spotlessly clean, and I knew that Diana had been proud of the stars and certificates she regularly acquired from various organisations ranging from the Food Standards Agency to popular travel websites. But however well looked after the tearoom was, it could do with an overhaul. Nothing drastic, but smartening it up was crucial if I was going to take it on and make it mine. My breath quickened as I started to absorb the implications of accepting the inheritance. I might have spiralled into panic, had I not heard a tapping on the glass door. I jumped, startled, and was about to call out that the tearooms were closed, when I saw who the visitor was and hurried to unlock the door.

'Tessa,' I said. 'Good to see you. Come in, please.'

'Are you all right?' she asked, taking down another chair to join me at the table. 'I didn't think we'd be opening up again so soon.'

'We're not.' I saw her face fall. 'I'm so sorry. I can't tell you when – or if – that might happen.'

'You might not open it again at all?' she said, her fingers clenching around the edge of the table. 'Are you going to sell?'

'I-I don't know,' I admitted, wishing I could conjure up the optimism I had felt at Peter Masterson's office the day before. 'I'm so daunted by it all. The plan is to open up, but...'

I trailed off miserably. I knew I was depriving her of her income and I felt terrible. But what had I been thinking: me, running a tearoom. I looked again at her worried face and rallied.

'Look, Diana had insurance set up which means I can pay business expenses – including your salary – for the next three months, whether or not I reopen. I promise I'll make a decision as soon as I can, but you won't be left out of pocket.'

She smiled, relief suffusing her expression.

'Thank you, that helps. I didn't want to ask, it seems so awful, with Diana gone...'

She trailed off and started to cry softly.

'No, it's not awful,' I said firmly, trying to stop my own tears, so ready these days. 'You have to think of yourself and your family.'

'Yes. My little boy, Noah, he's only just three and Caleb and I share our time to look after him. Caleb's setting up his own business, so it's tight at the moment.'

'What's he doing?' I asked. 'I think that last time I was down he was working in Dorchester.'

'That's right,' she said. 'He was working for an agency as a contractor, but he was fed up with it. We managed to scrape together enough money to buy the old bakery in the village. It was pretty cheap because they figured it would go to a developer, who would rip out all the old fixtures and redevelop it, but we're getting it working again instead.'

'That's amazing,' I said.

'I love watching him doing it all,' she replied, smiling. 'He's like some sort of bread whisperer, so patient with it, nursing it into shape, waiting for it to grow and then proud when it comes out well. His sourdough is to die for.'

'You make him sound like a very good father to that bread,' I joked.

'That's exactly what he is,' she said. 'And he's a lovely daddy to Noah as well. I'm a lucky woman.'

I pushed away an image that had taken up comfortable residence in my head for a couple of years, but had to be firmly evicted now: an image of Matt with our child.

'You are,' I said. 'And maybe I could talk to him about supplying bread for sandwiches and rolls for The Coastal Kettle, if we get up and running again?'

Tessa's face lit up.

'Would you?'

'Of course, but I can't say when it would be.'

'I understand. I hope you manage to open it again. It's always been such a happy place, and full of customers. I'm sure you could make it work.'

I pulled a face.

'At the moment I don't know one end of a jam tart from the other, but thank you.'

'Diana didn't do all the baking for it. I helped, too, and she had other local suppliers. Mind you, her scones sold out every day and her lemon slices will be sorely missed.'

This conversation was edging towards my being persuaded into moving faster than I felt comfortable with. I stood up.

'I promise I'll let you know as soon as possible.'

Tessa, taking the hint, also rose.

'Of course. Well, see you soon then.'

After she had left, I pulled all the blinds down again and retreated to the house. I went to look through Diana's desk, hoping to find her account books or other paperwork relating to the house or business. The desk was in a small office room behind the front door, which had probably been a boot room originally. Now, it featured a stylish mid-century bureau, on which sat Diana's laptop. The cubbies behind were stacked with letters, notebooks and stationery. A small filing cabinet stood to one side, a printer on top, and there was a low cupboard underneath the window. I started with the bureau, as I thought her most recent or relevant information might be there.

The letters were organised into sections that pertained to the house, the tearoom and her ocean conservation involvement, with a couple of more personal correspondences, including a card from Mum sent only a couple of weeks ago, and my wedding invitation. An older-looking envelope – slightly yellow and foxed, with worn edges and nothing written on the front – contained a photograph I had never seen before. I took it out and studied it curiously. It was unmistakably Diana, as a very young woman of maybe eighteen or twenty. She was standing in front of a huge house, holding a very small baby. I turned it over, but there was nothing written on the back to say where she was or who the baby might be. I studied the picture again. Diana was wearing a loose cardigan with black, red and yellow geometric patterns, leggings and ankle-length boots with turned-over tops. Her hair, which I had only ever seen short and stylish, was a fluffy, permed cloud. The photo screamed the nineteen eighties. I didn't know whose the baby was or where the house was, and didn't give it much thought. I was much too taken with the authentic vintage fashion of a few years before my birth, and wondered if any of it might be stashed away in the house. Maybe I should have a look.

I put the photo back in the envelope and tucked it into my back pocket, to look at again later, then tried the drawers, where I found a file containing the teahouse's recent accounts. This was more like it. I took the file to the sitting room, looking forward to combing through it. I could come back for the laptop if I needed to, but something told me that Diana would have printed everything out, anyway.

Settling into the pink and white striped chair, I started inspecting the paperwork and was soon engrossed. Despite being employed by Matt's parents as the office dogsbody, and paid accordingly, I had taken on their messy accounts and billing and sorted them out completely. Matt's father insisted on writing everything out by hand in ledgers, which had become hopelessly muddled over the years, but I had enjoyed unravelling them and producing neat rows of figures that were correct to the penny and saved them from a nasty run in with the taxman. I may have had no formal training or qualifications, but I understood and enjoyed accounting, finding the puzzles satisfying to solve and the work absorbing.

None of this had resulted in a pay hike, and I was still referred to as 'Belle, who helps out around the office', but I had enjoyed learning and self-teaching a great deal, and had been in such a happy bubble with Matt, sure of our future, that I hadn't ever challenged his parents. Their pride would never have allowed them to admit that I had saved their skins, and was brighter than either of them when it came to business, and I'm sure they would have been surprised if they had seen me scouring my contract so closely. Sadly, I had to imagine rather than enjoy in person the looks on their faces when they received my email reminding them that my contract stated that I should receive *two* months' salary in lieu of notice, rather than the one Celia had so condescendingly offered me. A cheque for the full amount arrived at my parents' house, the address I had given, a day later, with no accompanying note. The parking ticket mentality again, I supposed, and they probably thought it was a cheap price to get me out of Matt's life forever.

I was pleased but unsurprised to find that Diana's books were kept as immaculately as her house and tearooms. There wasn't a teabag unaccounted for, and Tessa had been right when she had said that The Coastal Kettle was popular: the figures showed a thriving business. This at once encouraged and further frightened me. On the one hand, I could step into a flawlessly run business without having to make any changes; on the other, I could easily bring the whole thing crashing to the ground with my inexperience and ineptitude. I might be able to make the numbers work, but it was an entirely different matter as to whether I could do the same thing for the lemon slices. But the choice was stark: I could change my mind, hand the keys back to the lawyer and return to Mum and Dad until the money from the sale of the house and business came through, or I could do what that spark of excitement had told me I could. Grab this opportunity with both hands and make it work.

I closed the folder and put it on the coffee table. There was another idea that had been knocking at my brain, and I wanted to walk it through to try to decide if it could work. I went from room to room of the ground floor, paying particular attention to those that were currently unused, then did the same upstairs. My unofficial survey confirmed it: the layout and size of the large house were perfect for running a B&B. I could put a second sitting room downstairs as well as a breakfast room and there were four large bedrooms besides my own. One of these already had an en suite bathroom, two were right next door to the main bathroom and there was plenty of room in the fourth to add a small shower room and bathroom. I would need to speak to Gloria, to make sure she wouldn't mind me opening somewhere else for visitors to stay in Spindrift Bay, but I was imagining a different set-up from her guesthouse and anyway, hadn't she said that she wasn't planning to stay forever?

Buoyed up by this idea, and more sure that staying was the right thing to do, I grabbed my own laptop and started making a rough budget for the potential renovations of both the tearooms and the house. I began with excitement, but that soon dampened as the figures stacked up. It wasn't only materials and labour I would need to pay for, but safety checks, food hygiene training, insurance, fireproofing and even planning permission. The technicolour image I had allowed to form in my mind of not only one but two prosperous businesses, faded into grey. Any money left in the bank after inheritance tax would never be enough to cover it all.

The doorbell stirred me from my ruminations, and I closed the laptop sadly, only cheering up slightly when I saw it was my shopping that had arrived. I received the bags gratefully and went to unpack and make myself something to eat. I was sliding a cheese omelette out of the pan when my phone rang: my friend Lottie.

'Hello! Good to hear from you!'

'Hi, Belle, how's it going down by the sea?'

I told her about everything that had happened since we had last spoken, and how I couldn't see a way to make the changes I'd had in mind, other than with a loan, which I wanted to avoid.

'I believe this was all meant to happen,' she said, her kind, familiar voice comforting me. 'I know you'll find a way through. But Belle, there's something else I need to tell you.'

My stomach dropped. I had been on the receiving end of so much bad news recently; I couldn't take any more.

'Not your mum?' I asked, hearing the tremble in my voice. Lottie's mum had heart problems and was often in and out of hospital.

'No, she's doing well at the moment. It's not that bad, nobody's ill.' She paused. 'Belle, it's Matt.'

'What about him? Is he okay?'

'Yes. Oh dear, I'm so sorry to be the one to tell you this, but I didn't want you to find out any other way. Matt's engaged.'

'*Engaged?* As in "engaged to be married"?'

'Yes.'

I pushed away the omelette untouched, my stomach rolling with nausea.

'Who to?'

'Somebody called Jessica.'

I took a deep, ragged breath. Jessica was one of the architects who worked with Matt's family company regularly. She had always been friendly, if not exactly warm, and I had never picked up on any kind of vibe between her and Matt that worried me.

'Belle? Are you all right?'

With a monumental effort, I managed to speak, my words staccato.

'Yup. I'm fine. Sounds crazy. Hope they're happy. Thanks for telling me – it was better that it came from you.' I forced a note of careless cheer into my voice, knowing perfectly well that Lottie wouldn't be fooled, but also that she would be kind enough to let me have my little deception. 'Anyway, better go, my dinner's getting cold and I was thinking of going to the pub quiz this evening to meet some of the locals. Thank you again for telling me.'

After a few more words, we hung up. I scraped the omelette into the garbage, threw a couple of slices of bread into the toaster and opened a bottle of wine. The last vestiges of optimism I had about my new life ebbed away, and even the evocative evening calls of the seabirds couldn't ease the bleakness that suffused my soul.

SIX

The next morning, I didn't feel much better and had a dull hangover to add to my woes. I'm not a big drinker, and only had a couple of glasses, but I could feel the effects. I made myself a large, strong coffee and mixed some porridge ready to cook on the stove; the one thing this kitchen lacked was a microwave. If I was going to stay, I would need to get one. I wandered out into the small garden with my drink and gazed at that spectacular view. It was early, and the sky was a soothing streak of pale pink and blue over the calm sea. I wriggled my bare toes in the cool grass and shut my eyes for a moment to listen to the waves. They lulled me into an almost meditative state, and the grief and anxiety that had been tussling for attention in my head stepped back for a moment. They were replaced by drifting thoughts of the words of the women in my life who, I knew, only had my best interests at heart. Diana, who had left me an inheritance that was not only generous but was intended to change my life. Mum, who wanted me to value my freedom and prove what I was capable of. Lottie, a steadfast friend who believed in me. Gloria, who I had only met recently but who had shown me a robust approach to life and its whims. *What would they do?* I opened my eyes to see a new, golden hue in the sky. Or, maybe, *what would they want me to do?* That was easy: they had all urged me to give running the tearooms a go and would want me to dig deep to find the determination I needed, not let frantic, panicky feelings win the day, when they would surely pass.

I drained my cup and wandered back inside to make the porridge. As I stirred it, the memory of the money I would need resurfaced to crush the fragile feelings of hope that had started to bloom. I gazed into the milky depths of the saucepan. *Come on, Belle. You'll have to do things as they are for now and worry about changes later.* This gave some relief, and as I sat down to eat, my mind felt clearer. I picked up the supermarket magazine that had come with yesterday's shopping and started idly flicking through it. That was when the idea came dancing into my head, like a joyful burst of sunshine: *what about the engagement ring?* My heart picked up pace as I tried to keep eating calmly, despite my whole body tingling with excitement. When Matt had called off our wedding, he had told me magnanimously that I could keep the ring. I had barely taken it in at the time, and it was only later, when he had left, that I had seen it sparkling on my finger, releasing a new torrent of crying. *But what had I done with it then?* Having tried so hard to force the memories of that time out of my head, I now had to bring them back. He had left the house and I had gone back to the sitting room and curled up on the sofa. Yes, then I had noticed the ring. I'd ripped it off my finger and stuffed it into my pocket. After that, I hadn't seen it again. *Was it still there?* I rushed upstairs and hunted for my jeans. Nothing. *Did I leave them at Mum and Dad's?* My jangled brain couldn't think straight. I sat back on my heels and took some breaths. No, I wouldn't have left them behind, they were my favourites: well-worn and soft. Then I remembered, and laughed at myself. I'd put a wash on last night; they were in that. Back downstairs I ran, to pull the damp clothes out of the machine. I had meant to hang them up but forgotten all about it. Yes, here they were! I pushed my hand into both front pockets, groping around in excited anticipation. But they were empty. The back pockets were the same. *Had it gone down the side of the sofa?* No, I was sure that I had put it in my pocket. *Maybe it had fallen out into the washing machine?* I pulled everything out and shook the items, then felt about in the drum and around the rubber seal: nothing. Energised by my mission, I opened my laptop and googled the problem. Instantly, a flurry of advice appeared, with the main thrust being that I should check the filter. I found a little door on the front of the machine, arranged some tea towels on the floor to soak up any spills, and prised it open. Carefully, I extracted the filter and there, caught up in some soggy fluff and rubbing shoulders with a penny, glinted the fabulous diamond.

I sat there, amongst the sodden debris of washing and tea towels, and looked at the ring as it sat on the palm of my hand. It was beautiful. A flurry of feelings collided inside me. I was elated that I had found it, but it also brought all the memories of Matt flooding back. I had worn that ring for nearly a year and loved him for every single day of it. But no tears came – I was tired and empty. I put it carefully in an envelope and tucked it at the back of one of the kitchen drawers, then opened my laptop and put in a search: 'Matthew Henshaw Jessica Jones engagement'. I had expected the first result, after I had scrolled past various TV programmes with characters of the same names, to be the announcement in *The Times*, but this didn't appear. What I did get was much worse: an entire website dedicated to their wedding, complete with soppy professional photos of them gazing lovingly at each other and a gift list full of ludicrous items that surely could only have been added by Jessica or by Matt's mother. When had he ever shown interest in electric salt and pepper mills or a small grains colander? As I trawled through the site, my anger and despair grew exponentially, but I couldn't stop. I clicked on a tab called 'Our Story', wondering what on earth I was going to find there. Maybe: "Jess and Matt had been together for – ooh – all of five minutes before deciding on this ridiculous wedding. Matt's previous fiancée, Belle, was swiftly despatched so that Jesski and Matt-Matt (their cute pet names for one another) could proceed with this meaningless insanity."

But no. Instead of finding something I could get my teeth into, the knife was only twisted deeper as I looked at photos of them misty-eyed in the Seychelles. So much for Matt going away for a while to heal, as Celia, his mother, had claimed. They had gone away on *our honeymoon*, and that was where Matt proposed to her. A series of soft-focus shots showed him down on one knee, her pressing her hand to her chest in wonderment and them entwined in each other, watching the sort of glorious sunset that I had been looking forward to. The only minute compensation was that the ring he had given her was significantly smaller than mine.

My breakfast porridge was threatening to make a reappearance, and I closed down the browser and shut my laptop. My feelings were no longer fuzzy and mixed but crystal clear. And right now, there was only one: rage. Any noble thoughts I might have once had of returning the ring were banished. No. I would take it to a jeweller, today, have it valued and then sell the damn thing. I hoped that it wouldn't turn out to be as fake as his feelings for me had been.

An hour later, I was standing outside a double-fronted shop in Dorchester, with a sign in the window announcing themselves as diamond experts. A quick internet search convinced me that they were a reputable and long-standing family business, so I pushed open the door and went inside. There was a reverent sense of hush inside the shop that settled over me like a velvet mantle as I gently closed the door and stepped onto the thick, purple carpet. The shop was lined on three sides with cases of not only jewellery but also porcelain figures and silver christening gifts. I was about to go and look at a particularly glamorous emerald necklace, when a door opened silently at the back of the shop and a small, neat figure glided out.

'Good morning,' the man intoned softly.

'Hello,' I said, then lowered my voice, which had sounded jarringly loud in the cushioned quiet. 'Hello. I was wondering if you could value a ring for me, please.'

'Certainly. Do you have it with you?'

'Yes.'

I hurried over and handed it to him.

'Do you wish to have it valued for insurance purposes?'

'No. I, er, I want to sell it.'

'I see.'

'Does that... matter?' I asked timidly.

'We charge for insurance valuations, for the certificate and so on,' he said, putting a small magnifying lens into his eye socket and inspecting the ring. 'But not if you plan to sell with us.'

I stayed silent as he looked at the ring from every angle, then weighed it. After a minute or two, he removed the lens and went over to a computer, where he tapped away. I had the strange sensation that I was in a headteacher's office, waiting to discover my punishment for breaking a school rule. I would be mortified if the ring turned out to be worthless. Eventually, he finished his investigations and came back over to me.

'Everything all right?' I couldn't help asking.

He gave me a small smile, and I saw a twinkle in his eye that was reassuring. Maybe he was used to jilted brides bringing in their rings to flog.

'Very much so. I had to run some checks, but they were clear. You have a very valuable ring, and I would be pleased to buy it from you.'

'Great!' *I think.* I glanced at the ring and suddenly wanted to snatch it back from him. I took a breath. 'How much?'

'The stone is exceptionally fine, and I would be glad to give you seven thousand pounds.'

Seven thousand pounds! I only just managed to keep my cool and refrain from leaping across the counter and hugging him, any remaining sentimental ties to the ring forgotten. Instead, those wonderful women friends of mine flashed through my head, and I managed a small frown.

'Hmm. I was hoping for a little more. It is, as you say, exceptionally fine.'

And not glass, as I had half expected.

He screwed the magnifier back into his eye and inspected it again.

'Very well. I can offer eight, but that will be my final offer.'

I dropped all pretence at froideur and beamed at him.

'That would be amazing. Thank you.'

With the transaction complete, I floated over the carpet and out of the door, then went to get a celebratory coffee. As I sat in the window seat of the café, watching people hurry past, I checked the receipt again and looked at the new, gigantic balance on my banking app. If the jeweller had given me *eight thousand pounds*, then, presumably, it would have cost a lot more to buy. I had never imagined that it was worth so much. Well, I'd never given the value much consideration; I was just happy to be engaged. Where on earth had Matt got that sort of money? From his parents, maybe? I pondered for a while on that thought, surprised that Celia hadn't tipped up on my doorstep demanding the ring back. Had I been wrong to sell it? I remembered the proposal and the excited wedding preparations, followed by the sudden cutting off of all my dreams and plans. I thought about the way Matt's parents had treated me. I brought to mind, still painfully, the photos of him on our honeymoon with Jessica. No, I had not been wrong. It was my ring to do with as I wished, and the proceeds were going to an excellent cause. I finished my coffee and decided that my next stop would be a bookshop. If this new start was to have any hope of a bright future, I was going to have to learn to bake.

Back at home, I unpacked my purchases. I had skimmed through the recipe book after buying it and chosen a couple of things that sounded fairly simple and familiar: millionaire's shortbread and butterfly cakes. I also found the recipe for Diana's lemon slices in my emails, that Tessa had sent me, and bought the ingredients for all three bakes. I was excited. I hadn't baked since getting my Brownies badge twenty-five years ago, and the thought of producing some delicious treats that people would want to buy and eat was very enticing. I started with the cakes. I put on some music and began carefully weighing and mixing. Of course, the kitchen had every possible baking tool I could need, and I was soon spooning mixture into paper cases neatly laid out in the holes of a tin, ready to go in the oven.

'Nice job,' I said as I slid the tin on to the top shelf. 'Now, they take about fifteen minutes, so I can start on the shortbread in the meantime.'

Again, I followed the recipe carefully and was soon pressing the mixture firmly into a rectangular tin. I popped it in the oven, very pleased with myself. Mary Berry, eat your heart out! I sang along to the music as I read the instructions for my final bake. This, too, started with shortbread, which I was an old hand at now. The tray joined the others in the oven and I was looking at how to make the toppings when the fairy cake timer went off. I grabbed an oven glove and took them out. They were an even golden colour, but they had baked into pointy little mountains of cakes, rather than having smooth, even tops.

'Now, why have you done that?' I asked them, then shrugged. 'Never mind, you can cool off and then I'll make some wings out of you. It probably won't even notice.'

The lemon mixture looked ridiculously easy, so I attacked that next. All I had to do was zest and juice a few lemons, then mix that up with some flour, sugar and eggs. How long could it take? Fifteen minutes later, my hands drenched in lemon juice and my thumb sore where I had caught it with the grater, I was less sanguine. But at least I had what I needed. At that moment, the first shortbread alarm went off, so I quickly washed my hands and went to take it out. The moment I touched the pan I realised my mistake: I had forgotten oven gloves. I dropped it on the floor and rushed to the sink to run cold water over my rapidly reddening skin, tears of pain and humiliation in my eyes. How could I have been so stupid as to forget to use oven gloves? My newfound enthusiasm for baking was quickly waning as I carefully bandaged my hand – Diana had kept a full first aid kit, although she probably never needed it – and took some painkillers. I tentatively picked up the pan, cool now, and put it on the side. The shortbread, by some miracle, was largely unaffected by being dropped; even if it was a bit broken, it would still do for my first efforts. Determined not to be demoralised, I decided to finish making the lemon topping and reached over for the bowl of juice and zest, but my bandaged hand was clumsy and I fumbled with the bowl before knocking the entire thing over.

'Noooooo!' I howled, scrabbling in vain to rescue some of the juice, which was now dripping off the worksurface and onto the floor. 'I don't believe this!'

I took big, gulping breaths, trying not to cry as I mopped up the mess with a kitchen towel. It was all very well having the money to get things going, but how on earth was I going to run a tearoom when I couldn't even complete one bake successfully?

I had more lemons, but I decided to work on the millionaire's shortbread for now. The thought of lemon juice seeping through my bandage on to my burnt skin was too wince-inducing to contemplate right now. To my own surprise, I made the caramel layer with little incident and was soon smoothing it over the shortbread. This was more like it! I popped it into the fridge, then opened some chocolate and put it in a pan to melt. As I stirred it, I smelt something worrying. Could it be burning? Oh no, I had forgotten all about the second pan of shortbread! Remembering this time to grab the oven gloves, I flung open the oven door and waved away billowing clouds of smoke to yank out the pan. I threw it onto the stove and gazed at it in despair. What should have been golden shortbread was a charred, inedible lump. I sighed deeply, threw the oven gloves on the table and returned to my chocolate. I peered into the pan and poked the molten mass with a wooden spoon. It didn't look right. I had expected to find a glossy brown pool, ready for pouring, but instead the saucepan contained a lumpy, grainy concoction that even I knew didn't belong atop a millionaire's shortbread. I switched off the heat and prodded it with the spoon again. What had gone wrong? Maybe I should cool it and try again? I pushed the saucepan to the back, wearier by the moment.

'Come on, Belle,' I said out loud. 'You can't let this get you down. What about those butterfly cakes? At least they're not burnt.'

I returned to the recipe book.

'Cut out the centre of each cake at a forty-five-degree angle. Right.'

I contemplated my pointy cakes.

'Shouldn't be too hard.'

Five minutes later, I had sliced off the mountains and had a set of crumby-looking, decapitated cakes in front of me. I refused to be discouraged.

'Place a small amount of jam in the middle of each cavity,' I read.

This I did without incident.

'Now, dollop or pipe some freshly whipped cream over the jam.'

There was clearly no point in even getting a piping bag out, so I whipped the cream until my arm got tired, then used a spoon to add some to each cake.

'Good. What next?' I studied the book. 'Cut the loose pieces of cake in half to resemble butterfly wings.'

I studied the loose pieces of cake. They were never going to resemble butterfly wings, however extensive the surgery, so I followed the process as described and decided not to worry too much about the product. After all, surely the taste was the most important thing? I chopped each piece in half and stuck two in the cream of each cake, then stood back to admire my efforts. They were, perhaps, a touch naïve, but they were cakes. Maybe a shake of icing sugar would give them a more professional finish? I found Diana's sifter, half-full, and shook it over the cakes, upon which the lid promptly fell off, dislodging half the wings and dumping a pile of sugar over the rest.

The situation was now beyond tears or self-recrimination.

Calmly, I went to the fridge, took out the half-full bottle of wine, found a glass and sat down at the table. I filled the glass to the brim, then took a large swig as I gazed at the destruction before me: the burnt shortbread, ruined chocolate, squashed and heavily powdered cakes, lemon juice congealing on the cupboard doors where I'd missed it. What the hell was I going to do?

I might have sat there forever if a tap hadn't come at the outside door. I looked up, hoping it might be Tessa or Gloria: someone who would join me in a glass of wine and make me see the funny side of the culinary catastrophe. No such luck. It was Tessa's mother, Beverly, her neat grey bob gleaming in the afternoon sunshine and a look in her eye like a hungry wolf who has spotted dinner. I put down my wine glass and unglued my reluctant bottom from the chair, to open the door.

'Hel-*lo*, Belle,' she said chirpily, taking a step forward.

I stood my ground.

'Hello, Beverly. What can I do for you?'

She peered over my shoulder, making no effort to conceal her nosiness.

'Just a neighbourly visit, I wanted to personally welcome you to Spindrift Bay. Seeing as you're sitting at the table and not busy, I'd love a cuppa and a chat to get to know you.'

She held up a small basket, lined with gingham fabric. I could see homemade biscotti – perfect, of course – and various sachets of tea.

'Coals to Newcastle for the owner of a tearoom, I'm afraid.' She gave a little titter. 'But one does what one can to be neighbourly.'

I could hardly stand there blocking the door any longer, so I stepped back.

'It's very kind of you. Please, come in.'

'Been baking?' she said, turning off my music, then picking up the kettle and filling it at the tap. 'Oh dear!' The little laugh again.

'I'm not sure you've got the knack, have you?' She took two mugs out of the cupboard, letting me know that she was perfectly at home in Diana's – *my* – house. She went to put them down, then looked pointedly at the wine glass. 'Oh, sorry, looks like you already have something. It's a bit early for me...' Little laugh. 'I can make you tea if you think it's a good idea?'

'I'm okay, thanks,' I said more breezily than I felt. I sat down again and pushed a few things aside to make space for her. I was not usually in the habit of being such a graceless hostess, but Beverly took the biscuit. Well, she brought the biscuits, but anyway. She didn't say anything else, just made her tea, then joined me at the table, brushing it off unnecessarily before setting down the biscotti, which she had put on one of Diana's plates. I took one and bit into it. It was depressingly delicious.

'So, you're taking on the tearoom, then?' she asked. 'I can see that you've started baking. How's it going?'

She looked at me with far more fake sympathy than she had been able to manufacture at Diana's funeral.

'It was a disaster,' I said bluntly. 'As you can see.' I drank some wine and took another biscotti. 'But I'll figure it out.'

'Will you?' A concerned tilt of the head. 'Would you like some help? I would have loved to help Diana and Tessa with the tearoom, but they were far too competent to need me, apparently.'

Diana had never mentioned Beverly to me, but I wasn't surprised to hear that she had rejected her help. She was exactly the type of woman who would immediately try to take over everything, and while her offer of help seemed on the surface to be kindness itself, I doubted her motives.

'I'll keep trying, thank you,' I said. 'I'm sure I'll learn. Most of the things that went wrong today were down to inexperience, bad luck and taking on too much in one go. I can already see what I need to do differently next time.'

The wine was giving me confidence, but as the words came out, I found myself believing them. Yes! What I needed to do was try again, but stick to one of the recipes, and think ahead about what had gone wrong. Most of it was easily fixed.

'Oh.' Beverly's mouth tightened. 'I'm not sure it's as easy as that. You can't open a tearoom with burnt shortbread and cakes drowned in icing sugar, you know.'

'Yes, I know,' I said. I stood up. 'I've got plenty of work to do. No time like the present!'

I started clearing away the mess, energised by my new plan as well as by the urge for Beverly to leave. She didn't take the hint and carried on talking as I noisily scrubbed pans and scraped things into the garbage.

'Any more ideas on why the Talbots were at the funeral?' she asked loudly. 'I was wondering if maybe the tearoom belonged to them, and Diana was leasing it. I suppose not, if she left it to you.'

'Nope, it's all mine,' I replied cheerfully. 'And I've still got no idea why they shouldn't have been there.'

'Well, *I* think it's very odd,' she continued. 'But I suppose it's good for those two young men to mix with the village. Although Luke seems to mix with it more than he does with his own people, living down here and having the surgery. I've always found it most strange. What's going to happen when he inherits?'

I turned off the tap.

'I'm sorry, but I haven't got a clue. I don't know these people.'

'Mmm. I thought Diana might have said something.'

'No.'

My terse reply temporarily silenced her. I started drying the clean things and she looked pointedly at the disordered side. We both spotted the photograph of Diana in front of the house within a split second of each other. At least I had remembered to take *that* out of my jeans before I put the wash on, but I didn't want Beverly nosing at it. I gave a sharp intake of breath and made a move to grab it, but she was too quick for me.

'What's *this*? Oh! It's Diana. Gosh, she's very young. Who's the baby, and what's she doing up at Spindrift House?'

Curiosity overcame irritation.

'Is that where she is?'

'Yes – haven't you ever been there?' I shook my head. 'It must be at about the time the family moved in – a few years before I came to the village. Well, I never. I'll have to ask Luke about it next time I see him. You don't mind if I take a snap, do you?'

She went to get her phone out of her bag, putting the photo down. I snatched it up.

'I'd rather you didn't.'

'Oh come, come,' she said irritably, holding out her hand for it. 'It's only a photo. Luke and Diana were very good friends, so I'm sure he'd be interested to know that she had been in the area – at his family's house – all those years before he met her.'

'Sorry,' I said, feeling childishly irrational but also protective of Diana's picture. I tucked the photo under a recipe book on the table, then stood quietly, giving Beverly little choice but to thrust her phone back into her bag.

'I suppose I'll be on my way, then. I'll stop by again, in case you change your mind about having my help with the tearoom, or sharing that photo. I'll mention the tearoom to Tessa, and the photo to Luke, when I see them. Bye then.'

Fuming at her interference, I mustered enough manners to wave her off. I don't know *why* I didn't want her mentioning the photo to Luke – after all, she was probably right about him being interested – but it felt like she was forcing my hand in some way. Huffing a bit, I once more turned my attention to baking, in the hope of working away my annoyance. I decided to try the lemon slices again as, while the zesting and juicing had been pretty miserable, nothing too difficult had gone wrong. Fixing the grainy chocolate or the pointy fairy cakes was going to take some research. I flicked the radio back on, pushed Beverly to the back of my mind, and got to work.

SEVEN

The second batch of lemon bars I made on the day of Beverly's visit turned out perfectly, and spurred me on to try some other bakes. Next, I discovered why chocolate splits when you melt it and carefully used a *bain-marie* to create a thick topping for the rest of the millionaire's shortbread, which had survived. The end result was crumbly from when I had dropped the pan, but I shared it with Gloria one day when she came over, and she declared it delicious.

When the things I had ordered to spruce up the tearooms arrived, Tessa turned out to be completely invaluable, and she often brought her little boy, Noah, who hoovered up my fairy cakes, which I was still struggling to make with flat tops, no matter how much I tinkered with the temperature of the oven.

'They're yummy,' he said, sampling my latest effort, which contained little chunks of fudge.

'If you were my only customer, I'd be winning,' I said, grinning. 'Paying clientele might be a little more fussy.'

'Less than you'd think,' said Tessa, climbing down from a chair to inspect her painting efforts. 'People like a tearoom like this to be homely; as long as the prices are what they expect and things taste delicious, they'll embrace a bit of wonkiness.'

'They might have to! That paint looks fab, by the way; you were right about the colour.'

I had been going to play it safe and paint the walls over white again, but Tessa had persuaded me to choose a softer ivory, which paired beautifully with the pale blue accents we were using to enhance the coastal décor. We didn't want to overhaul the tearooms completely, more freshen them up, while keeping the feel that Diana had gone for.

'I'm glad,' she replied. 'There was a danger of it looking too yellow, but it works.'

'I'm going to start sanding down the chairs,' I said. 'Then we can get those painted, too. Want to help, Noah?'

He agreed enthusiastically, so I set him up with a little face mask and a piece of sandpaper, which he rubbed determinedly over the seats of one of the chairs.

The three of us worked happily in this way for days, mostly on our own as we scrubbed, sanded and painted. I drew the line at sewing, but commissioned some pretty, new curtains, as well as seat pads to tie to the chairs. I also discovered that I was surprisingly handy with a hammer. I had learnt from my baking mistakes, and checked out plenty of online advice before hanging some of Diana's pictures and a few new ones I had bought locally. I was pleased with my new gadget that showed me where electrical wires ran through the walls before I banged a nail straight through them.

'I like that one,' said Tessa, nodding at a large black and white photo of the village from around a hundred years ago. 'Spindrift Bay hasn't changed much, has it?'

'Barely at all,' I replied, carefully straightening it. 'That's what I loved about this photo: you can see exactly what everything was. The post office is still a post office, and this blacksmith's is the vet's surgery, isn't it? Nice that it's still something to do with animals.'

As I spoke, an image of the handsome village vet at Diana's funeral, calmly collecting my tear-soaked tissues, came to mind, and I smiled to myself.

'Have you seen Luke Talbot since the funeral?' asked Tessa, as if she had read my mind.

I shook my head and my cheeks became warm.

'He's such a great guy,' continued Tessa. 'My mum's cat was poorly the other night, and he came over to the house to check her over. Nothing's ever too much trouble for him when it comes to animals and he cares about the owners, too.'

'I wouldn't mind having a cat,' I said. 'I'm not lonely, exactly, but I'd like another heart beating under my roof.'

'You should ask Luke to keep a look out for you,' she said. 'He does occasionally rehome strays.'

A tap on the door saved me from answering. Seeing that it was Caleb, Tessa's husband, I went to open up.

'Hello,' he said, with his shy smile. 'I've come for Noah – but I also brought you some of my latest batch of sourdough. I'm pleased with this one.'

Tessa climbed down from the stepladder and greeted Caleb with a kiss.

'Thank you, love, I'll go and cut some of this for lunch. Are you and Noah staying to eat?'

'If that's okay?' he replied. 'Then I'll take him home for what I call his nap, but he seems to think is "climbing on Daddy time".'

He scooped up the little boy, who screeched with delight and demanded to be turned upside down again and again, until I was dizzy watching him.

'You two have done wonders with this place,' said Caleb, eventually putting Noah upright. 'It was always nice, but you've breathed new life into it.'

I looked around. It was true. While the tearooms had been clean and well-kept, some of the décor had grown a little tired, and its fresh new look worked well.

'Thank you,' I said. 'It's been more fun than I anticipated. Tessa's great to work with and I hope Diana would approve of our changes.'

'I'm sure she would. Oh, let me help you with that, love.'

He jumped up and took a tray from Tessa, while she disappeared back into the kitchen. I pushed a couple of tables together, and soon we were all eating Caleb's bread with local butter and blue cheese and some strawberries I had bought from a stall on the side of the road, a common sight around here.

'This bread is amazing,' I said, taking another bite. 'How on earth do you get it so soft in the middle but with such a crunchy crust? And the flavour!'

'I'm glad you like it. I've tried so many different techniques, but I might have finally cracked it.'

'He's not exaggerating,' said Tessa, giving his hand a loving squeeze. 'This must be attempt two hundred and four! They've all been good, but I think this one does have a special something.'

'It's all to do with timing and the flour-to-water ratio,' said Caleb. 'There are a million different things to try.'

'Well, I think it's perfect,' I said. 'And I'd like you to supply the tearooms when we reopen. Could you?'

'Definitely,' he said, holding out his large hand for me to shake. 'And I might have to have some of your lemon slices for the bakery when it opens. I hope Diana isn't anywhere she can hear me, because the truth is they're even better than hers.'

'Do you think so?' I said, pleased. 'I had such an awful time at first with the baking, but I'm getting the hang of it. I did change her recipe slightly, which felt both sacrilegious and pretty daring, given my inexperience, but I think it's worked.'

'I *thought* they were different,' said Tessa, taking a bite. 'Have you added lime?'

'No, it's yuzu,' I said. 'The first time I tried it the flavour was far too strong and overpowering, but I think it's about right now, don't you?'

'Definitely,' said Tessa. 'And Diana would approve. She loved trying new recipes. She scandalised my mother one year by submitting scones with strawberry and rosemary jam, rather than plain strawberry, to the village fête.'

'Poor Beverly!' said Caleb, licking lemon curd off his fingers. 'She wanted Diana disqualified, and then she won!'

'So you see, you're the right person to have taken over The Coastal Kettle,' said Tessa. 'Although I do wish Diana was here. We could have had so much fun together.'

I sighed.

'I know. I was really looking forward to seeing her.'

My voice broke and I stared awkwardly at my plate, not wanting to upset Noah. Understanding, Caleb took his hand.

'Come on, son, time to go home.'

We said goodbye and I went to make some tea.

'I'm sorry you didn't get to see Diana again,' said Tessa. 'I'm grateful that I was with her right at the end.'

'I'm grateful for that too,' I replied. 'I'm sure it was a comfort to her.'

A small silence fell between us, until Tessa broke it, her words tumbling out quickly.

'Look, Belle, Diana said something to me before she died, and you should know about it. I have no idea what she meant, but maybe you do. She said: "He should know. Find the box." That was all. I asked her who 'he' was, but she didn't speak again.'

She started crying as she relived the trauma of Diana's final moments so, for a few minutes, I was more concerned with comforting her than with giving any thought to what she had said. But eventually her sobs subsided and she took some wispy breaths.

'Sorry, Belle, I'm okay. It was remembering, you know...'

'Of course. It must have been so shocking to find her like that. Please don't apologise for being upset.'

We both drank our tea and then Tessa said, 'Do you have any idea what Diana meant? About the box and someone needing to know something?'

'None at all,' I replied, frowning. 'I've known her my entire life, and my mother knew her long before I was born, and I've never had wind of any sort of secret. The only thing I've wondered—'

I paused. My curiosity had been whetted, but I didn't want to gossip about Diana, and I couldn't forget that Tessa was Beverly's daughter.

'You can tell me,' said Tessa, then added, as if she had read my mind, 'I won't pass anything on to Mum. I love her, but I know she's much too interested in other people's lives. She said she'd tried to persuade you to let her get involved here.'

I bit my lip. Did Tessa mind that I had refused?

'It's fine,' she said, smiling. 'I like having something that she can't get in on, to be honest. She's too free with her advice and she can't stop herself being critical. Of everything. I've had to have some pretty strong words over Noah with her. Would you believe that she disapproved so strongly of the way I was weaning him that I found her about to give him some chocolate when he was four months old?'

Her face was a picture of horror, but I had to laugh as I replied.

'I know less than nothing about weaning babies – I'd probably have given him a curry!'

'And Mum knows nothing about twenty-first century weaning, but that didn't stop her knowing best,' she said, with a comical grimace. 'Anyway, all I want to say is that I promise not to pass anything you say on to her.'

'I know you won't,' I replied. 'And anyway, there's not anything to tell. I found a photo of Diana when she was very young... I didn't think much of it at the time, but I've been wondering ever since I saw it. She was standing by a huge house, holding a baby. Maybe she was a nanny?' Tessa bit her lip, her eyes clouding with anxiety. 'Your mum's already told you about the photo, hasn't she?'

She nodded.

'Yes. I didn't tell you because I didn't want you to think I'd been talking about you behind your back. It's none of my business and I said that to Mum.'

'What did she say?'

'She was annoyed, because she was hoping to gossip about it, or that you'd told me something. She was very cross that you wouldn't let her take her own picture of it, but I said it was your right.'

'Thank you. Do you mind me telling you now? Does it put you in a difficult position?'

'No,' said Tessa decisively. 'Like I said, I promise I won't pass anything on.'

'Thank you. I'll go and get it.'

I ran through the tearoom kitchen and into the house, where I found the photo and took it back to show her.

'Your mum said that's Spindrift House?'

'Yes, that's right, where the Talbots live. I didn't know Diana knew them, other than Luke, of course.'

I took the photo from her and studied it, looking more closely this time at the house behind Diana than at her.

'So Diana was in Spindrift Bay when she was young,' I said. 'I'll have to ask Mum if she knew; Diana was living in France when they met. Perhaps she was Luke's nanny? The photo looks about the right period.'

Tessa shrugged.

'Maybe. But if she was, she never said anything. She was friendly with Luke – he came in here a lot. I'm kind of surprised it wasn't mentioned.'

My brow creased as I turned my attention back to the face of the young woman in the photo. She had a small smile, but looked tired more than anything.

'Your mum said she was going to ask him, but maybe I'll try to get there first,' I said. 'Although it feels weird to go charging up to someone I've met once and start demanding details about Diana's past – and possibly his.'

Tessa giggled.

'Yes, I suppose it might seem odd. But it might be your best bet; you can hardly go knocking on the door of the manor house and asking Lord and Lady Talbot. I'd say go for it if they were more friendly, but they keep their distance from the village. That's why Mum was so surprised to see them at Diana's funeral.'

I pulled at my thumbnail with my teeth, a bad habit I had fallen into in childhood, and never managed to shake.

'Put like that, I get it too,' I replied. 'Although if she had worked for them forty odd years ago, then it would make sense. But wouldn't people in the village have known? There are plenty who were there then and are still here now.'

'I'm not sure they've been there that long,' replied Tessa. 'I might be wrong, but I've got a feeling they only moved in when the old baronet died.' She tapped the photo. 'It was probably around this time. So maybe Diana came with them as their nanny, but didn't stay long enough to get to know anyone in the village?'

'That sounds plausible. Well, look, I'm sure that there's not much of a mystery. I was going to see about continuing some of Diana's sea pollution work, anyway. She was so passionate about it, and as she was so generous to me in her will, I feel sort of honour bound to do something in return. Maybe I'll get to know Luke a little better and then I can ask him.'

Tessa grinned.

'Getting to know Luke better won't be too painful, either. He's lovely and a great vet – really kind, and gentle. If I wasn't madly in love with my husband, I could easily have my head turned in that direction.'

I snorted.

'Lovely he may be, but I've had enough of men to last me a life-time. Well, a few years at least. No, if I get to know him, it'll be all about ocean plastics, nothing else.'

'I believe you,' said Tessa teasingly, standing up and collecting her painting things together. 'Although thousands wouldn't.'

I started stacking our lunch things on to a tray.

'There is one thing I've always been curious about,' I said. 'Diana loved animals, didn't she?'

'Yes,' replied Tessa, stretching up to reach a part of the wall she had missed. 'All animals, not just sea creatures. That was some-thing else that she and Luke had in common. She used to help him at the surgery sometimes, when he'd taken in more waifs and strays than he could handle before he managed to rehome them. He's far too kind to turn any animal away.'

'Exactly. So, why didn't she have a pet of her own? It surprised me, but I asked her once and she was short with me.'

'It's a good question,' said Tessa. 'Diana didn't talk about it much. In fact, you're right, she was touchy with me, too, when I suggested she took in a cat that Luke was struggling to rehome. She said that she preferred animals in the wild and would be terrible at looking after a pet.'

'She'd be amazing!' I blurted out. 'She was the kindest and most conscientious person I know!'

'Right?' said Tessa. 'But she wouldn't have it.'

I took the lunch things back to the kitchen and washed them up, then went into the house to return the photo. I didn't want it getting lost or damaged during the refurbishments. I stared once more at the young woman in front of what I now knew was Spindrift House.

'What secrets were you hiding?' I said aloud. 'I'll do my best to find the box and let "him" know, whoever he is. I promise.'

EIGHT

After all our hard work in the tearooms I was too tired that evening to start hunting for mysterious boxes, but Diana's final words as recounted to me by Tessa lingered in my head. The following day, I had put aside the morning for a more difficult bake, but one I hoped might be popular, so I started on that and would make some time later to look for the box. By now, I had a good stock of ingredients in the house and of course Diana had every baking tool imaginable, but I had run out of coffee and I wanted the filling of my cream horns to be mocha and hazelnut flavoured. Not entirely sorry to be postponing the tricky bake, I stepped out into the warm spring morning and took a huge breath of the fresh, salty air. I was going to try to make my own puff pastry, which I knew would be difficult, but my confidence in the kitchen was growing as I produced more and more successful creations. Sometimes, especially when I was using recipes that she had written out, or annotated, I could feel Diana by my shoulder, gently guiding me. Even when I did make mistakes, I could usually figure out what had gone wrong and produce something better on my second attempt. The cream horns would be my first patisserie bake, the recipe taken from one of Diana's French cookbooks and translated using my phone.

I went to the small supermarket and bought the coffee, nodding hello to a couple of people I recognised, then started to head for home. As I walked past the post office, a photo amongst the advertising cards jostling for space in the window caught my eye, and I stopped. It was a picture of two tiny kittens, one jet black and the other a soft, grey tabby. Underneath was written:

CAN YOU GIVE US A HOME?

We are two friendly brothers who were left on the doorstep of the vet's surgery. We're happy and healthy and old enough to go to a real home now. We would like to stay together, so please adopt us both.

I took a photo of the ad with my phone and quickened my pace home. The baking could wait; I had a strong instinct that these kittens were meant for me. After all, it had been only yesterday that Tessa and I had been discussing it, and here they were. I tapped the number from the ad into my phone, then wrote a quick message:

> Hi, I saw the picture of the two kittens in the post office window, and I would love to adopt them. Thanks, Belle (The Coastal Kettle)

Now, I had to wait for an answer. Full of excitement at the thought of my new pets, I got started on the cream horns. I had looked up various tips for making puff pastry successfully, but it was going to be a long morning. I switched on the radio and got to work.

I had put the pastry into the freezer for the first of its several chillings, when my phone chimed. Quickly wiping my hands, I picked it up, to see a reply to my earlier message about the kittens. I opened it eagerly.

Hi Belle, great news about the kittens, I have reserved them for you. They're a very friendly pair, I'm sure you'll love them. We do have a policy of home checking all potential adopters. Would you mind if I stopped by? I could come today at lunchtime? Luke

For some reason, I hadn't thought that it would be him handling the adoptions personally, but it would be a good opportunity to break the ice with him, and maybe find out a little more about Diana and her connection to Spindrift House, if there was any. I replied, saying that I would be at home all morning, then tried to focus on my pastry, pushing away worrying thoughts that, after the home visit, perhaps I wouldn't be considered a suitable owner for the cats.

I had brushed the horns with glossy melted chocolate – I was quite the pro at this now – when there was a knock on the front door. I put them in the fridge and hurried to open the door. There was Luke, as handsome and smiley as I remembered him from the funeral.

'Hi,' I said, dusting awkwardly at my floury apron. 'Thanks for coming so soon. Er, come in.'

'Thanks.'

I led the way through to the kitchen, only now seeing it through fresh eyes. I had been so engrossed in my baking that I had barely noticed the mess I had created.

'Oh, gosh, sorry about this. I've been baking – a difficult recipe – and I didn't realise how awful it looked.'

Luke grinned.

'It doesn't look awful at all. It looks like it did most of the time when I visited Diana. I would have been sorry if it had been pristine.'

'Thank you. I was suddenly worried that you wouldn't let your cats go to someone with such a disastrous home. Oh, please, sit down. Coffee?'

'Yes please, I'd love a coffee.' As he went to take a chair, I saw the photo of Diana on the table, where I had left it after showing Tessa. Panic darted through me, and I practically threw myself over the table in order to scoop it up, gabbling all the time about what a terrible mess everything was. Luke didn't seem to notice my odd behaviour and continued chatting. 'You don't need to worry about this home check – I'm not looking at the house, how tidy it is or anything. I know you have plenty of space and a secure garden. We have a few questions that we run through with potential owners to make sure that you understand exactly what it means to take on cats.'

'Wonderful!' I said, a trifle too enthusiastically, shuffling together everything I had swept off the table into a presentable pile, the photo discreetly tucked away. Now it was hidden, I kicked myself for not just asking him about it, but the adrenaline was seeping from my veins and the moment had passed. I poured hot water into the cafetière. 'That bit I can do; we had cats at home.'

We chatted for a few minutes about the cats, until Luke said, 'You're perfect for them, and them for you. Is there any chance you'd be able to pick them up today? We're short on space at the surgery. I can lend you everything you'll need until you have a chance to get stuff yourself?'

'Of course! I can't wait to meet them! It will have to be later, though, if that's okay? I'm expecting a delivery this afternoon that I must be here for.'

'That's fine. I'll be at the surgery until at least six.'

'Thank you so much. Oh! Would you like to try a cream horn in celebration? It's my first attempt, so I'm warning you that they might be horrible. In fact, you'd be doing me a favour if you taste-test them.'

Jokingly, he sat up straight and saluted.

'At your service. I have form for this as a friend of Diana's, so you can trust me.'

I took the horns out of the fridge and filled a couple with the cream I had mixed up with chopped hazelnuts and coffee. We chatted as we ate them, mostly about marine conservation. I was beginning to find it genuinely interesting, rather than something I was investigating as a link to Diana, or because I wanted to find something to talk to Luke about. It crossed my mind to show him the photo then, but it was too awkward a non sequitur, so I left it for another time, hoping Beverly didn't beat me to it.

'Those were delicious,' declared Luke, pushing his plate away. 'Your customers will devour them.'

'They'd better not be too popular,' I said, pulling a face. 'They took hours to make. Maybe I'd better keep them as a "first Monday of the month special" or something.'

I waved him off, then went to clear up the disarray in the kitchen and wait for my delivery.

When the parcel finally turned up, I had a quick look. It contained samples of thirty unusual teas, and I was planning to choose three or four of them to offer in the tearooms, alongside the English Breakfast, Earl Grey, camomile and peppermint that Diana had sold. They offered a welcome distraction from the question of the photograph. I knew I could simply have shown it to Luke while he was sitting at my kitchen table, but I still barely knew the man, and it had seemed an oddly intimate thing to have brought up out of the blue. I turned my attention to the intriguing, colourful little packets that lay in the flat box, taking some out to inspect. Alongside the several green varieties, chai and some fruit teas, there were some I had never heard of. I plucked out one called pu'er, another called *Coastal Breeze*, which had sea buckthorn as one of the main ingredients and a third called *My Bonny*, which was made from rose petals and seaweed. Following Diana's example, all were unbleached and plastic free. I wasn't sure how adventurous my average customer would be, but these ocean blends would surely tempt some people? I decided to try one, and put the kettle on.

. . .

It was only when I went to turn on the kitchen light that I realised it was later than I had thought, and the sky was turning ominously dark. The kittens! I glanced at my watch. The surgery would still be open, if I hurried. The day had changed completely from the sun of earlier and as I strode down the path, the wind plucked at my hair and pulled at the thin jacket I had put on. As I reached the vet's, fat raindrops were starting to fall and I was relieved to get indoors. There was nobody on reception, so I tapped on an internal door, hoping that Luke hadn't waited behind for me. It quickly opened.

'Hi,' I said. 'I'm sorry I'm so late.'

Luke's face was serious, but broke into a warm smile when he saw me.

'Belle, hello. You're not late at all; it's me who's late. I was operating on a rabbit and it went on longer than I had expected, then I've been catching up on paperwork. I've sent my nurse and receptionist home because of the storm.'

I remembered the thoughtfulness that Tessa had mentioned; it obviously extended beyond his patients and their owners.

'Yes, it's horrible out there,' I said, peering through the window. 'Such a change from earlier.'

'The weather's unpredictable on the coast,' replied Luke. 'This was forecast, although it's turned much sooner than expected.'

'I haven't seen a weather forecast,' I said, unwilling to divulge to Luke that in my current fragile emotional state I was avoiding the news completely and living on a diet of cheerful reality TV and familiar films. 'I had no idea about a storm.'

'It's going to be a bad one. Did you drive?'

'No, I walked down.'

'Then I'd better give you and the kittens a lift back. Why don't you come and meet them while I finish up for the night?'

Excitedly, I followed him through the consulting room and into a small corridor. He opened a door and we went into a warm room lined with cages.

'This is where we keep our inpatients and any strays we're trying to rehome,' he explained. 'Your kittens are over here.'

He indicated a cage at eye level, and I went and peered in. Four lively green eyes stared back at me and my heart leapt.

'Oh, they're sweet, and so tiny!' I exclaimed.

Luke opened the cage, reached in and picked up the two kittens, then handed them to me. They immediately started clambering over me, their tiny, pin-sharp claws scrabbling for a hold on my jacket. I chattered nonsense to them, giggling as one disappeared under my hair around the back of my neck and the other embarked on a speedy descent down my leg.

'You're going to have your hands full,' remarked Luke, with a smile. 'I won't be long – have to make sure this lot are settled for the night.'

As I played with the kittens, I half watched as he went around each cage, talking softly to its inhabitant and giving food and medicine. How kind he was; no wonder Diana had liked him. While the kittens settled and became drowsy, I was mesmerised as I stroked their minuscule bodies and listened to Luke's gentle voice reassuring his patients. It was a long time since I had been so relaxed; although I was happy in my new home and preparing to open the tearooms, I had pushed myself since the day I had arrived. I wanted to keep busy to try to keep memories and pain at bay, but also, I knew, to try to prove – whether to myself or to others – that I was a person of value, that I had more to offer the world than being merely a jilted bride with a knack for numbers. It was only when I heard Luke whispering my name that my eyes popped open. Like the kittens, I had drifted off to sleep.

'I'm so sorry,' I said in a quiet voice, not wanting to disturb the animals. 'I didn't realise how tired I was.'

He smiled gently, not at all embarrassed or annoyed.

'It is peaceful in here. I have a camp bed I often use when an animal needs care through the night, and I always sleep well. Do you want to pop those two back in their cage for a few minutes while I show you what they'll need?'

I did so, then followed him back through the consulting room to the reception area, where the wind and rain were lashing furiously against the windows.

'What a night,' said Luke. 'I'll give you a lift back home – you'll need it, anyway, with all this.'

He showed me a large heap of items for the kittens.

'I am stupid,' I said, my face reddening. 'I should have brought the car. I was so busy thinking about the kittens; I'd kind of forgotten everything you were lending me.'

He frowned at me.

'Not stupid at all. You could have carried what you needed for the first night and come back for the rest in the morning. Anyway, you're only up the road; it's no trouble to run you home. Although' – he screwed up his face as he looked out of the window – 'it won't be a pleasant journey.'

'I'm not sure I could have done it in my little car,' I said.

He went to reply, as the phone at the desk and his phone rang at the same time.

'Excuse me,' he said. 'I'll get this, it's the emergency line.'

He picked up the phone behind the desk and spoke for a few moments as I gazed out into the stormy evening.

'I'm very sorry, Belle, but I have to go and collect a patient. It's nearby but in the opposite direction to you, I'm afraid.'

'Of course,' I replied. 'Would you like me to help?'

He hesitated, then said, 'If you don't mind going out in this?'

I shook my head.

'Then thank you. I have to collect Edward Burns' dog – Edward was at Diana's funeral.'

I remembered the gentleman who had been a friend of Diana's.

'He's going to be very worried about his dog,' continued Luke. 'It sounds to me like some sort of obstruction in the digestive system that I can operate on, but obviously success is never guaranteed. I don't know if you might be able to distract or comfort him a little?'

'I'll do my best,' I said, trying not to let my doubt sound in my voice.

Even walking the few steps from the surgery to Luke's Land Rover was miserable, and I was relieved I wouldn't be going home on foot. The drive to Edward's house was only a couple of minutes and, as we pulled up, the front door opened and he appeared. We hurried to meet him.

'Thank you so much for coming, Luke,' he said. 'Doris is through here – she's in so much pain, and she's been sick.'

We followed him through to a tiny, cosy sitting room, where a large golden retriever lay on the floor. As we walked in, she lifted her head, then her whole body crunched up in pain and she let out a shrill whimper.

'Okay, girl,' said Luke calmly, kneeling down beside her and stroking her. He looked back at us. 'Belle, can you help Edward find some of her favourite food, a lead and so on? I'll need to take her in.'

'Can you show me?' I asked Edward and, reluctantly, he tore his eyes away from his dog and we went to the kitchen. He started rummaging in cupboards, and I could see his movements becoming more panicky. I put a hand on his shoulder.

'Sit down,' I said. 'I'll find everything. Why don't you tell me about Doris? She's a beautiful dog.'

'She is,' he said, his voice unsteady. 'I've had her since she was a puppy, so nearly eight years now, and she's been a loyal friend. You'd think I would have noticed sooner. I've spent my career studying fish guts, but I didn't spot the problem with my own dog. I just hope I wasn't too late.'

His voice broke. I wanted to hug him, but I wasn't sure if he would welcome that. Instead, I tried to keep my voice calm and cheerful.

'Luke will sort her out, I'm sure. What kind of work has had you studying fish guts?'

He nodded to a photo pinned to a noticeboard: him in a laboratory, a metal dish in front of him with a large fish on it, and a scalpel in his hand.

'I'm a marine scientist. The debris you find is shocking: microplastics, mainly.'

We heard a yelp from the next room, and I quickly started talking again.

'What sort of things might she need for a trip to Luke's surgery? This is her food, isn't it – and are these treats she likes?'

I held up a couple of packets and Edward nodded.

'Yes, those are her favourites, the ones in the green packet. She'll need them.'

'I'll make sure Luke knows,' I said. 'And shall we take her blanket?'

I pointed to a plaid woollen blanket in the dog bed by the back door.

'Yes, her blanket, and her lead is hanging up in the hall.'

I went out to fetch it, and put my head in the sitting room.

'How is she?' I whispered.

'It's an obstruction, as I thought,' said Luke. 'Golden retrievers will eat the silliest things. Have you got everything? I'd like to get her in as soon as possible.'

'Yes,' I said. 'I'll go and get Edward.'

I went back to the kitchen and told him what Luke had said, then found a large carrier bag to pack up Doris's belongings. When I went into the hall, Luke was carrying the large dog in his arms.

'Can you take my keys?' he said to me. 'They're in my coat pocket. And open the back, please.'

A little shy at the sudden proximity, I slipped my hand into the large pocket of Luke's wax jacket and quickly found the keys. I turned to Edward and put a reassuring hand on his arm.

'Doris will be well looked after,' I said. 'We'll phone as soon as we have any news.'

'Please do,' he said. 'I won't sleep a wink tonight, so do call. You will, won't you?'

'I will,' I said, realising that all thoughts of going home myself any time soon had evaporated. 'And the treats in the green pouch; she'll have one of those as soon as she's allowed.'

'Thank you,' he said.

I hurried out into the foul weather and opened up the back of the car, where a large cage was fitted. My cold, wet fingers fumbled at the catch, but Luke didn't hurry me, although the dog must have been heavy and we were all now drenched. I supposed his patience was one of the things that made him so good with animals. I was certainly grateful for it; Matt would have been fussing and tutting by now. Eventually, I pulled open the cage door, and he placed the dog inside. With a final wave to Edward, who was standing outside his door, apparently oblivious to the driving rain, we got in and drove the short distance back to the surgery. Once there, I helped again with the car doors and opening up the surgery, and soon Luke had Doris lying on the table.

'Is she going to be all right?' I asked, looking doubtfully at her. I don't know much about dogs, but even I could see that she was weak and in pain.

'I don't know,' replied Luke, his expression serious. 'It depends on how long it's been there and how easy it is to clear. Edward adores her, so I'm sure he'll have picked up quickly on any change in her behaviour. I'm going to X-ray her. Would you mind staying to help?' I shook my head. 'Thanks. You'll need to read and sign a form and wear a lead apron. Here.'

He took a sheet of paper from a tray and handed it to me, then started setting up. I read quickly through the questions and ticked 'no' to everything, then signed. Next, Luke handed me a heavy tabard, helping me put it on over my head.

'Great. Hold her head, please, talk to her and try to make sure she lies still.'

I wasn't confident about any of this, and a million worries and questions ran through my head as I muttered soothingly to Doris.

What if I held her wrong? What if I couldn't stop her moving? What if, God forbid, I hurt her in some way?

'All done.'

'Really?'

I had been so busy trying to hide my agitation that I hadn't noticed anything else.

'Yup. Can you carry on talking to her while I look at the X-ray?'

Happy to be of use, I continued chattering nonsense to the big dog, telling her about the new kittens and reassuring her that she would see her master soon. A few minutes later, Luke spoke.

'Yup, she's managed to swallow something that's blocked her up completely. No wonder you're uncomfortable, old girl.'

'Will she be okay?' I asked. It sounded serious, and my throat constricted with sadness at the thought of Edward losing his companion.

'She should be,' said Luke. 'The object is in a fairly straightforward position. But I'm going to need to operate immediately. There's no way I can get my nurse to come out in this weather.' I knew what was coming. 'Would you be okay to stay and help? I can manage most of it, I'll just need to hand things to you and for you to keep an eye on the numbers on the machine.'

I willed the tears of sadness and fear to subside. What choice did I have but to help? I nodded, rather than risk speaking.

'Good, thanks. Right, let's get you some scrubs, a mask and gloves.'

Within minutes, we were both togged up and I had some simple instructions for what numbers to look for on the machine Doris was hooked up to. Luke talked in a low voice through everything he was doing and this calmed me, even as he administered an anaesthetic and shaved then slowly cut open poor Doris's tummy.

'Ah, that's what I'm looking for,' he murmured, then turned to me. 'Can you hold out a tray, please?'

There were some ready nearby, and I proffered one, intrigued now, despite the blood, to see what he extracted.

'Oh, it's huge!' I exclaimed, as he placed a split tennis ball on the tray.

'Crazy, isn't it?' he said, his eyes smiling above his mask. 'I once had a dog that swallowed an entire tea towel – heaven knows how it managed. Right, everything else looks good, so I'm going to stitch her up. How are her stats?'

I looked quickly at the screen and confirmed that the numbers were still where they should be, then watched as he deftly stitched up the wound. Once it was bandaged, she was lifted carefully into one of the large cages in the same room as the kittens.

'Will she be okay?' I asked for the third time that evening.

'I don't see any reason why not. Would you like to call Edward and update him?'

'Me?'

'Yes. I'll speak to him as well, but you can deliver the good news.'

He handed me his phone, ready with the number. The phone was snatched up on the first ring.

'Hello? Luke?'

'Hello, Mr Burns, it's Belle. I'm ringing to tell you that Doris had to have an operation' – he gasped and I hurried on – 'but she's done brilliantly and is recovering now. She had swallowed a tennis ball.'

'Is she going to be all right?' he asked, his voice faint.

'Yes,' I said. 'Let me hand you over to Luke and he can explain.'

I gave him the phone and went over to check on my kittens, who were fast asleep, entwined together, and utterly enchanting. A few minutes later, I heard Luke saying goodbye, and I turned back to him.

'I bet he's pleased,' I said.

'Very,' replied Luke. 'Doris is so important to him.'

'When Doris is back on her feet, I can see if he wants someone to go on dog walks with him,' I said. 'And he might like to taste-test some of the bakes for the tearooms.'

Luke smiled, his tired eyes warm.

'He'd like that. Doris will need close observation for a little while longer, until she wakes up, but then I'll run you home. It's nearly three in the morning. What are you going to call the kittens?'

I looked in at them.

'I don't know. Given the storm, they should probably be Thunder and Lightning or something, but they're not cute enough names.'

'What about something to do with baking?' suggested Luke. 'Um, Cookie and Cakey?' He groaned as soon as he'd said it. 'No, they're awful. Sorry, I'm too tired to come up with kitten names. Maybe you should wait till morning.'

'No, I've got it!' I said. 'And tell me if this is madness due to lack of sleep, but what about Bubble and Squeak? It's not strictly what I'm learning to bake for the tearooms, but there's a connection, and they're sweet names.'

'Bubble and Squeak,' said Luke thoughtfully. 'Love it!'

Once Doris had woken up and Luke was satisfied that she could be left for a short time, we put Bubble and Squeak into their travelling basket and went back outside to the car. It was still blustery and raining, but the ferocity of the storm had lessened, and we made it back to my house without incident.

'Thank you for the lift,' I said. 'Would you like to come in for a coffee?'

'I would,' he replied. 'But I'm going to go back to the surgery to check on Doris and grab a couple of hours' sleep before I head down to the beach for my regular Saturday morning litter pick.'

'That's what you used to do with Diana?'

'Yes. I try to advertise it, but it was the two of us more often than not. Edward too, sometimes.' He shrugged. 'And I can guess that this morning, given the weather, I'll be on my own.'

'I'd like to join you sometime,' I said. 'But today I'm going to get these two settled and, hopefully, get some sleep.'

'You'll be very welcome,' said Luke. 'But your new babies are top of the list for now.'

I let myself into the dark house, only turning on side lamps in the hope that the kittens would think it was still nighttime, and continue snoozing for a while yet. And despite the time and the dark and the chill and my exhaustion, I couldn't ignore the creeping thought that this, maybe, was a better place to be than married to Matt.

NINE

By the time I got to sleep, after settling the kittens, it was nearly half past four, and the sky was lightening. I pulled the thick bedroom curtains shut and snuggled down in bed, listening to the crash of the waves and flurries of pattering raindrops on the window. I had wondered if I would be able to sleep after all that had happened, if maybe my brain would gallop around the events of the night too excitedly to allow me any rest, but exhaustion took over and it was several hours later that I awoke, to bright sunshine leaking in around the edges of the curtains. I stumbled downstairs and immediately checked on the kittens. The black one was awake and started mewing and trampling all over his brother when he saw me.

'Hello!' I said, smiling. 'Are you ready for some breakfast?' I opened the cage and took him out. 'You'd better be Bubble, and your sleepy little brother there can be Squeak.'

I got their breakfast ready then my own, and I chattered away to them happily as we all ate, already knowing that it had been one of my best ever ideas to rescue the two of them.

'Now, boys,' I said, draining my coffee cup. 'I'm feeling distinctly better than I did half an hour ago, but I'm not sure I'm up for any more baking right now. Would you like to help me on a treasure hunt instead?'

They followed me as I went to have a shower and get dressed, both of which simple tasks took me far longer than usual as the kittens wanted to play with everything, and I wasn't going to stop them. It was too enchanting seeing them surprised by water droplets, determined to scale the duvet that hung off the unmade bed and transfixed by the moving reflection of the sun off my small mirror. Eventually, however, I tore myself away, and went downstairs to open up the room I had barely entered since moving in, the one where I had put my own belongings that I didn't know what to do with, and which housed what could only be Diana's archives: boxes, a couple of packing crates, an antique desk and an upright piano covered by a dust sheet. I opened the curtains and looked around.

'What do you think, boys?' I asked Bubble and Squeak, who had followed me and instantly discovered an old ping pong ball, which they were now batting around. 'What kind of box are we looking for?'

For a moment, I was frozen with indecision. All I had to go on was a request Diana had made with her dying breaths – "find the box" – and a gut feeling that whoever "he" was, whatever "he" should know had been important enough to her that I should find out.

'Okay,' I said out loud. 'There are plenty of boxes here; maybe it's one of them. I've got to start somewhere.'

I knelt down and opened the cardboard box nearest me, sneezing as dust rose. All that was inside was tightly packed fabric. I delved down to make sure there was nothing hidden within its folds – after all, I could be looking for something as small as a matchbox, for all I knew – but my search yielded nothing. I closed the box up again and moved on to the next. This looked more promising: it was full of lumpy items wrapped in old, brittle newspaper, and could easily hold an interesting box. I took out the first thing and carefully unwrapped it. It was an ugly, to my mind, porcelain statue of two people riding a horse with the words 'Returning Home' painted across the bottom. It was only moulded on the front, and the back was completely flat and plain; there were no identifying marks of any kind on the base. I took it to the kitchen, where I had left my phone, and took a photo of it which I then searched, my heart beating a little faster in the hope that I might have found something of value that could shore me up further as I got the tearooms up and running again and paid my inheritance tax. The result pinged back instantly with several identical items being sold on eBay. Apparently, it was a Staffordshire flatback, with a value of around twenty pounds.

Grinning at my own treasure-seeking excitement, I returned to the room and unwrapped everything else in the box, all of which seemed to me to be very similar, and equally unattractive. No wonder Diana kept them stuffed in a box in here; it was barely worth the effort of selling them, but she would never have displayed them in her tasteful home. Maybe she had inherited them herself. I rewrapped everything, shut the box up again and put a sticky note on the top saying: 'charity shop/eBay' and moved on to the next one. Immediately, it seemed to hold possibilities. On the top were some papers and a blue cardboard file, labelled 'Letters' in Diana's strong, spiky handwriting. I had now been working on the boxes for over an hour, so I took a break to make a cup of tea and encourage the kittens to use their litter tray, before returning.

I have to admit that a flush of excitement coursed through me as I unpacked the box, along with a certain thrill of trepidation. What was I going to discover? It might be nothing more than old gas bills, but there might be the key to some secret from Diana's past and, if this did turn out to be the case, was it okay for me to delve into it? Diana was dead, of course, but the sense of intrusion I felt, which had only recently started to fade where the house was concerned, came back with full force. I sat back on my heels and looked at Bubble and Squeak, who had snuggled up together in a patch of sunlight.

'I wish I could be as carefree as you two,' I muttered.

I nearly put everything back and went to do something simpler – I even considered some more baking – but I thought of Tessa and her confidence that Diana had something urgent to impart, something she wanted to be discovered before her sudden death. Maybe it was something she had been intending to share herself, but had missed her opportunity in life. I looked again at the papers and the box I had begun emptying, and sighed. Was it more that I was shying away from *what* I might find, rather than being squeamish about intruding into Diana's life and affairs? If someone needed to know something and I found out what it was, I would then have the responsibility for telling him, or not, and for whatever fallout ensued. After being jilted by Matt, my eagerness to engage with any sort of personal drama was at an all-time low, and the urge to batten down the hatches and be alone – which I had shaken off since my first days in Spindrift Bay, when Gloria would have allowed nothing of the sort – threatened to return. Timid and frightened was not who I was: time for some action. I picked up my phone, walked back through the kitchen and out into the garden, being careful not to let the kittens follow me as they were too young to be allowed out yet. I tapped into my address book.

'Hello, darling. How are you?' Gloria's voice was warm and welcoming. 'I'm cleaning up after the *strangest* guest. He brought me some toffees to thank me for the stay – *quite* unnecessary – but left grass clippings over everything. Heaven knows where he picked them all up.'

'Probably best not to ask,' I said, grinning.

'What can I do for you?'

'Well, I do want you to come over and meet my new little friends...'

'Oh! What have you got?'

'Kittens, and they're adorable.'

'I would love to meet them. They might cheer me up after that awful storm last night. It's left a terrible mess.'

I took a proper look at my garden. It was true that there were lots of twigs and a couple of bigger branches scattered about, but otherwise I seem to have got off lightly. I hoped the same could be said for the roof.

'I saw some of it this morning. When can you come?'

'This evening? I'll bring pizza.'

'Perfect. But before then, I was hoping you could give me some advice.'

'Always.'

'Thank you.'

I explained about what Diana had said to Tessa, and my qualms over prying into her personal papers.

'I understand that it's something you might resist, for all sorts of reasons, all of them good, but you don't have much choice,' said Gloria. 'You don't know what this box is – whether it's a big box stuffed with papers or a little thing – so you can't avoid checking through what you have. Go for it. You'll know if you're looking at something she wouldn't want seen, and you'll be discreet about anything like that.'

'Thank you,' I said, relieved, and touched by her confidence in my integrity. 'Yes, that's true. I'm not being prurient, but I'm dying to know – and it is a sort of duty.'

'Exactly,' said Gloria. 'And tonight, I'll bring some duty free and you can tell me anything you decide would be okay to tell.'

'Great,' I said. 'And you can tell me about your toffee-wielding, grassy guest!'

I hung up feeling much better and returned to the box, taking everything out and sorting it into more or less logical piles: personal letters, official letters and documents, notes and so on. As I did so, one envelope in particular caught my eye. It was A5 sized and had 'Birth Certificate' written on in pencil. It looked like Diana's writing, but a slightly softer, maybe younger, version. It was the first thing I opened once the box was empty and, as I had wondered if it might, revealed a long-hidden secret. The name of the new baby on the certificate was Diana's, without a doubt. I remembered her and my mother laughing together once about their middle names, both of which had been given for their grandmothers, and both of which they hated. My mother's was Josephine, which struck me as glamorous, but she couldn't bear, and Diana's was the same as the one on the certificate I now held: Lettice.

'It's all right, I suppose, if it's pronounced correctly,' she had said, rolling her eyes. 'Luh-*teece*. But everyone talks about you like you're salad. There was a girl at school – Pamela Hetherington her name was. She got hold of it and taunted me for weeks.'

And there it was, in blue fountain pen: Diana Lettice. My eyes moved across the columns. Sex: girl. Name and surname of father: Sir William Talbot.

My heart pounded. *What?* I read on.

Name and maiden surname of mother: Lady Margaret Talbot, formerly Chamberlain. Rank or Profession of Father: Baronet/Landowner.

I sat back on my heels and stared into the room, frowning. Sir William and Lady Margaret must, I supposed, be the current baronet's parents – and Luke's grandparents. And this meant that Diana was their daughter – Luke's aunt – although her surname was different. Could this be what she wanted 'him' to know – that the woman he considered a friend was, in fact, a close relative: his father's sister? Or could it be that his father didn't know himself, for some reason? I was here to solve mysteries, but the questions were stacking up. Spurred on by this discovery, I put the birth certificate back in its envelope and placed it carefully to one side, then started to look through the other documents. Most of the official-looking letters were easy to discount as they were bills paid long ago or other formalities, including notice of the changing by deed poll of Diana's surname from Talbot to Dalton.

The personal letters were sure to be of more interest, so I collected these up and, tired of sitting on the floor, took them through to the sitting room, where I installed myself on the comfortable sofa to get reading. Bubble and Squeak instantly clambered up beside me and promptly fell asleep again. I stroked them gently as I started on the letters, many of which had their French addresses scribed in familiar handwriting: that of my mother. It was fascinating to read her words from over thirty years ago. She wrote of meeting my father, later thanking Diana for coming to the wedding and her gift. There was poignancy there, also, in hindsight, and although she described an attentive and flattering beau, her sympathetic descriptions of his difficult childhood and occasional bouts of jealousy and temper waved red flags at me across the decades. She had believed that by loving and caring for him, she could heal his wounds, and I wished that I could go back in time and warn her that some people thrive on being broken, their only succour coming from the relief that inflicting control and pain on others could bring them. But then, of course, she would never have had me. Reading of the joy I had brought her as a baby and beyond made me sob with a tumultuous mix of love for her, sorrow for the cruelties my father inflicted on her and grief for the babies I never had with Matt, and to which I had looked forward to with such longing.

The overspill of emotion brought with it an intense hunger and, checking my watch, it was no surprise: it was nearly two o'clock.

'Come on, boys,' I said to the kittens, scooping them up gently. 'You need some lunch, too. We'll all feel better for it.'

I carried them through to the kitchen and prepared us all something to eat. Needing a break from the intensity of the past day and night, I opened up my laptop and found a cheerful, anodyne programme about people rescuing old furniture from the dump and 'upcycling' it for resale. This fulfilled the purpose of taking my mind off storms, vets, sick dogs, kittens and old secrets for the forty-five minutes it lasted, and afterwards I was sufficiently refreshed in mind and body to return to the letters.

Those I had read from my mother made no reference to Diana's past, so I tried something else. There was one sheet, folded into quarters but not in an envelope, and I opened this next. It was from Diana to Mum, and was unfinished. I started reading.

Dearest Vivienne,

Thank you for your recent letter and the photograph of little Belle. She looks so like you, and I am so happy and honoured to be her godmother, although this responsibility, and the trust you have placed in me, compels me to be honest with you. In all the years we have known each other, there are secrets I have kept about my past. I know you know this, and you have been respectful and kind enough never to ask questions. But I have always understood that I can tell you anything, no matter how difficult. I worry, though, that my motives are selfish and that, once hidden things are brought out in the open, I will destroy lives. And I don't want to do that, even though my own life's suffering may, to some degree, be alleviated.

That was where the letter ended. I sighed loudly and Bubble stirred, then gazed up at me with his luminous green eyes. Being careful not to disturb Squeak, who was still sleeping peacefully, I picked up the tiny black kitten, and he snuggled under my chin as I stroked him.

'I'd better give Mum a call,' I said. 'Maybe Diana told her in person rather than putting her secret down in writing.'

Eager to stretch my legs after spending most of the day sitting down, I took my phone into the garden again, breathing in the soft air and gazing out at the sea, so calm and innocent, as if it had never raged a few hours before.

'Hello, darling.'

My mother's warm voice made my heart lift the moment I heard it. With her in the world, nothing could ever be as frightening as it was when I was alone.

'Hello, Mum, how are you?'

We chatted for a few minutes as she told me about the garden and the poetry translation she was currently working on, and I brought her up to speed on the renovations and the kittens.

'I'd love to meet them,' she said. 'They sound sweet.'

'They are, and they're tiny, so do come sooner rather than later, won't you? There's loads of room here, you know that – you can come and stay whenever you want.'

There was a tiny pause, and then she said, as I feared she might, 'I'll see.'

I'll see. That was what she had said for as long as I could remember. *I'll see* meant 'if your father lets me'. I wanted to push and nag her to *come*, but I knew it was futile. The only thing I could do was repeatedly say how welcome she was and to leave her to make her decisions in her own time. The last thing she needed was anyone else haranguing her.

'Okay. Mum, there was something else I wanted to ask you about.'

I told her Tessa's story and explained about the documents I had found, skimming lightly over the fact that I had read several of her own letters. Instead, I read out the birth certificate and then the unfinished letter from Diana.

'I am flabbergasted,' she said. 'In all those years, I had no idea, no idea at all, about her parents. I mean, I knew she was hiding something because she refused to speak about her family. I assumed that there had been abuse, which was why she had cut herself off from them.'

'Didn't she talk about them at all?' I asked.

'No. The most she ever said was "I don't see my family, we don't get on" – that was it. We were close friends, but she could be secretive about all sorts of things, and I could tell that she had been traumatised. She would cut herself off, even from me, for days or even weeks at a time. Sometimes, when we were out having a coffee, chatting about this and that, her eyes would suddenly fill with tears, but she wouldn't tell me what had upset her, just wave my concerns away and say that sometimes things were too close to the surface and she was probably tired.'

'Poor Diana,' I said. *I knew how that felt.* It could be exhausting, keeping going, when at any given moment one could succumb to the urge to lie down and sob with misery. 'I wonder why she came back to live near them?'

'I can't imagine. Do you think anyone knew, anyone in the village? Do those boys know she was their aunt?'

'I don't know,' I replied, flipping through all the variables in my head. 'Her surname was Dalton, not Talbot...'

'Which I suppose she changed,' interjected Mum.

'She did, I found the paperwork. It sounds kind of similar. The Talbot family came to the funeral, and that caused some interest.'

I explained to my mother about Beverly and her gossip. Looks like she had a nose for a secret, after all.

'So, Sir Henry and Lady Talbot must have known who she was?'

'Yes. Unless my explanation at the time was right, and they were simply supporting Luke, who had been friendly with Diana. Oh Mum, what a mess. What do you think I should do?'

'I don't know. Secrets, especially old secrets, are often best left undisturbed. On the other hand, it sounds as if Diana wanted somebody to know something, if it was that important to her that she mentioned it in her dying breaths.'

Mum's voice caught as she spoke and I desperately wished I was there to give her a hug.

'I won't just sit on it,' I said decisively. 'But I will give it some space for now. If whatever it is has been hidden for nearly forty years, surely it can wait a little longer.'

But even as I said the words, I was aware that Diana may well have thought the same thing.

TEN

After I had said goodbye to Mum, I was twitchy. The tiredness after my long night was dragging at me, but with all the questions whirling around in my head, I knew it was pointless trying to nap. I had no appetite for returning to Diana's papers. I was worried that I might uncover painful truths, but also felt the weight of responsibility for fulfilling Diana's final wish. What I needed, I knew, despite my exhaustion, was to keep busy, and where better place than the tearooms? I went back into the house, encouraged the kittens to use their litter tray, gathered together the things I needed and went through. For the first time in a long time, I didn't feel like shutting myself away; I had spent long enough that day in silence and rumination. So I drew the curtains, put up the blinds and opened the front door wide, to let in the fresh spring air and ever-strengthening sunshine. The area outside the tearooms was littered with sticks, leaves and other debris, but I seemed to have escaped any serious storm damage. I fetched the remaining four painted wooden chairs that hadn't yet been refurbished and stood them outside. Then, dust mask in place, I began sanding them vigorously, revelling in the physical work that required no thought, yet was utterly absorbing.

I was halfway through the second chair when I saw Tessa approaching, pushing an empty pushchair as Noah ran around next to her, pausing every few seconds to pick something up, or look closely at a fragment that had caught his interest. I waved.

'Hello!'

'Hello,' said Tessa warmly. 'I didn't realise you were working today; you should have given me a call.'

'I wasn't planning to,' I said. 'And I wouldn't call you to work at the weekend. Looks like you're having a fun walk, anyway.'

'We are,' she said, smiling at Noah as he frowned in concentration at a half-broken stick he had found that was too soggy to snap properly. 'This always happens. I intend for us to come out for twenty minutes and it turns into two hours because Noah *needs* to inspect every speck of dust he finds.'

'Sounds like you need a cuppa. Let me finish this chair and I'll put the kettle on. Do you want to try one of the herbal teas I'm thinking of for the tearooms? Caffeine free?'

'Perfect,' she replied.

For the next ten minutes or so, I rubbed away at the chair, while she helped Noah collect treasures, then I brewed some of the sea buckthorn infusion and poured Noah some milk.

'Ooh, it's a pretty colour,' said Tessa, looking at the golden liquid.

'Gorgeous, isn't it? And I like the taste, although I'd like a second opinion as to how it might go down with customers.'

She sipped it, looking thoughtful.

'I like it,' she said. 'It's citrussy, quite tart.'

'Try with a drop of honey?' I suggested. 'Or add a little freshly squeezed orange juice?'

I had brought both out along with the tea, and she opted for some juice.

'Oh yes, that's delicious now! You should try selling it. Diana was always trying new things, and she was aware that these days people often want something different.'

'Yes, I'm getting more and more of a picture of how dynamic

she was. All right, I'll give it a go!' I tapped a note into my phone and took a sip of my own tea. 'Tessa, I'm getting closer to finding out what Diana meant about the box and telling "him" something.'

'Is it connected to the photo?'

'I think so. I'm not going to say what it is right now, I hope you understand. I'm not sure myself yet of the details or the implications. The thing is—'

I broke off and watched Noah as he added three more stones to his treasure trove. I pulled at my thumbnail with my teeth.

'The thing is, it feels kind of dangerous.'

She frowned.

'Dangerous? What do you mean?'

'I don't mean that anyone is *in* danger. More that I might be lighting a fuse, in a way. Uncovering things that are none of my business. At worst, bringing to light things that people want to stay secret. At best, maybe making myself unpopular in a village I'm still beginning to get to know.' I turned my troubled face to her. 'I have no idea what the right thing is to do, but the more I think about Diana, the less I want to let her down.'

Tessa nodded gently, then stared out to sea. She didn't speak for several minutes and, when she did, her voice was full of compassion and strength.

'Belle, you are guardian now of some sort of mystery, something Diana obviously wanted to be brought into the open. Do you – did you – trust Diana?'

'Yes, completely. Mum did as well.'

'Well then. Do you think she would have used her last scraps of life to urge something destructive, or cruel, or wrong?'

'No.'

'Neither do I. I trust her as well. Diana wasn't someone who shied away from uncomfortable things...'

'So, neither must I?'

'I'm afraid not. And Belle, you can use your own judgement. If you find something out that you truly believe is better to remain secret, then you don't have to tell a soul. But you can't decide that now, not until you know. Diana trusted you, too, with her entire inheritance – and that includes the secrets.'

I sighed.

'You're right. And thank you.' I looked at Noah, so happy as he pottered around peacefully in the sunshine. 'If only life stayed that simple, eh?'

'Maybe,' replied Tessa. 'Now, can I help you with these chairs?'

For the next hour, we sanded the chairs, then rinsed them with soapy water.

'I can't believe we've done all of them!' I said, standing back to appreciate our hard work. 'Thanks so much for helping. I'll leave them to dry completely and paint them another time; I've had enough for one day.'

'You're not the only one,' said Tessa, nodding over at Noah who had climbed into his pushchair and fallen asleep.

'Thank him for me when he wakes up,' I said. 'He was very helpful.'

She grinned.

'If he carries on getting so much joy from washing stuff as he gets older, then I'll be happy,' she said.

I waved them off, moved the chairs back inside and locked up, then went back to the house and spent a happy half hour playing with the kittens. I could have spent four times that long; it was utterly enchanting to watch them chase a piece of string, then cling to it for dear life, or pounce on the reflection of the sun off my watch as I moved it around the floor. But I had one more job to do that afternoon.

'All right, lads, that's it for now, but I'm sure Gloria will have a game with you later.'

I found a plastic box and packed some of my recent bakes in, then headed off to the village. As I got closer, I could see that the storm damage here was much more severe. Several windows of homes and businesses had been broken and were patched up; roof tiles lay smashed on the pavement. Debris had been pushed off the road, but lay in gloomy, damp piles to be dealt with another day. The small florist's shop was shut, with a 'closed' sign on the door saying that the owner's home had been so badly damaged that they couldn't open up for several days. There weren't many people around, and those I saw hurried past with a brief greeting. The whole place had a feeling of bleakness, and I knew I was incredibly lucky to have avoided any significant damage myself. Glad to see Edward's house apparently unharmed, I rang the doorbell. I heard him inside reassuring Doris, and urging her to stay in her basket, but she was by his side when he opened the door.

'Hello,' I said. 'I hope you don't mind me coming by, but I had some cakes and things left over from the baking I've been practicing and I wondered if you might like them? I wanted to check on poor Doris, too. It's good to see her home already.'

'How kind of you,' he said. 'Please, come in. Luke is finishing up.'

I stepped inside and followed him through to the sitting room, where Luke was packing up his bag.

'Hello,' I said, oddly shy at seeing him again after the intense time we had spent together. 'I didn't think Doris would be home so soon.'

'It is quick,' he said. 'But Edward convinced me that they'd both be better off here, together, and I agree. She's not to have a single crumb of those, though,' he added, nodding at the box of cakes I still held. He crouched down to ruffle Doris's fur, and I thought what a calm, steadying presence he was, working his magic on us as much as on the animals he tended.

'No, no, I promise she won't,' replied Edward. 'Plain diet until further notice, I know.'

'Splendid. Now *call*, won't you, if there's the slightest concern?'

'I will. Thank you, Luke.'

He saw him off, then came back through.

'Will you stay for a cuppa?'

'Thank you, but why don't you sit down and I'll get it?'

'No, no, you're my guest. I won't be a minute.'

I handed him the box, and he disappeared into the kitchen while I sat next to Doris, stroking her gently and telling her about Bubble and Squeak. I had hoped she wouldn't hold a grudge against me after my part in her surgery last night, but she was the sweetest dog.

'Here we go,' said Edward, bringing a tray through and placing it on a small table by the window. 'Now, you come and sit down.'

For a few minutes, we spoke about the operation and the storm.

'You weren't affected, were you?' Edward asked, concern in his face.

'No, I seem to have been lucky,' I said.

'Luck and good management,' he replied. 'Diana's, that is. Because she was so exposed up there, she took extra care that everything was sturdy and safe. I bet there was barely a blade of grass out of place.'

I grinned.

'You're right. Once I got home, I was perfectly snug, and I didn't realise how bad it had been for everyone else until I came to see you.'

He shook his head sadly.

'I'm worried for this village. People here often feel forgotten by the powers that be, and this will do nothing for morale. I hope no one else gives up and sells up, just as we're getting some new blood, what with you and with Caleb getting his new bakery off the ground.'

'Well, I'm not going anywhere,' I said firmly.

'Good,' he replied. 'We need more like you. And Luke. He's run himself ragged since the storm, checking on livestock and pets. Won't leave anyone to suffer or worry. He's a good man.'

'I want to get more involved,' I said. 'I don't know how I can help with the storm damage, but what do you know about Diana's work in ocean conservation?'

'She cared so much about the coast here. She would have made a good marine scientist herself, and I tried to persuade her to explore it, but of course she brushed that off and said she was perfectly happy with the tearooms. That didn't stop her pouring her time and energy into her conservation work, though.'

He was glad to talk about his friend. I only realised how late it had got when Doris started stirring, her tummy telling her that her dinner was due. He leant over to stroke her lovely head.

'Hungry, are you, girl? It's plain rice for a while, I'm afraid. Better than half the things I've found in fish stomachs over the years.' He gave me a quick, rueful smile. 'Forgive me – I see the world through a rather fishy lens.'

I grinned, standing up.

'I'd better go. But maybe you'd do me the favour of helping with some of my other trial bakes another time?'

'It would be my pleasure,' said Edward, clasping my hand briefly. 'You've been kind, coming here to see me and Doris.'

The big dog thumped her tail, as if seconding the sentiment.

I left them boiling some plain rice, and hurried back home, hoping to have a few minutes to tidy up before Gloria arrived with the pizza.

When I opened the door to Gloria half an hour later, I couldn't stifle the shock and concern, and it must have been written across my face.

'Darling girl,' she said, hugging me with the arm that wasn't balancing the pizza box. 'From your expression I can tell that I look exactly how I feel.'

In one way, she looked as she always did: her hair and make-up were done, and she wore her usual fabulous clothes – today, some wide black satin trousers and an electric blue chiffon top, with lots of chunky gold jewellery. But she looked exhausted and her manner lacked its usual *joie de vivre*.

'Would you like a drink?' I asked. 'I've got a delicious rosé.'

'Please,' she said, getting some plates out of the cupboard. 'Sounds like it would hit the spot. Oh!'

I turned around.

'What?'

'Are these the kittens?'

She had spotted them, fast asleep as they were most of the time, and entwined in the most appealing little bundle.

'Yes, that's them. I've called them Bubble and Squeak. They'll wake up soon and we can have a cuddle, but shall we eat first?'

'Good idea.'

She asked me about the kittens, and I told her the whole story of the previous night.

'How's the guesthouse?' I asked, ashamed that I hadn't checked up on her sooner.

She shook her head.

'I'm afraid she's suffered somewhat. It looks like I've spent too much time choosing wallpaper and gossiping with my guests, and not enough time thinking about what's going on outside. The roof is in pieces, and I've lost a couple of windows. Looks like the frames were rotten, so when the strongest gusts came, they disintegrated.'

'I'm so sorry,' I said. 'Can I help you get it sorted?'

I was horrified to see her eyes fill with tears.

'Oh, Belle, you've no idea how good those words sound. Georgie has already sent me the money for the repairs, so it's not exactly a *problem*, but...' She sighed. 'I don't want to complain, I'm so lucky.'

'What is it?' I asked. 'You can tell me – I won't think it's silly, or ungrateful, or whatever. God knows I've got nothing to complain about, but I still feel low half the time.'

'You *will* understand,' she said. 'It's just that however happy I am – and I am – it does get hard sometimes doing everything myself. Even with the money sorted out, the tasks of calling the window and roof people, coping with the mess, dealing with insurance... Maybe it's time to join Georgie in Spain.'

'I know,' I said quietly. 'It's a cliché to say that "a problem shared is a problem halved", but it's true. However competent we are – and we are – it's much better to do all this stuff with somebody else. Tessa's made the whole tearoom business so much better for me. I meant what I said: I'll help. You don't have to do this on your own.'

ELEVEN

The week passed quickly as Tessa and I continued working on the refurbishment of the tearooms and I helped Gloria navigate the process of fixing up the guesthouse. She wasn't wrong when she said that she had neglected the care of the fabric of the building. I organised quotes from three separate roofing companies, all of whom shook their heads dolefully and pulled faces when confronted with her roof.

'It's more than a few tiles,' was the repeated refrain. 'That whole roof needs replacing and it's a miracle the chimney stacks haven't collapsed. We won't know about the rafters and joists until we've got everything off.'

Thankfully, Georgie seemed to be able to send over seemingly bottomless funds, so that eliminated one major worry, but I could see that Gloria struggled with organising the works. Each day I would leave her with some simple but crucial tasks – ringing someone up or researching prices – and the next day I would find that the jobs were, at best, half done.

'I'm sorry, darling, I did mean to do it, but the valance in Seaspray' – all her rooms had beachy names, rather than numbers – 'is looking tired and it took me ages to find something perfect.'

As well as these logistics, we had to find a time, and soon, for the roof to be replaced, and that meant cancelling guests. Gloria hated letting people down, so this process usually began with me putting in the call and breaking the bad news before she took the phone from me and chattered away for the next twenty minutes about how sorry she was and how she could help them book something else.

Between Gloria, the tearooms and the kittens, I barely had a moment for myself, but that didn't stop me worrying about the secret of Diana's past that I was guarding. I kept reminding myself that there was no hurry to do anything, tell anyone, but my indecision about what or who that should be weighed heavy on me. If I got it wrong, I risked causing a great deal of upset, but doing nothing wasn't an option I was willing to take. Diana deserved better than that. As the weekend approached, I started feeling jittery. Tessa would be busy with her family and Gloria had decided to pop over to Spain for a few days to see Georgie. I planned to visit Edward and try a couple of new bakes, but that still left too many hours stretching ahead of me with only my own thoughts to keep me busy. It was when I was in the small village shop, stocking up on eggs, that I saw a flyer pinned to the noticeboard:

Beach Clean-Up

Come and join us every Saturday from 9 a.m.
Together we can reduce sea pollution and help protect marine wildlife.

The phone number on the flyer was one I recognised from when I had enquired about the kittens: Luke. My stomach did a little jump. This was exactly what I had been looking for. I had wanted to continue Diana's work, and I was in desperate need of activities to help keep me busy over the weekend. As I walked home, my steps lighter, I also couldn't deny that the opportunity to spend more time with Luke wasn't the most dismal of prospects.

· · ·

The morning air was fresh and invigorating and I took big, deep breaths of it as I walked down to the beach. There was nobody about, and the view of the sea, sunlight sparkling across it, would have raised anyone's spirits. A gentle breeze lifted my hair, and I might have launched into a sudden, glorious spin to rival the opening credits of *The Sound of Music*, had I not at that moment spotted Luke on the beach below. I commuted my whirl into a slightly too enthusiastic wave, and he waved back.

'Good morning!' I said, when I arrived on the sands. 'Perfect day for it!'

'Have you come to help with the clean-up?' he asked.

'Yes. I've been meaning to, but I'm afraid last week I was wiped out by the night we had.'

'How are Bubble and Squeak settling in?'

I was touched that he had remembered their names.

'Brilliantly. They spend a lot of their time asleep, but when they're awake, they're so funny. They like scaling Diana's floor-length curtains, but then they get confused about how to get down again and sit there crying until I rescue them. I have to tie the curtains up out of the way when I'm not home.'

'It sounds like they're keeping you busy. Is the training going okay?'

'Yes. I'm surprised how quickly they've taken to it. There's the odd accident, but it's not too bad. Oh, I've bought them everything they need, so I must get your stuff back to you.'

'No rush – drop it by when you can. Er, there was something else I wanted to ask you about.'

My stomach dropped. *Beverly*.

'Mmhmm?' I said, as casually as I could.

'I saw Beverly yesterday and she mentioned that you had a photo of Diana up at my parents' house, when she was young?'

'That's right,' I said. 'I didn't know she had been here all that time ago.'

'Neither did I. I'd love to see it, if you don't mind showing it to me?'

'Of course,' I replied, wondering if I should mention the birth certificate as well. As I hesitated, Luke continued.

'Great, thanks! Shall we get on with our clean-up now?'

He handed me a pair of gloves, a long litter picker and a sturdy bag attached to a hoop.

'There are no rules, just grab anything you see and put it in the bag. When we empty them, we'll separate what we can for recycling.'

'Do you think it will be the two of us?' I asked.

'It's usually just me, and sometimes Edward comes along,' he said, biting his lip. 'I'm probably not advertising enough, but I wish more people would come. It's such a short time each week, but it makes a huge difference to the ecology of the ocean if we can collect up even a tiny fraction of the garbage that ends up there. Did you know that the equivalent of an entire truck of garbage ends up in the world's oceans *every minute*? Plastic bags alone are a terrible threat. Sea animals ingest them or get tangled up in them and drown, they smother coral reefs and when they eventually do break down, they enter the food chain as microplastics. Humans can end up consuming these, and they don't do our health any good, either.'

I had read some of this in the literature from Diana's desk, but hearing him speak about it with such passion lent it a whole new meaning. My horror must have shown on my face, because Luke frowned.

'I'm sorry, I didn't mean to bombard you with all of that. It's so *important*. I'm pleased you've come to help.'

'Not at all,' I replied. 'I agree. I wish we could find a way to get more people involved.'

'It's even harder than usual at the moment,' he said. 'The whole village is distracted by the havoc that storm wreaked, particularly to the church. There's barely enough money to patch up the damage, let alone do the proper repairs that are needed.'

'I've been helping Gloria with the guesthouse,' I said. 'It's a lot of work and money even for a building that size. I don't know where you'd begin with a church.'

'Well, let's get these bags filled,' said Luke. 'It's a grain of sand in the desert of need, but it's something.'

For the next hour, we worked. Although the patch of sand in Spindrift Bay was relatively small – we weren't talking about Bournemouth beach here – it yielded a shocking amount of garbage. In the end I managed to fill two of the large bags with plastic bottles, bags, squashed tin cans, lengths of green and orange rope and string that Luke told me came from boats, and various other bits of debris. My mind, having been given a new problem to chew over, temporarily put Diana's secret on the back burner, which was a relief given that Luke was probably, unbeknownst to him, her nephew, and I was terrified of blurting it out just to relieve my mental tension. Instead, I pondered ideas for what might be done to help the village, and by the time Luke called me over, I had a plan.

'What do we do with all this now?' I asked, nodding at the four bulging bags.

'Now, they need sorting,' he said. 'But don't worry about that, I normally take them back and do them at home, in the garden.'

'I don't mind at all,' I said truthfully. 'Let's take them back to my place; it's much closer and we can use the garden there. I've got some flapjacks that need eating and I should probably check on the kittens, anyway. Oh, and I'll show you that photo.'

We hauled the sacks into the back of Luke's car and drove the short distance home. Soon we were ensconced in the sunny garden with tea and flapjacks, and a kitten each.

'It won't be long until you can let them out to explore,' said Luke. 'But as long as we keep them with us, there's no reason why they shouldn't enjoy some fresh air.'

'It's much easier with two people,' I said. 'I haven't dared bring them both outside at the same time yet.'

'They're escape artists,' he replied. 'Look at this one trying to crawl under my arm; he's so determined. I see you kept the easy one for yourself!'

I laughed as I stroked the little tabby, who had settled peacefully on my lap.

'Squeak is calmer for sure.'

I stroked him and his purr would have rivalled the engines of the tractors that passed by every so often.

'Luke, I was having a think when we were on the beach, and there might be a way to help the village – the church – and get people involved in your regular clean-ups.'

'Sounds good. What did you have in mind?'

'Well, what about an event that would raise money but also get people down to the beach – maybe an early evening barbecue? Some local bands could come along and play as well. We could raise some money and morale at the same time, and if you talked to people about the beach clean-ups – well, it might be more effective than flyers.'

He scooped the kitten out from where it had burrowed behind his back and looked at me with such thoughtful intensity that I began to feel awkward. Did he think it was a terrible idea? I leant carefully over Squeak, still quiet on my lap, and began collecting together the tea things.

'Maybe everyone would hate it,' I said, unable to bear the silence any longer. 'It was silly of me, I barely know the village. I wanted to try to help...'

I tailed off, then risked a glance at Luke, sure that he would be either embarrassed or scornful. Instead, he was smiling.

'No, no, it's a brilliant idea!'

'Really?'

'Yes. I remember going to something like that years ago; it was good fun and everyone came. I reckon we could pull it off, although it'll take some organisation.' He paused, and it was his turn to look awkward. 'Sorry, I'm assuming you meant that we would organise it, but you probably didn't.'

'I'd like to,' I said. 'It's nice to keep busy. But I didn't mean to rope you in – although it would be good if you could...'

'I can,' he said firmly. 'I'll start by asking my parents if they've still got some barbecues they bought for an event at the house a few years ago. I've seen the effects of big storms several times, but this feels different. The church looks so pathetic and people are overwhelmed. A beach barbecue could give them back some oomph – and, even if it doesn't, *I'll* feel better knowing I'm doing something.'

'You're like me,' I said. 'I like to help. But it means I've been taken advantage of.' I thought back to my father and the way he exploited mine and Mum's good natures, and to Matt and his parents, who saved tens of thousands of pounds by paying me the salary of an office dogsbody while I did the work of a chief financial officer. 'When I moved here,' I continued, 'I wanted to rebrand myself, but it hasn't worked.'

'Some of us are doers. Speaking of which, shall we get these plates and kittens inside?'

We collected everything up, then returned to the garden to start sorting the garbage we had collected. Luke explained that it was simple – one pile for recyclables, one for garbage and one for plastic bags, which went to a separate place for recycling. We donned the heavy-duty gloves again, and got to work.

'If you don't mind my asking,' said Luke, peeling some seaweed off a tin can. 'Who has taken advantage of your helpful disposition in the past?'

My face burnt. Where Matt was concerned, I had been vacillating between grief, despair and self-blame since it happened, with occasional 'power moments', such as the one that led to me selling my engagement ring. As time had moved on, shame and anger had joined the party, and I was wary of revealing my ugly emotions to a man I barely knew. It had felt different with Gloria. My feelings about my father were also complicated, and currently bathed in deep guilt about leaving my mother alone with him so far away.

'I'm sorry,' said Luke. 'I shouldn't have asked.'

'No, it's all right,' I said. 'I brought it up. In short, my father is a bully and I was jilted by my fiancé. I worked at his parents' company and they didn't treat me fairly. I didn't mind too much because I was in love with their son and saw myself as helping out, being part of the family. When he called off the wedding, they all dropped me like a hot coal. The most I had ever been was useful: cheap labour, not the daughter they never had.'

I knew I sounded bitter, and I was, but injecting my tone with sourness was the best way I had found to stop myself crying.

'I'm so sorry,' said Luke, his voice soft. 'It sounds like you've had a bad time of it. People can be cruel.'

His kindness wrapped itself around me, and I didn't trust myself to answer. I could see why everyone said he was such a good vet: it wasn't just technical skill, but his gentle sympathy that made you feel safe. I took a few breaths, added yet another plastic bag to the correct pile, and changed the subject.

'How about you?'

He sat back on his heels and scrunched up his face.

'My parents have been great, but they inhabit a world that is out of date – well, for me, anyway. My father's entire life has revolved around the land and the house he inherited, and my mother took all that on when she married him. I know people in the village see them as distant, even unfriendly, but they don't know how else to be.' He gave a short laugh. 'My mother, would you believe, avoids coming to the village shop because she thinks it might make people uncomfortable to see her there. It's almost as if she feels she has a duty to play an anachronistic role as the lady of the manor.'

'And, one day, all of this will be yours,' I said with a grin.

Luke rolled his eyes.

'Indeed. Or maybe not.'

I frowned.

'Doesn't it all go to the eldest son?'

'Yes, well, usually, but it's been odd. I was brought up to be prepared to inherit the land and title, but when I was fourteen, my brother was born and suddenly all the training and expectation ground to a halt. I assumed it was because they were so shocked – pleased and surprised, yes, but also completely shocked – by Sam's arrival. Mum was forty-four and I don't think they'd expected another baby. Anyway, I had no interest in bringing the subject up. By then I knew that I wanted to go to university and study to become a vet, rather than do a degree in land management, which was what had been expected of me.'

'And that obviously happened.'

'Yes. Sam was only little when decisions had to be made. Mum and Dad were pretty distracted by being older parents to a toddler, so I sorted it all out myself and they agreed. I've got no idea what will happen when they retire or pass away. Sam's already interested in the estate, so maybe there's some way he can take it on. I don't want to – can't – jack in my whole career, but I don't know how I'm going to avoid it.'

He looked desolate, but I didn't know what to say to console him. For a few minutes, we sorted the rest of the garbage; maybe it was a good time to try to find out if he had any idea that Diana was his aunt.

'What about other members of the family?' I asked, cringing at the false nonchalance I could hear in my voice, and hoping he wouldn't notice. 'Isn't there an uncle or aunt or someone who might take it on?'

He shook his head.

'No. I don't mean to sound ungrateful – I know many people would be only too glad for such an inheritance – but it's all-consuming and not what I want for my life.' He paused. 'Inheritance has worked well for you, though.'

'Yes, although I wasn't all too sure about it at first, either. I didn't think I was worthy of it, so I suppose it's kind of the opposite problem.' I had almost forgotten about the photo, but the talk of inheritance reminded me. 'Oh, I'll get that photo to show you.'

I ran inside to get it, and handed it to him. He studied it.

'Look at Diana! It seems odd to see her so young, but she looks just the same, in a way.'

'I agree. I think that happens when people have strong personalities.'

'She's definitely up at Spindrift House. I wonder who the baby is?'

He turned the photo over, as I had, but of course found nothing there.

'I don't know – I thought she might have been a nanny or something?'

'Could have been, or visiting with a friend. It might have been before my parents moved in. It's funny she never mentioned it, but she'd probably forgotten all about it. I'll have to ask my parents.'

I made a noncommittal noise, and we moved on to chat about the teahouse and what I was planning on keeping and changing. Maybe it would be better to wait to hear what Luke's parents said. Any big reveal of a family secret would be far better coming from them than from me. For now, at least, I would have to continue to bear the burden of Diana's secret alone.

TWELVE

After Luke had left, I was tired from our morning's work and spent the next couple of hours quietly, having some lunch and reading my book. I must have been more tired than I realised, because I fell asleep on the sofa and only awoke when my phone pinged with a text. Blearily, I groped for it and saw that the message was from Luke.

> I spoke to my dad and they do still have the barbecues, but not sure of condition. Do you want to come up with me tomorrow to take a look?

I was wide awake now, and quickly tapped back a response, agreeing. We arranged the time with a couple more texts and then I rang Mum for a chat. She sounded cheerful, which I was pleased about, but when I asked her about it, she merely said that life was good and maybe she'd come down for a visit soon. After the call, I started to make some shortbread to take with me to Luke's parents tomorrow. I could whip some up without looking at a recipe now, and was experimenting with different flavours, although my current obsession was on creating shortbread flavoured with tea. There were scores of different methods for doing this, from infusing and straining butter, which then had to be left overnight to solidify again, to simply chucking a couple of spoonfuls of leaves in with the mixture. Results varied, but nothing had been inedible – yet. Maybe today would be the day, as I had the idea of using smoky lapsang souchong tea, given that we were planning a barbecue. *Ah well, nothing ventured, nothing gained.* I breathed in the strong, evocative scent of the tea. And at least it would keep me busy and my mind off Luke, my mum and other people's secrets.

Luke came by at ten o'clock the following morning to drive up to the manor house.

'What have you got there?' he asked, nodding at the paper-wrapped package I carried.

'It's shortbread for your parents,' I said. 'To say thank you for the barbecues.'

'And if they're rusty and useless, then maybe we can eat it ourselves.'

'I had some for breakfast,' I confessed. 'Purely as a final taste test, you understand?'

'But of course,' he replied. 'What was the verdict?'

'I made them with lapsang souchong, so I wasn't sure how tasty they'd be, but I was pleasantly surprised.'

'Sounds as if The Coastal Kettle is getting a dramatic makeover,' he said, turning up a narrow lane of the kind that proliferate in Dorset.

'I'm sticking to all the old favourites as well,' I said. 'But it doesn't do any harm to mix things up. I was even thinking of trying to develop some kind of online presence, so people could order from all over the country.'

We turned in through a pair of huge iron gates that stood open, flanked by tall stone pillars, and the large, elegant house I had seen in the photo of Diana and the baby stood before us. I began to feel nervous, but Luke's kind voice reassured me.

'Going online is a great idea. I have a friend who does web

design if you need any help. Diana would have been kicking herself that she didn't think of it. Ah, there's Dad.'

He stopped the car in front of the house, and we got out as a patrician-looking man strode over. He was tall – taller than Luke – and had thick, grey hair, brushed back from his face. His eyes were a clear, bright blue and swept over me appraisingly as he approached and first shook Luke's hand, then mine.

'Welcome to Spindrift House,' he said in a strong, deep voice. 'I'm Henry. I hear you're after those old barbecues.'

We started walking towards the side of the house.

'If they're still in working order, we'd like to borrow them,' said Luke. 'Belle and I are organising a beach barbecue to try and cheer people up and raise some money for the repairs the church needs after the storm.'

'Terrible business,' said his father, stopping at an outbuilding and pulling back a large bolt. 'Your mother and I are glad to help.'

Although his manner was brisk, his words were kind, and I began to relax as he ushered me ahead of him into the building and snapped on an overhead light. The room we stood in was filled with the bric-a-brac I supposed came with owning a large, centuries-old house. There were wooden chairs stacked on top of one another, rolled-up carpets and a couple of ladders. Henry pulled a table to one side, then exclaimed with delight.

'There they are! Give me a hand, Luke.'

The two men squeezed into the small space and hauled out three large barbecues. I helped pull them out of the building to the yard outside.

'They look pretty good, Dad,' said Luke. 'They haven't rusted.'

'No, it's dry in there. Give them a good clean and they'll be fine. Do you want to take them now?'

'Yes,' Luke replied. 'I'll bring the car round; it'll be easier than carrying them all the way to the front of the house.'

He jogged away, leaving me standing with his father.

'How long have you lived in the bay?' he asked.

'Only a couple of months,' I said. 'I'm taking over The Coastal Kettle – Diana Dalton was my godmother.'

'Of course she was,' he said. 'I remember seeing you at the funeral. My condolences.'

I gave a small smile of thanks as a flash of adrenaline zipped through me. Much as I had decided to keep out of it, I couldn't miss this opportunity to mention the photo.

'I found some interesting bits and pieces in her personal effects,' I said.

He frowned, and my resolve wavered.

'Is that right?'

He sounded wary.

'Mmm. There's a photo of her standing outside the house – your house – in fact. I wondered if you knew her?'

The colour had drained from his face, and I didn't dare push any further by mentioning the birth certificate.

He cleared his throat, then said, 'Plenty of people visit this house; I know few of them personally. Ah, look, here's Luke.'

He strode off to meet the car before I had a chance to gather my thoughts, let alone answer him. I helped put the barbecues in without saying anything else. When it was all packed, Henry turned to Luke.

'Are you going to come in and see your mother?'

Luke's eyes moved between us; sensitive as he was, I was sure he had picked up on something being wrong.

'Yes, of course,' he replied. 'Belle, would you like to join us?'

I risked flicking a glance at Henry, who was inspecting a speck of dust on his cuff.

'I won't, thank you,' I said. 'But please do take these with you.'

I retrieved the shortbread from the passenger seat of the car and gave it to Luke, who thanked me.

'Come along, then,' said his father. He went to walk away, then turned back awkwardly and tried to force a smile, although he struggled to meet my eyes.

'A pleasure to meet you, Belle. I wish you all the best for the barbecue – and the tearooms.'

He started to walk towards the house, but Luke didn't follow him.

'Are you all right?' he said, frowning. 'I'm sorry about Dad, he's in a funny mood. It was rude of him not to invite you in.'

'I think I might have upset him,' I said, kicking myself now for having said anything. 'I asked him about the photo of Diana, and he seemed cross about it.'

Luke frowned.

'I'm sorry, Belle. He can be quite... brusque. Are you okay?'

His kindness and concern were making me feel guilty.

'I'm fine, really. I shouldn't have said anything – it's none of my business.'

'Of course it is – it's your photo, so why wouldn't you ask about it? I'll see if Mum knows anything. You're very welcome to come in?'

'No, no. You go, I'll enjoy the walk back.'

'All right,' he said reluctantly. 'I don't see enough of them, or I'd drive you home. Now I'm here, I can't leave without stopping by.'

'It's no problem,' I said. 'Let's be in touch soon about the barbecue.'

Luke headed towards the back of the house, and I went back out the way we had come. I wasn't sorry for the solitary walk; although it had only lasted seconds and hadn't been particularly dramatic, the interaction with Luke's father had unsettled me. He clearly had no intention of discussing Diana or the photo. His comment about not knowing everyone who visited the house was probably true, so I suppose he hadn't lied outright to me. What he didn't know was that, as well as the photo, I also had the birth certificate, so I was as sure as I could be that he was evading the truth. *I suppose*, I mused as I climbed over an old, wooden stile to pass along a farm path and avoid walking in the road, *it could be possible that he had no idea whatsoever that Diana was his sister.*

That he was the person Diana referred to as needing "to know". But, then again, the family had turned up at her funeral which was, apparently, wholly unexpected. I reached a glorious part of the walk home, where the farmland rose and there was a wide view taking in the sea, the village and the undulating countryside all around. I paused to drink in the vista and attempt to calm my turbulent thoughts. Diana may well have asked with her dying breath for her secrets to be brought to light, but it wasn't straightforward. The burden of responsibility weighed heavy upon me, and I threw my head back in frustration. It was then that I heard pattering feet and turned to see Doris trotting towards me, Edward a little way behind.

'Hello, girl,' I said, bending to pat her smooth, golden head. 'You're feeling better, aren't you?'

'That she is,' said Edward. 'Luke worked wonders on her.'

I patted Doris again, still distracted by my thoughts.

'I hope you don't mind my asking,' went on Edward, 'but something seems to be bothering you. The way you were standing there when we turned up – well, let's say you're not the first person to try to get answers from the sea and the hills.'

I gave him a watery smile.

'And do they – give answers, that is?'

'Sometimes, sometimes, but not always quickly. Would you like a cuppa?' he went on. 'I'm heading towards my favourite bench, just up yonder.'

I chewed at my lip. In one way, I wanted to continue tramping the fields and the cliffs until I knew what to do, but the same things were sure to continue waltzing around my mind, with no clear answer in sight. Besides, I liked Edward and would be happy to have his company.

'Come on, then,' he said, before I had spoken. 'You'll as likely find your answer in the bottom of a cup of tea as you will standing here.'

We set off slowly, my confidence low. Where on earth might there be a bench on these windswept, lonely hills? It was hardly your local park. But, sure enough, a few minutes later, we were sitting comfortably and Edward was unpacking his knapsack.

'Who puts benches out here?' I asked.

He shrugged.

'Depends. Sometimes, the landowner – that might be private, or council, or National Trust. Sometimes, ramblers' associations raise money for them. I'm grateful; they seem to know how to pick the perfect place.'

He produced a Thermos flask and two china mugs and proceeded to pour out steaming tea. Next came a small, plastic bottle filled with milk, which he doled out.

'Sugar?' he asked, opening a box with some cubes inside.

'No, thank you,' I said, and he plopped one cube into his own tea, then stirred it with a metal spoon from the bag.

'Do you always bring two mugs?' I asked curiously.

'Always,' he replied. 'It's partly force of habit; Diana and I often came for a walk together. And it's partly hope of a chance encounter, like this one today. I prefer to share my tea, but I don't often get the opportunity.'

Next, he brought out a box and took off the lid to reveal some cookies, the luxury kind which have giant chunks of chocolate throughout. He offered them to me and I took one gladly.

'Not up to your standards, I'm afraid,' he said. 'Only shop-bought.'

'Sometimes, shop-bought is best,' I said. 'You can't argue with perfection, and this is what I needed.'

'Simple things,' replied Edward.

For a few minutes, we sat in a relaxed silence, eating cookies, sipping tea and watching Doris as she gambolled about like a puppy. I was so comforted by it all that I jumped when Edward spoke.

'Do you want to share your worries?' he asked. 'I don't pry, but usually it helps to talk, and you can trust me to keep it quiet, whatever it is. Although,' he added, with a gentle smile, 'I can't promise I won't tell Doris.'

I looked at him anxiously.

'The problem is,' I said, 'I'm not sure if it's my secret to tell.'

'To do with Diana, is it?' he said bluntly. 'You might find I already know; I might not.'

'I think she wanted this aired,' I replied, and explained what she had said to Tessa as she lay dying. His blue eyes swam with tears, and he mopped at them quickly with a handkerchief.

'Sorry, sorry, can't bear to think of Diana lying there, broken. The picture of it haunts me, Belle, I don't know how to shift it.'

I didn't know what to say, because I felt the same way. Every time I passed the stairs an image of Diana helpless on the floor, knowing she was dying, desperate to share her secret before the opportunity was lost forever, swamped my mind.

'I think—' I started to say. My voice caught and I paused and cleared my throat, took a breath and tried again. 'I think that I *have* to tell you. I can't keep turning it over by myself and getting no further. She didn't want it to stay a secret, and I know you were good friends. I know you won't tell anyone – other than Doris – and I'm happy to bring her into our circle of trust.'

We smiled weakly at each other, and I went on to describe the photograph and the birth certificate.

'I tried to speak to Sir Henry about it earlier,' I said. 'And he was so obviously uncomfortable that I didn't get far.'

Edward nodded slowly, then stared out to sea for a long time. I gazed at my hands, focusing on how much they had changed in the time since I had been in Spindrift Bay. I used to care for my hands and nails, having regular gel manicures and liking the way my nails looked as they flashed over the keyboard of my computer. Now, I had picked away at the varnish, not having been anywhere near a salon to have it professionally removed, and what I hadn't worried at myself had been assaulted by cooking, kittens and the beach. My skin was no longer creamy and smooth but slightly roughened and reddened, with several minor cuts and burns courtesy of the kitchen, as well as a few friendly kitten scratches. Matt had liked my pretty hands. As I contemplated them now, waiting for Edward to speak, I had an odd sense of pride in my neglected mitts. They had been working hard, and it showed. No shame in that.

Eventually, Edward spoke.

'Thank you for telling me,' he said slowly. 'I deeply appreciate your trust, and I will honour it. It may reassure you somewhat to hear that this is not news to me. I knew Diana when we were young, and I always had the feeling her family was somehow stifling her. She became estranged from them many years ago, then moved to France. But she never told me what happened. I believe' – he turned to me with troubled eyes – 'I believe that whatever secrets she – and they – were keeping, they cast shadows too long for her to confront.'

'But she came home.'

'Yes, if "home" is the right word. Although it is true that she did make Spindrift Bay her home again. And I also believe that the time was coming for her to bring everything out into the open. I felt that she was coming close to sharing more with me, but she never did.'

He stopped talking and stared out to sea again, his eyes moist. Doris trotted over and laid her beautiful head on his knee.

'Ah, you understand, don't you?' he said to the dog. 'You understand all about love.' He turned to me again. 'I cared for Diana all my life. More, I think, than she ever knew. She didn't only leave her family when she moved to France, she left me, and with no explanation. I was so *glad*,' he said forcefully. 'So very *glad* to have her back, if not for long enough.'

'I'm sorry,' I said quietly. 'I didn't realise.'

'Selfishly,' said Edward, 'I would dearly love to know what happened nearly forty years ago, if only to understand where I fitted in. And, as I said, I do believe she was going to let it out. You know that she had become close to Luke?'

I nodded.

'And that was a source of joy to her – to not only get to know her nephew but to become so close to him. Diana was hard to get to know, but he was a steadfast friend to her. They admired each other: he, her passion for the sea, and she, the fact that he would drive ten miles in a snowstorm rather than let a farmer lose a calf. As stubborn as each other, in their own ways. He would like to know, I think, that his friend was his aunt. I have never dreamed of speaking to him about it, because Diana swore me to secrecy, but it sounds as though she may have given permission, right at the end. You will have to tread carefully, though, as you discovered up at the manor house today.'

'Did anyone else in Spindrift Bay recognise her when she returned?' I asked.

Edward shook his head.

'I don't think so. She and I met before her family moved to the house, and it wasn't so long after that she left. She didn't have much of a chance to make friends in the village and those she might have known to say hello to would be unlikely to recognise a passing acquaintance after nearly forty years, if they were still here. Plenty have moved away.'

I sighed.

'All right. Thank you for talking to me. I have to take the action that Diana couldn't bring herself to.'

Even if it makes me feel sick thinking about it.

Edward grasped my hand.

'She'd be proud of you for that. She would be glad to know that you were brave enough to push forward with her wishes. My door's always open for you, Belle, if you need to talk more.'

We walked back to the village together and then I continued up to my house alone. The belief that I had to speak to Luke about Diana had now hardened into knowledge, and it sat like a stone in my stomach. What if he already knew, and he responded as his father had done? What if there was a good reason that the Talbots wanted their connection to Diana kept a secret? All I could do now was to find trust: trust that Diana wouldn't have left me with a legacy that would be destructive, and trust that, despite the pain that might arise, truth was usually the best choice.

THIRTEEN

Luke and I wanted to hold the beach barbecue as soon as possible and, with all the preparations, I couldn't find a good time to tell him about Diana's birth certificate. We had spoken briefly when our paths had crossed in the village.

'I asked Mum about that photo,' Luke had said. 'I think you were right about Dad: she was really odd about it, too. I think she was about to tell me something, but Dad came in and she changed the subject.'

'Maybe she'll fill you in another time,' I said. I was even more uneasy, now that I knew Luke's parents weren't going to readily admit that Diana was part of the family, but clearly knew *some*thing.

For a few days, I worried and was on edge, seeking the perfect moment but then, as is so often the case, I found peace by letting go. I decided that I wouldn't even consider telling him until after the barbecue and, for now, I would put all my energies into organising it as well as continuing the refurbishment of the tearooms and practising baking. I was achingly aware that Diana, too, had been working herself up to revealing her secret in some way, dying before she could, but I refused to let this haunt me, or shake my resolve. After all, Edward and Mum also knew the truth.

The proposition of the barbecue was met with interest in the village, but although people regularly told me they were looking forward to it, it was hard to rally them to help. After all, they may be concerned and upset about the church, but most of them had to focus on rebuilding their own homes and businesses after the devastation the storm had wreaked, and lacked the energy to do much else.

'It's all right,' said Tessa one evening, as we sat at the kitchen table in Seaspray Lodge. She, along with Caleb, Gloria, Edward, Luke and me, had formed what we had delighted in calling the "BBC" – Beach Barbecue Committee. 'The six of us can pull this together and it will be a sort of gift to the village.'

'And although people are short on time and money,' added Caleb, who had finally sat down after making sure that Noah was fast asleep upstairs, 'pretty much all of them have offered something.'

'They've been incredibly generous,' I said. 'But we still can't afford enough food. At this rate they'll get half a burger bun and some lettuce, maybe some ketchup if we see some on offer. And I don't see how we're going to *make* money, even if we do find enough to hold the event.'

Tessa and Gloria both started talking, then stopped and laughed.

'You go on, darling,' said Gloria. 'Mine can keep.'

'I've got good news and bad news,' said Tessa. 'Which do you want first?'

'Always the good,' said Edward.

'So, Mum has offered to sponsor the food – well, the buns, burgers and salad,' she went on. 'She's been shaken by what's happened and by seeing her beloved village and church looking so broken. She'd normally be the first one on a committee like this,' she added, grinning. 'But I'm afraid I told her that it was practical help we needed more and that the committee was full. I do love her, but having her at these meetings wouldn't help.'

We all gave small smiles and glanced at each other in guilty acknowledgement.

'That's incredibly generous of her,' said Luke. 'Please do thank her from all of us. But what's the bad news?'

Tessa grinned.

'I also mentioned that we were thinking of having some entertainment and Mum is insisting, as a quid pro quo for the food, that my cousin Dean's band plays. And they're awful. She sees him as the son she never had and doesn't believe that her brother and sister-in-law "encourage" him enough. The truth is that they're realistic. Jon Bon Jovi he ain't. Look.'

She picked up her phone, which she was using as a baby monitor for her sleeping son upstairs, and opened a video, which we all leant in to watch. A good-looking young man was strutting around on a small stage, giving his all to a cover of *Livin' on a Prayer*, while the drummer, guitarist and keyboard player tried pluckily to keep in time with him and each other. The overall effect made you wince, but I'd seen worse. It was Edward who broke the stunned silence.

'It's not my sort of music,' he said diplomatically. 'I must say, the lead singer has plenty of charisma.'

'Well, I vote yes,' said Gloria firmly. 'They're not so terrible and we can claim there's a law about volume and turn them right down. I presume we don't have to pay them?'

'No,' said Tessa. 'They want the exposure and to hand out a few flyers. Is that all right, then?'

Everyone nodded.

'Well, thank you, Beverly,' I said. 'Thanks to her that's food *and* entertainment ticked off. What's next?'

'I had an idea for raising some money,' said Gloria. 'Well, it was my Georgie's idea, something he said goes down well with the expats in Spain. He suggested we hold an Auction of Promises.' She looked around the table and was met with five confused faces. 'No, I'd never heard of it, either. I'll explain. You get people to make a promise to do something or give something, and people bid on it. So, Belle, you might offer to bake something of the winner's choice, or give them afternoon tea once The Coastal Kettle is open again. Or Luke, you could offer to dog walk. People often auction their time rather than things: babysitting, hair or make-up, an hour of odd jobs around the house and so on. I'd be happy to take on the organisation, if you all like the idea.'

'It's brilliant,' said Caleb. 'And it's a good way for people to feel involved, without having to commit too much time.'

We all agreed, and Gloria smiled.

'Good. I'll start with you lot, so get your thinking caps on!'

'We're sorted for the main food,' said Tessa. 'But what about puddings? Can we afford to buy them now?'

I bit my lip.

'I'm afraid the budget is still horribly tight. We have to buy public liability insurance, fuel for the barbecues and consider hiring toilet and handwashing facilities, although I have wondered if the loos at the tearoom would be close enough? They haven't been refurbished yet, and there's a second, separate entrance, so I don't mind at all.'

'You and I should go and see the vicar,' said Luke. 'He holds plenty of lunches and so on, so he might have some tips.'

'That's an excellent idea,' said Gloria. 'Apart from anything else, the poor man needs to rally. When I told him about the barbecue, he could barely raise a smile. In my experience, *doing* something, however hopeless you think the situation is, is a surefire way to feel better about it.'

And, with her galvanising words, we closed the meeting. As I walked home, I could only pray that "hopeless" wasn't the truth of the matter.

That evening, I steeled myself to do a job I had been putting off: sorting out Diana's clothes to donate to a local charity shop. When I opened her wardrobe, the waft of her familiar, fresh, slightly sharp-scented perfume reached my emotions before it reached my nose, and I doubled over as if I had been physically hit. I groped for the bed and sat down, gasping for breath as my suddenly reawakened grief caused a torrent of tears. I had been keeping so busy, so distracted, that it had been surprisingly easy to bury my upset, but the scent had unlocked that tight compartment in my heart, shocking me that the pain I thought I had managed so well was, in fact, so very near the surface. The sobs, for all their ferocity, didn't last long, and soon I found myself out of breath and trembling, staring at the open wardrobe. Could I carry on with the job I had assigned myself?

'Come on, girl!' I said out loud, my voice a wobbly impersonation of Diana at her most brisk. 'No time like the present.'

Slowly, I stood up and started pulling clothes off the hangers to fold up. I wasn't surprised that everything in the wardrobe was clean and in good condition, or that there wasn't very much of it. Diana always looked smart, chic and very much herself, but she didn't need piles of clothes to achieve it. I put aside a couple of soft, cashmere jumpers that I would like to wear myself, and a couple of other items to photograph for Mum. Soon, all the clothes were sorted, and I moved onto bags and shoes. Again, Diana didn't have large amounts of these items and, before too long, I was pulling out the final handbag, a simple black one that was tucked right at the back. It was timeless in style but, when I opened it to check for any bits and pieces, I realised from the label and soft chamois lining that it was vintage – maybe sixties or seventies. There was a small mirror tucked in the interior pocket, and behind it a stiff piece of paper, folded in half. I took it out and unfolded it, then drew my breath in sharply. For here was another photograph of Diana holding a baby, but this time the set-up was very different. She was sitting on a bench in a garden, without make-up and with her hair pulled loosely back in a ponytail. She was wearing a dressing gown and bedroom slippers and trying to smile for the camera. Was this a snap of a nanny with her tiny charge? It didn't look like it to me. It looked more like a photo of a young mother holding her own baby. But if Diana *had* given birth, what had happened to the baby? Did

Luke and his brother have a cousin they didn't know about, who had been adopted? Or maybe, and my breath caught in my throat at the thought, maybe the baby had died. I gazed into Diana's eyes, but didn't know what to read there. *What secrets were you holding?* I wondered. *And what terrible sorrows?*

The photo had upset and overwhelmed me, and I didn't know what to think. The next day, when I received a text from Luke saying that he had arranged for us to see the vicar at three that afternoon, if it suited me, I was at once terrified that I would blurt out something about Diana at the wrong moment, but also looking forward to seeing him – and to getting out of the tearooms. The workers I had in at The Coastal Kettle had discovered some underlying damp problems and I had thrown myself into moving all the chairs and tables out of the tearoom and into the house, followed by the entire contents of the shopfront cupboards, which had exhausted but also distracted me. Luckily, the kitchen hadn't suffered too badly, needing mainly cosmetic work inside, or I could have been looking at a great deal more expense and upheaval. As it was, I was worried that some of the painting Tessa and I had done would be ruined, and we'd have to start again.

For now, I busied myself stacking the dishwasher with cups and saucers, mugs and glasses and what felt like four thousand teaspoons, and writing an inventory of everything. I was finding it difficult to decide if I should keep Diana's mishmash of utilitarian items or invest in crockery and cutlery that lent more of a sense of style to the tearooms. The current things had the advantage of being cheap and easily maintained, which I knew would have appealed to Diana's practicality, and I wasn't ready to throw them out yet. Maybe changing them would be a "nice to have" rather than an "essential". Regardless, I had let the debate about them fill my head, pushing out the photo and the worry over if, or when, I should say something to Luke. The fact that his parents had avoided the subject so determinedly unsettled me. There was clearly some secret being kept, and I wasn't at all sure that I wanted to poke the wasps' nest any more than I already had. At half past two I hung up my rubber gloves, said goodbye to the kittens and headed over to the vicarage.

I was doing a lot of walking since I had moved to Spindrift Bay and rarely now got the car out unless I was driving to Dorchester or Weymouth. Instead, I loved discovering the myriad paths you could use to get from A to B. Some of them were clearly sign-posted, well-worn and easy to pass along whilst others had to be discovered by the regular walker, or shown by a friend. These could be almost invisible at first, and require significant intrepidity in terms of pushing past overgrown and often prickly bushes, or navigating areas still muddy even at this time of year. But, despite these drawbacks, they were often worth it, revealing treasures you would never see from behind the wheel of a car or on the more regular paths. I had spotted little lizards flicking their tails as they fled from me, and more varieties of butterflies than I had ever imagined possible. Town living seemed far away, and I had even started noting down some of the nature I saw on an app on my phone, finding unexpected joy when it flagged up 'an unusual sighting!' and congratulated me.

I had left plenty of time for my leisurely stroll, and arrived at the vicarage a couple of minutes early. I perched on a conveniently placed bench outside and closed my eyes to enjoy the sunshine while I waited for Luke.

'Falling asleep on the job?' came a teasing voice, as a shadow fell over me. I opened my eyes to see Luke and grinned at him.

'I've had a busy morning. Who would begrudge a girl a quick snooze?'

He held out his hand, which I took, and he pulled me up. I admit, it wasn't at all unpleasant to feel his strong hand in mine, and I could easily have gone on holding it. Although I still thought about Matt daily, and the pain I felt at his loss hadn't fully abated, I knew I was moving on, however impossible that had once felt.

'Nice place he's got, hasn't he?' said Luke, as we walked up a curving, gravelled drive towards a huge, red-brick house.

'I'll say. Didn't the church sell off all the decent vicarages and put the clergy in poky newbuilds?'

'Not here. I'm sure they would have done, but there probably wasn't anything suitable nearby. And anyway, the house is as badly in need of repair as the church, so unless someone's looking for a passion project in the middle of nowhere, the vicar of Spindrift Bay will probably be allowed to live here until it falls down. Half of it's shut up as it is, and they use at least one of the downstairs rooms for parish meetings and other community stuff.'

'Maybe he should start taking in paying guests?' I suggested, picturing all the unused rooms at Diana's house, and the plans I had considered for them.

'Maybe, but the vicar's wife isn't well,' Luke said quietly, as we approached the front door. 'He's got enough on his plate without launching his home on Airbnb.'

He lifted the huge brass knocker and tapped it as gently as he could. I still heard a rousing boom echo through the hallway beyond, and a few seconds later a small, balding man in a cardigan that must have been far too warm for a day like today opened the door.

'Luke,' he said, trying to raise a smile to his morose face. 'And you must be Belle? I'm Fergus.'

'Yes,' I said, holding out my hand, which he shook listlessly. 'Thank you for seeing us.'

'Oh, it's fine,' he said distractedly. 'Please, come in, sorry about the mess.'

The black and white tiled hallway was strewn with shoes, boots and toys, and I could hear the shouts of children playing somewhere. We followed Fergus into a large kitchen, every surface covered in books, toys, packets and interesting-looking pieces of church ephemera and I saw, past the kitchen sink piled with unwashed dishes, two young children of about six and eight years old playing on a swing and slide set. A woman sat near them in the shade, a rug over her lap. Fergus's eyes followed in the direction of mine.

'My children, Grace and Ben,' he said, pushing a saucepan aside to fill the kettle and causing greasy, tomatoey water to splash over the draining board. 'I'm afraid my wife, Gillian, has little energy much of the time, but they're good kids.'

'I'm sorry to hear that,' I said, then went to take the mugs from him that he had extracted from a cupboard. I could see his hands were shaking. 'Why don't I do that? I need to keep getting in the practice for the tearooms. I brought some madeleines as well. It's a new recipe and I was hoping you'd help me out by tasting them. The children, too, if they're allowed? I hear that they're the most discerning critics.'

'Oh yes, yes, I'm sure they'll love them.' He suddenly looked as if he was going to cry. I glanced at Luke who, thankfully, appraised the situation quickly.

'Come and sit down, Fergus. I thought you might like me to take a look at your insurance, and then Belle and I have got a suggestion.'

They started tapping away at their phones while I made tea and found some juice for the children. I took out a tray to the garden and, while Grace and Ben ran over and chattered excitedly about their favourite cakes, their mum barely moved, other than to give me a tiny smile when I put her tea on the table next to her.

Back inside, Luke, looking pale, handed me his phone. The details of the church's insurance were open and I scanned the information quickly. No wonder Fergus was worried; the policies weren't fit for purpose, and he would only be able to claim a fraction of what I had understood the damage to be. I pasted on my brightest smile.

'Okay, these need to be updated, for if anything happens again, but that can wait. So, Luke and I – and lots of other people in the village – would love to help raise some funds for the church to be fixed. We're organising a barbecue on the beach. Beverly has been super generous in saying she'll sort out the main food, but we need your help!'

Fergus looked at me listlessly.

'I'm not sure what help I can be.'

Privately, I wasn't too sure, either, but I ploughed on.

'Well, we were wondering if you might be able to ask some of your congregation to make the puddings. We need at least ten.'

'Yes,' continued Luke. 'I've been telling Belle how amazing you are at organising community events, and you will get results where we won't.'

Thankfully, the vicar brightened.

'It is true that we have had several *most* successful lunches for the needy in the parish – and surrounding areas,' he said. 'I have more than one congregation, you know?'

I shook my head.

'It is common for country vicars to serve more than one parish – declining numbers, I'm afraid – and many of my flock won't have seen for themselves what we have suffered in Spindrift Bay. I'm sure that I can be confident of their help, if I explain. They have never failed me.'

His gaze drifted to the window; maybe he felt differently about his wife.

'Thank you,' said Luke. 'It will make all the difference.'

'It is I who should be thanking you,' replied Fergus. 'I'm afraid I have lost my spark these days, but I feel that you have been sent to ignite it.'

A little while later, our tummies full of tea and cake and our metaphorical cups overflowing with the vicar's fulsome gratitude, we were heading away from the rectory. We soon reached the war memorial, which was where I went left to walk up to my house, while Luke turned right towards the village.

'That went well,' he said. 'Better than I had hoped.' He paused and, unusually, looked awkward. 'Er, are the kittens all right?'

'Yes, they're fine,' I said, a little surprised at the sudden change of subject. 'Desperate to go outside, but otherwise well.'

'Good, good. I was going to say, if you ever want me to stop by and check them over or anything, I'd be delighted to.'

I frowned. Didn't he think I was looking after them properly?

'You're welcome to,' I replied. 'But they *are* fine.'

'No, no, good, good, I'm sure they are.' He paused again. 'All right, then, well, I'll see you soon. We're nearly there with the barbecue. Unless you think we should get a drink and go over the details?'

He flushed red and the penny dropped. He wasn't suspicious of my kitten-caring capabilities... he was asking me out... wasn't he? Now, it was my turn to feel flustered. I wasn't sure if I had understood correctly and, if I had, how I felt about that. Luke was undeniably handsome as well as being clever and kind, but was I ready for a date? I stared at him as panicked, excited thoughts rushed through my mind, and he was looking ever more embarrassed.

'Look, it's okay,' he said. 'I'm sure you're busy with the kittens and the tearooms and everything. We're having another BBC meeting in a day or two, anyway.'

A combined rush of disappointment and relief surged up my body.

'Yes!' I said with a strangulated laugh. 'Yup, better get back to those monkeys – that is, the kittens, I mean, of course – and give them some dinner. And I'll have a look at the insurance. Don't say I'm not in for a fun night!'

I scuttled away up the cliff to my house, not sure whether I had been extremely sensible or utterly stupid.

FOURTEEN

'So that's three cakes – one an occasion cake – two babysitting, a haircut, a pet health check, several dog-walkings, gardening, a loaf of bread two times a week for a month, French tuition, three carwashes, afternoon tea at The Coastal Kettle when it reopens, a lift to the airport and a pickup home again, dinner for two in Dorchester and two nights at Seaspray Lodge.'

Gloria finished with a flourish, gasped for a breath and then curtseyed as the BBC – gathered around her on the beach an hour before the barbecue was due to begin – applauded her heartily.

'It's not even been two weeks – I can't believe how many promises you've managed to collect,' I said. 'Surely we'll make good money from that?'

'I hope so,' said Gloria. 'And I'm going to put reserves on some of the lots so that nobody gets a bargain.'

'My father has given me a bid for the afternoon tea,' said Luke, holding out an envelope. 'He and Mum can't make it tonight, but they wanted to help.'

Gloria took the envelope, opened it and took out a cheque. As she read it, her eyes grew round and her smile wide.

'What is it?' asked Luke. 'He didn't tell me how much he was bidding.'

'And neither shall I,' said Gloria primly, closing the envelope again and tucking it into her bag. 'You can wait and see later.'

'Ticket sales have been excellent,' said Tessa. 'The vicar not only got his congregations making puddings, but lots of them are coming tonight. It was a good call going to see him – and it is his church, after all.'

'How many are coming?' asked Edward.

'Eighty-three tickets sold,' said Tessa. 'And hopefully a few more on the door.'

'I've got some friends to help with the barbecues,' said Caleb, who had taken on that job. 'They've bought tickets themselves, but they're happy to cook for most of the evening.'

'And Doris and I have done our bit,' said Edward. 'I promised decorations and here they come.' Two smiling men carrying enormous bags were approaching us and waved at Edward, who introduced them as Michael and Chia-hao. 'I work with Chia-hao,' he explained. 'Another one who's usually up to his elbows in fish guts.'

Chia-hao grinned.

'Yup, I'm afraid I'm pretty useless here, but Michael is much more talented and doesn't reek of fish.'

We all laughed.

'Indeed,' said Michael. 'I run an interiors business from our home in Coombe Keynes. This is all made from scrap fabrics. We try to use deadstock as much as possible; it's shocking how much goes to waste.'

He started to pull out bunting from one of the bags, with triangle after triangle of beautiful colours and patterns.

'Oh, it's gorgeous!' I said. 'I'd love to buy it for the tearooms once tonight is over! Can we arrange it?'

'It would be my pleasure,' said Michael, smiling broadly. 'Now, shall we get this put up?'

By the time the first guests arrived, the beach was looking fabulously festive. The bunting danced cheerfully in the warm breeze, and we had intertwined it with solar-powered lights, which would come on as the daylight faded. Tessa and Caleb had built a fire for people to sit around, which burnt merrily. We had carried down some chairs and small tables, but it was likely that most people would want to sit on rugs on the sand, so we had begged as many as possible from everyone we could think of. These were strewn about higgledy-piggledy, with solar lamps on stakes next to them. Beverly's nephew's band had brought with them a makeshift stage created from pallets and rigged up a surprisingly sophisticated looking arrangement of speakers and instruments.

'The guitarist's dad is as big a fan as my mum is,' whispered Tessa, trying not to giggle. 'And he's kitted them out with all the gear. I hope they know how to use it.'

'The warm-up sounds professional,' I said. 'All that twanging. I mean, I assume that *is* the warm-up and they haven't started playing yet?'

We collapsed in laughter as Luke walked past us, looking amused.

'Don't enjoy yourselves too much,' he said teasingly. 'You're first behind the bar and the customers have started arriving.'

We scuttled over to the trestle table that was serving as our bar that evening and quickly started setting out paper cups.

'I don't think I've seen so much wine and beer,' I said, looking at the boxes and coolers stacked up beside us. 'It was clever of Gloria to get it all on sale or return.'

'The place she went to has never been known to be so generous,' said Tessa. 'She could charm the birds out of the trees. She's on the bar later herself, isn't she?'

'She is,' I replied. 'And she's given herself a personal challenge to return no more than a single case of each thing, which would help our profits.'

An hour or so later, the barbecue was in full swing. The band made up in enthusiasm and energy what they lacked in musicality and plenty of people were dancing and singing along with gusto. I had finished my stint on the bar and was having a quick bite to eat before I went to help Gloria with the auction, when Luke came over. He smiled at me and my stomach flipped. *You should have gone for that drink the other night*, whispered a little voice in my head. I shushed it, and smiled back.

'It's going well, isn't it?'

'Very,' he said. 'We've had another twenty or so people turn up on the door, so that's already a thousand pounds just in ticket sales.'

'And the bar's been doing brisk business,' I said. 'As long as the auction goes well, we're going to have a respectable amount to give the vicar. He looks a lot happier than he did the last time I saw him.' I nodded over to where he was sitting on a rug with his two children. 'I don't think his wife is here, though.'

'She's not,' replied Luke. 'But for a good reason.' He looked searchingly into my eyes, and my stomach did somersaults again. 'I can trust you, can't I?'

'Yes, of course.'

After all, I was stunningly good at <u>not</u> *telling people things, even when I knew I needed to.*

'The truth is that she's an alcoholic. It's got worse over the last few years, and Fergus has been trying to cope, trying to carry it all by himself. But when we went along and rallied him to help with the fundraising, he seemed to have some sort of epiphany.'

'How appropriate for a vicar.'

'Well, quite. Anyway, he managed to persuade her to go to rehab, which is why she's not here tonight.'

'Good for him.'

'Yes. I hope it works. Oh, look,' he said. 'Gloria's going up on stage; it must be time for the auction.'

'See you later,' I said, and walked away, feeling sorry for Fergus, but basking in a happy glow that Luke had trusted me enough to share sensitive information. When I climbed up onto the stage, I saw that he was still looking at me, only breaking eye contact when a young man who looked vaguely familiar came over to speak to him. Gloria and I were perfecting the order of the auction, adding in some last-minute lots, when they both came over.

'Belle, Gloria, this is my brother, Sam.'

'Of course it is,' said Gloria warmly. 'Glad you could make it.'

'I wanted to do more than just come along,' said Sam, his eyes gleaming with fun. 'I've got another auction lot.'

'Wonderful,' I said, flipping through the pages on the clipboard. 'What are you putting up?'

He opened his arms wide and grinned mischievously.

'Me!'

I laughed and Gloria pretended to fan herself vigorously.

'My, my!' she said. 'We'll make some money for sure! But you had better specify exactly what the deal is.'

'I'm not bad at jobs around the house,' said Sam. 'So I thought I could be sold by the hour to help out in any way people like – within reason. Four lots of an hour each?'

'That's a great idea!' I said, scribbling it down near the end. 'Are you going to do the same, Luke?'

I stood with my pen poised, a look of innocence on my face.

'Only if you promise to be the highest bidder,' he said, holding my gaze.

For a moment, the cheque the jeweller had given me for my engagement ring flashed into my mind. If I didn't need it for the tearooms, I'd be only too tempted to spend the lot. Instead, I pulled a pout.

'Ah, what a shame, I can't stretch to much more than a cup of tea and some shortbread.'

'Sold!' said Luke, bringing down an imaginary gavel. 'A very fair price.'

Our eye contact broke as we laughed, but the tingle I had felt continued rippling through my body.

'Right, if you've all had enough fun,' said Gloria, grinning. 'It's time we got started.'

She stepped up to the microphone and called everyone's attention, then started on the lots. It had been a good idea to hold the auction later in the evening, when many people had enjoyed a few drinks, and the bids came thick and fast. Cakes were being sold for twenty-five pounds each, window cleaning went for fifty and Caleb's bread for a hundred and five pounds, which he was thrilled with. When it came to my lot, I was intensely curious. What had the Talbots bid?

'And now for lot twenty-seven: afternoon tea at the newly refurbished *Coastal Kettle*, on a date of your choosing, once it reopens,' announced Gloria. 'Now, I have to tell you lovely people that I already have an opening bid right here in this envelope, made by Sir Henry Talbot. I'd love to see one of you beat it, but he may have it sewn up.' She opened the envelope with a flourish. 'The bid is for seven hundred and fifty pounds!'

The audience, thoroughly enjoying themselves, all said 'oooooooh!', then laughed.

'Are there any further bids, or must I accept this maiden offer?'

Little pockets of excited chatter broke out as people playfully encouraged each other to bid, but, unsurprisingly, no one put their hand up.

'Very well then. Sold! To Sir Henry and Lady Talbot!'

I scribbled their names down on my clipboard, dizzy with pleasure and shock. I was delighted that my lot had made so much money, but why on earth had the Talbots bid so high? I didn't have time to consider the possibilities before Gloria had moved on to the next lot: Sam.

'Now, ladies and gentlemen,' she announced in her ringing tones. 'A super special late lot for you! Here we have the young, strong and – may I say? – devastatingly handsome Sam Talbot. He's come all the way down from the big house tonight to offer you his services. He tells me he's handy around the house if you need some pictures putting up or the dishwasher filter unblocking, in the garden if you need a spot of weeding, behind the wheel if you'd like a chauffeur or in the kitchen – although here, he admits, his skills are limited to making the best cup of tea this side of Weymouth.' There were laughs and catcalls as Gloria's big build-up ensured plenty of interest. I might have felt awkward for Sam, but he looked like he was having the time of his life, hamming it up as he flexed his muscles and mimed serving tea. 'Sam is available in four lots of one hour each, so let's see who's going to snap him up!'

Bidding started coming in thick and fast, and at first I couldn't keep up, but as the price rose, the bidders thinned out, and I was soon able to name the first winning bidder as Lacey Macintyre, who ran the little gift shop and spent ninety-five pounds on her prize. The next hour of Sam's time went for eighty pounds and the third for ninety-one. I scribbled down the numbers, thrilled at how much everything was totting up to. When Gloria announced the fourth and final parcel of Sam's time, a voice rang out above all the others.

'Two hundred and fifty pounds – and I'll make him earn every penny!'

Heads swivelled and voices muttered curiously, but Gloria and I had instantly known who it was.

'Sold!' shrieked Gloria. 'To Luke Talbot!'

The murmurs turned to laughter as Sam grinned and bowed dramatically before going over to clap his big brother on the back.

The final lots were also bid for generously and, although I didn't have time to do complete calculations, my mental maths told me that the vicar was going to be very happy indeed. With the auction finished, the evening began to wind down. As people left, many of them grabbed bags of garbage and recycling, or paused to help the band dismantle their gear and load it into the van. An hour or so later, it was the six members of the BBC left on the beach.

'I know that Belle will come back to us tomorrow with the final figures,' said Gloria. 'But we can be confident that this evening was a huge success.'

'I agree,' said Edward. 'And even if we hadn't made as much

money as it feels that we have, did you see people's faces? So happy, talking to their neighbours, bidding like mad, helping with the clear-up. The community spirit that has been raised is worth more than anything. If we had any energy left to raise a glass, it would be to Belle and Luke, for coming up with this in the first place.'

'Belle and Luke,' said the others, raising imaginary glasses. My skin tingled with pleasure and pride, and I smiled at Luke. He put a hand on my shoulder, which only exacerbated the tingling, in the best possible way.

'It was Belle's idea,' he said warmly. 'I know the circumstances could have been happier, but your arrival in Spindrift Bay has been a godsend.'

Dear though the little group had become to me, I suddenly wished for nothing other than for them to all vanish, leaving me alone with Luke. I gave myself a little shake.

'Thank you,' I said, then cleared my throat, which was treacherously giving away my emotions. I saw Gloria smirk knowingly. 'Thank you. Now, we'd better get the rest of these things packed in the trailer. Edward, Gloria, you can leave this to us, why don't you head off?'

Twenty minutes later, everything was packed into the trailer behind Luke's car.

'Just the fire left to deal with,' said Luke. 'Belle and I can see to that, since you two have to be up with a small child in the morning. I'm sure you could do with some sleep.'

'He's at my sister's,' said Caleb. 'But we will have to get him pretty early. If you're sure?'

We promised that we didn't mind, and they headed off towards the village.

'Would you like a nightcap before we put the fire out?' asked Luke. 'I'm sure it won't dent the budget too badly if we finish off one of those open bottles of red. I'm leaving the car and trailer to take home in the morning, anyway.'

A dart of excited anticipation shot through my stomach. This time, I wasn't going to run away.

'As official treasurer of the BBC,' I said, trying to keep my voice steady, 'I can formally sanction that.'

Luke grinned and went to the trailer, where he dug out the bottle, a couple of glasses and a rug. We sat down near the remains of the fire with its glowing embers and low flames. It still radiated warmth, and it was undeniably sexy, sitting close to Luke in the flickering shadows, the gentle plashing of the waves nearby and the indigo sky above with its gloriously uninhibited display of stars. We clinked our glasses gently together and took our first sips in silence.

'I've loved getting to know you,' said Luke quietly, gazing into the fire. 'I know—I know you've been through a bad break-up, and I don't know if you're ready for anything new—'

He turned his face towards me, and I allowed myself to gaze into his eyes, which were as mesmerising as the reflection of the firelight dancing in them. A soft smile touched my lips and my fingers crept across the rug until they reached his.

'I don't know, either,' I whispered. 'But I think I am. I don't want to go back, that's certain, only move forward.'

With our faces so close, it barely required a tilt of the head for our lips to meet and all the fizzing and flipping I had felt before to be confirmed as nothing but a warm-up act. But a few minutes later, I pulled away slightly. If I didn't, then the headiness would overtake me completely, and that wasn't what I wanted. Not yet. Luke put his arm around my shoulders and I snuggled into him, taking another sip of wine. Then, through my peace, a thought cut that shattered my mood completely. How could I sit there, embark on *something* with Luke, when I still kept such an important secret about his family? How could I simply have forgotten? I sighed.

'Are you all right?' he asked.

I pulled away slightly and turned to him.

'Yes. Very much so.' The kind concern in his eyes made me want to kiss him all over again, and forget what I was carrying for another day, but I knew that if anything was to grow between us –

and I so hoped it would – then honesty and trust must be there from the start. 'But there's something I must talk to you about.'

'Your ex,' he said dully, turning back to the fire.

'No,' I replied. 'Not him. God no, not him. It's about you.'

'Me?'

'You and your family, yes.'

I went on to explain about Diana's final words and the new photograph and birth certificate I had found. His brow creased.

'I can hardly believe it. Diana – my aunt? My father's sister? And you think she had a baby? But why didn't any of them *say* anything? Why did it need to be kept a secret all these years?'

His voice was rising and edged with anger. I could hardly blame him.

'I think that Diana was working up to telling people before she died. Edward knew that she was your father's sister – I haven't shown him the photo – and he firmly believed that. And given what she told Tessa, we have to believe that she, at least, wanted the secret out, even if your father doesn't, for some reason.'

I didn't add that Edward suspected there was more to the story, but it wouldn't take Luke long to work that out for himself.

'It explains why Dad was so cut up about her death, and why he and Mum attended the funeral. I *thought* it was odd, when as far as I was concerned, they barely knew her. Stupid: I told myself they were upset on *my* behalf, because she had been my friend. Why the hell didn't they tell me we were related? And what caused her to disappear to France, to change her name? Something terrible must have happened.'

I shook my head.

'I'm sorry, I don't know.'

'I *wish* I had known we were family.' He stared into the fire, chewing his lip in agitation. 'We got on so well, you know? With the ocean conservation stuff, but in other ways as well.'

A silence fell, then Luke spoke again.

'I don't suppose that *I* could be the "he" that she wanted to be told? Those were her last words, you said?'

'Yes, that's right,' I replied, and repeated, 'She said "He should know. Find the box." That's all. I don't know if she meant you, or Sam, or your father – or someone else altogether. Maybe she meant the baby; I did wonder if it had been adopted.'

'I'm going to go up to the house tomorrow and ask Mum and Dad again. They can explain everything.'

His voice was harsh now.

'I don't know,' I said, speaking firmly in a way that was unusual for me, thanks to Dad's training. But this was too important to shrink away from. 'They didn't want to talk about it last time. I think we should check the other boxes and see if we can work out exactly what Diana wanted to be found. There's no point in wading in with what we've got; we'll probably end up causing more pain and being further away from finding the truth.'

Luke's face softened and he took my hand.

'You're right. I'm not usually impetuous, I'm just so shocked. Yes. Show me what you've already found and we can take it from there.'

'Of course. I can do tomorrow, if you can?'

'I can.' I smiled as a shiver also went through me. 'You're cold.'

'A little. Maybe it's time to call it a night?'

'Okay. We have to put this fire out.' He stood up and grabbed a bucket he had kept out for the purpose, as I started to fold the rug. 'Belle?' he said. I stopped and looked over at him. 'Thank you – for being honest with me.'

A few minutes later, we were at my front door. The night air had become chilly, and I was looking forward to a warm shower. Luke tucked a stray piece of hair behind my ear, then bent his head and kissed me again. Every atom of my body screeched at me to open the door and lead him inside, let the evening go where it may, where we both wanted it to... but I didn't. I had put Matt firmly behind me, but it was still recent, and raw, and I didn't want to hurry into anything new until I was sure I was ready. Even – or especially – when it felt as viscerally right as it did with Luke.

'Good night,' I whispered. 'See you tomorrow.'

He squeezed my hand and kissed me one final, lingering time. 'Good night.'

I fell through the front door to be greeted by my two mewing, gambolling kittens. The best thing I could do, right now, was to focus on them, however much my mind wandered back to Luke and his kisses.

FIFTEEN

The next morning, I was woken by both kittens scaling the bed, digging their tiny claws into the duvet cover and making little mews of determination. I threw an arm across my face.

'What are you two doing? It's far too early for this.'

I felt first one, then two featherlight weights start the wobbly journey up my thighs towards my torso and I flung my arm back to look at the clock.

'I'm sorry, I was wrong, you were right,' I said, as the kittens reached my tummy and were distracted by a mote of sunlight coming from between a crack in the curtains. 'It's late, you two must be hungry.'

I played with them for a little while, teasing them with the soft fleece end of my dressing gown belt. It was endlessly charming, the way they believed themselves to be such fierce lions, pouncing on and savaging the fabric, whereas I could pick them up as they clung on and take such cute photos that the Instagram page I was starting for The Coastal Kettle would surely explode in a flurry of 'likes'. They were happy to be distracted, but soon my stomach was rumbling, too.

'Come on, fellas, time to go down.'

I climbed out of bed, my limbs heavy and tired, and pulled on my dressing gown, which had to stay open as Bubble and Squeak were still busy killing the belt. I picked them and it up in a bundle to carry downstairs, where I finally managed to claim it back by offering them some breakfast. Fastening it around my waist, I filled the kettle, then picked up my phone. I saw that there was a message from Luke which I had missed earlier when I was taking pictures of the kittens. Through my sleepiness, I felt a thrill as I remembered our two kisses from the previous night. Of course! He was coming round today. I glanced at the messy kitchen and down at my own dishevelled state; hopefully, he wouldn't be here too soon.

> Morning. Hope you slept well :) Is it still okay if I come over? I've got an emergency coming in soon, so it won't be this morning. Afternoon all right? L x

It had been sent an hour and a half ago, and I was glad I wasn't the one who had needed to get up so early after last night. I made a coffee and sat down to reply.

> Yes, any time is fine. Is 1 too early? I can make some lunch x

I didn't expect a reply quickly, so was surprised – and yes, pleased – when the phone buzzed a couple of minutes later.

> 1 is good. What can I bring? L x

I had an idea of what I was going to make, a traditional plough-man's lunch, but with a twist. I was planning on serving it in the tearooms, and I wanted a guinea pig. I resisted the temptation to reply suggesting he brought a ready meal in case my idea went wrong, so simply said:

> Just yourself. See you later x

The messages perked me up and, once I had eaten my breakfast, I got showered and dressed quickly. I then got down to work in the kitchen, enjoying the creativity of crafting something new as the sun streamed in through the window and the kittens tumbled about happily. When a knock came at the door, I ran happily to answer it. Luke looked tired, but smiled warmly as I stepped aside to let him in, then drew me into a hug when I closed the door.

'Did it go well this morning?' I asked, waving him towards a chair. The kittens immediately bounded over to him, and he scooped them up in one hand.

'It was touch and go,' he said, as Squeak settled contentedly on his lap and Bubble began a mountaineering expedition towards his shoulder. 'A cat that had been attacked by a fox.'

'Does that happen a lot?' I asked, horrified at the thought that my darling boys might be in danger, once they were allowed out.

'No,' he replied, wincing as Bubble dug his pin-sharp claws in. 'They attack rarely, and then usually kittens or weakened adult cats. The patient I had this morning was elderly and shouldn't have been out at night. Her owners hadn't been able to call her in and were beside themselves with worry. They were relieved to find her still alive the next morning, but in a bad way. She had lost a lot of blood and most of one ear and had some nasty bites to her back and haunches.'

The tears that were so near the surface these days sprang to my eyes.

'Oh, the poor thing, and the poor owners. Will she be all right?'

'I hope so,' he said. 'I managed to patch up the wounds and, thankfully, there wasn't any damage to any of her organs, or her throat. She's dosed up on antibiotics and has had plenty of fluids, so now we have to keep our fingers crossed that no infection sets in and that she's strong enough to pull through. She's gone home with my nurse, Addy, so she's in good hands, and Addy will call if there's any sudden deterioration.'

'Weren't you exhausted, doing all that after last night? I had a very slow start to the morning.'

'I'm tired a lot; you get used to it. It's impossible to turn patients away when they need my help, and seeing the animals recover, and their owners so relieved... It's worth it.'

'It's about the owners as much as the pets for you, isn't it?' I asked, remembering how considerate he had been of Edward when Doris was ill.

'Absolutely. Some vets would rather stick to the technical stuff and never meet an owner, but that's not me.'

'What about when the pets die?'

'It happens, of course, and it's always awful. But it helps to know I've done all I could, and I've learnt a lot about how to break the news. It doesn't get easier, but it's part of the job.'

I smiled at Squeak, who shifted slightly in his sleep.

'I hate the thought of anything happening to these two.'

'I know. It's a tough part of having a pet.'

'Anyway,' I said, pushing aside the uncomfortable thoughts. 'Lunch is ready. It's simple, but I want to serve it in the tearoom, and I'd love you to be honest about whether people will be put off by the variation on a classic. Also, I'm trying out a few different things on you, so can you tell me what you like best?'

'I must say,' said Luke, leaning back in his chair and repositioning Bubble, who was in danger of abseiling with no rope, 'I like this sideline I have in tasting things for the tearoom. Bring it on!'

I put out a plate for each of us with some of the traditional elements of a ploughman's lunch: a hunk of local cheddar, tiny onions I had quick-pickled myself, tomatoes, homemade chutney and two thick slices of one of Caleb's delicious sourdough breads. Then I brought out some of my ideas for adding 'a twist': cheese straws that I had made with Dorset Blue Vinney, some almond pesto, a puy lentil and thyme pie and some turmeric spiced piccalilli.

'I'm talking to a local supplier about offering some of their ham as well,' I added as I put a bottle of chilled apple and pear juice on the table, with two glasses. 'With a fig and shallot chutney. But I didn't have time for that today.'

'This is amazing!' said Luke, adding some of everything to his plate. 'I can't believe you've only been doing this for a few weeks.'

'I found the baking hard to get to grips with, but this sort of thing is much more straightforward. I love eating, so it's not hard to come up with ideas – I think about what I'd like to try. And I've discovered now that if I turn my mathematical mind to recipes, they're much less intimidating. I don't have the confidence to try a pinch of this or that and then taste things, but I do understand that the ratio of dry ingredients to fat in a cake is crucial.'

'You're doing something right,' said Luke, digging a cheese straw into his pesto. 'Maths or no maths, these are incredible.'

'Will people buy them?' I asked anxiously. 'They're not too much of a departure?'

He looked at me seriously.

'Belle. It will take one person to buy and eat one of these and they'll tell everyone else. You'll be sold out every day. Are you planning on selling them separately, as well as to be a side to the ploughman's?'

'I might,' I replied. 'And if people like the chutneys, I might offer them in jars to take home.'

'The Coastal Kettle was always popular,' said Luke, balancing a pickled onion on top of a piece of cheese. 'And Diana liked trying new things. But you're going to take it to another level.'

He popped the food in his mouth and raised his eyes to heaven in a dramatic show of ecstasy.

Soon, both our plates were clean, and I knew that I didn't have any room left for another crumb.

'Would you like anything else, or shall I show you those things now?'

'Much as I'd like to eat you out of house and home, I can't manage another morsel right now. I'd love to see them, please.'

I led him through to the unused room and first handed him the two photos – the one he had already seen and the one I had found later. He studied them for a few moments in silence, then frowned.

'In this photo she looks – well, she looks like she might be the baby's mother, not a nanny.'

'That's what I thought,' I said.

'I cannot understand why my parents have never said anything, why there is this secret.' He looked at me with troubled eyes. 'I hope nothing awful happened to her or the baby.'

The same thought had crossed my mind, although I had barely wanted to acknowledge it.

Next, I gave him the birth certificate and the half-finished letter to Mum, and he studied them carefully, then screwed his face up in confusion.

'What on earth's going on?' he said. 'She says here' – he tapped the letter – 'that she doesn't want to "destroy lives". That's strong stuff. But given what she said to Tessa, just before...' He faltered, paused and took a deep breath. 'Just before she died. She wanted the secret out.' His voice rose with emotion. 'We *have* to find out what it was, Belle. You will help me, won't you?'

'Of *course* I will,' I said, taking his hand. 'I've been so scared of telling you, of stirring things up.'

'I'm glad you did. Can we go through some more of these?' He indicated the various crates. 'We need to find whichever "box" it was she was talking about.'

I was deeply uncomfortable as I agreed and started work on one of the crates, but I knew underneath that my instinct was – as it always had been – to seek out the truth.

An hour later, we had both searched through nearly two crates each and turned up nothing more than old paperwork relating to the house and tearooms. There had been a momentary thrill when Luke pulled out a carved wooden box with a lock.

'Look, this *must* be it,' he said, shaking it gently. 'We need to get it open.'

A hunt through the rest of the crate yielded nothing, so I went to get a small toolbox.

'It's a simple lock,' I said, jiggling a small screwdriver inside it. 'It won't be hard to open.'

I was proved right when, a few seconds later, the latch popped.

'You open it,' I said, handing the box back to Luke. 'I'd like you to.'

Slowly, he opened the lid and I'm sure his heart was beating as fast and insistently as mine, only for the adrenaline to drain away in disappointment.

'It's nothing,' he said, turning it to show me. 'A couple of books of matches and some old tickets.'

'They may have meant something to Diana,' I said, my voice flat at the pathos of the worthless items. 'But I doubt we'll ever know what. Shall we carry on looking, or do you want to stop for a break?'

'Let's finish these two crates,' said Luke. 'Then maybe we should have a breather.'

My zest for the project had waned considerably, but if we wanted answers, there was nothing for it but to carry on.

When I found the box, I didn't at first realise. I had finished sorting through the contents of a fat cardboard envelope file, checking each piece of paper carefully only for one after another to be a bill for curtains or a delivery slip for bowls. My mind had almost entirely turned to the cup of tea and cake I had to look forward to when the crate was empty, and a yellowing Tupperware box roused no interest. Other such containers had only yielded receipts or been empty, so I pulled the lid off this one without expectations. The contents, however, made me draw in my breath sharply.

'What is it?' asked Luke, looking up. 'Have you found something?'

'I think I have,' I whispered, holding the box out to him.

He took it and slowly sifted through the poignant contents. It held two hospital wristbands, a small pile of photos, the first of which showed a newborn baby, and a curled lock of hair in a little plastic bag. I saw his hand shake as he took out the smaller wristband and read the faded biro writing. Then he turned pale and handed it to me.

'Baby boy,' I read out loud. 'Son of Diana Talbot. 2nd March 1989.'

I felt the blood drain from my own face as I looked up at him.

'Is that you?' I whispered.

He seemed to have been turned to stone. I took the box out of his unresisting hand and looked at the rest of the paltry contents. The second bracelet showed Diana's name, with the surname "Talbot" and stated her own date of birth. There were five photographs in total, four just of the baby and one of Diana sitting in an iron-framed hospital bed, holding the little bundle and looking utterly bleak. I started to speak, but my throat constricted. I had to clear it and try again.

'Diana's your mother,' I stated. My shock at the discovery must have been microscopic compared to Luke's. He stared at me blankly. 'Unless there's another baby?' I said. 'With the same birthday...' I trailed off. But we both knew it was him. I reached for his hand again, but it lay limp and cold under mine. Then, seeming not to notice my touch, he stood up and ran a hand through his hair.

'I need some space,' he choked out. 'I – this – I don't know. I have to go.'

He strode from the room and was opening the front door in seconds. I caught at his arm.

'Luke, please...' Tears were now trickling down my face and my voice caught in a sob. 'Please, stay, we can talk about this...'

He stared at me, his eyes wild.

'How could they? How could my parents and Diana have lied about this, for all these years?' His voice rose, now, in anger. 'And she died and no one had ever told me. I could have known her as my mother.' He choked out a rough, sour laugh. 'Obviously, she never wanted me *then*, when I was born, but she didn't want me as an adult, either. Well, not as a son. Rather ghoulish, don't you think, that she made a friend of me? Wonder how she felt, keeping that secret? Do you think it gave her some sort of feeling of power?'

'No!' I shouted. 'Of course not! Diana wasn't like that, she wasn't!'

He shook off my hand.

'Doesn't look like any of us knew her that well, does it? I've got to go, Belle. I'll be in touch.'

And, with that, he half ran to his car and was soon out of sight.

I shut the door gently and went back to the room, scrubbing at my wet face. I picked up the box's contents and carefully replaced them, pressing the lid shut. I went through to the kitchen as though I were in a dream and made a cup of tea, although what I wanted was a large gin and tonic. The box sat on the kitchen table, innocent enough but emanating some invisible threat, as if it might suddenly explode; in a way, it already had. I took out a tin of amaretti and went through to the sitting room where I curled up in my favourite chair. The kittens immediately climbed up and settled down on my lap, their little purrs rumbling comfortingly. After a couple of amaretti and a few sips of tea, I was less shaky and my head started to clear. I took my phone out of my back pocket and rang Mum.

'Darling, what's wrong?' she said the minute she heard my voice.

'Oh, Mum,' I said. 'We – Luke and I – we've discovered Diana's secret.'

I described the contents of the box to her, and when she next spoke, her voice was full of emotion.

'Poor, poor Diana. What a terrible thing for her, to give up a baby and then not be able to speak to anyone else about it for—for the rest of her life.' We were both now weeping freely, and her words came in fits and starts. 'You know, Belle, that having you – it is without doubt the most incredible thing that ever happened to me. You're not a child anymore, you know that things with your father... aren't easy, they never have been. But for all of that—' Her voice took on a fierce note. 'For all of that, I wouldn't change a second, because I have you. It was hard, when you were born. The lack of sleep, getting over the birth, the fears and guilt that tumbled in from nowhere, your father's behaviour... good God, it was hard. But it was all laced with a love that was powerful and unexpected and something I had never come close to feeling before. A visceral, almost violent, love that changed my whole being and informed everything I did from then on. When we think of babies, we picture pastel colours, smiles, coos and softness – and those things *do* exist. Yet the reality is also pain and blood and mess and despair and rage. But I went through all of it also feeling this raw, passionate love that superseded everything, and still does.' She paused, and I could hear her ragged breaths. I was also wracked with sobs, the one tissue I had with me now sodden and slimy, my half-drunk cup of tea going cold, the kittens looking apprehensive. I tipped them gently off my lap and staggered to the kitchen where I broke off a couple of pieces of kitchen towel to mop my face and wipe my nose. I then took a bottle of wine out of the fridge. This was no time for cold tea.

'Are you still there?' asked Mum.

'Yes,' I stammered. 'I love you, too, Mum, so much.'

'I know you do, darling. I'm so desperately sad for Diana. What if she spent her entire life with all those feelings and nowhere to put them? It must have been agonising. I can only think that she must have believed it was the best thing for Luke. Rightly or wrongly, parents are usually prepared to make any sacrifices they believe are necessary for their beloved children.'

I nodded speechlessly, knowing that she was thinking of herself and how she had stayed with my father all these years because she thought it offered me the best chance in life.

'What about Luke?' I said. 'He was so angry when he left.'

'He needs some time to process it,' said Mum. 'He'll be back when he's ready. For now, I'm worried about you. Will you be all right?'

'I'm okay,' I said. 'Better for talking to you. I did—I did do the right thing, didn't I? Finding all this out?'

'Without a doubt,' said Mum firmly. 'It was what Diana wanted, and she wouldn't have made that clear with her final breaths if she hadn't believed it was important, rather than selfish. Give it time.'

We spoke for a few minutes before ringing off. My tears had stopped now, and I looked at my empty wine glass in surprise, then refilled it and took out the remains of mine and Luke's lunch. I carried everything through to the sitting room and switched on the TV. But I barely took in the reality show that was on as, reluctant as I was to allow it, my mind wandered to Matt and how we had talked with such joy and eagerness about the children we would have together. I had looked forward so much to motherhood, imagined exactly the same hospital photo I had seen of Diana, but with such crucial differences. In my mind, I would be blooming, rosy-cheeked, content and complacent. I had never considered that having a new baby could look any different. I had certainly not stopped to think about the things my mother had described, the painful, messy side, but now that she had described them with such passion and clarity, the pity for what I had lost returned with a new intensity. I knew, now, that the relationship with Matt, as grown-up as it had seemed, had been little more than a schoolyard romance. Real love, real life, was more than a neat, picture-perfect set-up, but was as deeply challenging as it was satisfying. And this realisation, humbling though it may have been, helped me to understand, to know, that for the first time since he had told me he was leaving me, I was truly healing.

SIXTEEN

The following morning, I woke up drained and unrefreshed but feeling, nevertheless, a new, if slightly unsteady, sense of peace. Rather than throwing myself into any kind of physical work, which would tire me even more, I checked that the workmen were all set in the tearooms, then returned to the house. I decided that I would immerse myself in the gentle and enjoyable task of designing menus. I had been putting off this particular job because, given that it was something I knew I would enjoy, I didn't see it as 'proper' work. Rationally, I knew this was ridiculous as the menus were a crucial part of the tearooms. Where along the way had I absorbed the idea that if it was something I liked doing, then it didn't count as work?

'You wouldn't be so silly, would you?' I said to Bubble and Squeak, who were stretched out in a patch of sunshine. 'I'll take you into the garden later and we can all have some fresh air.'

I had been working for about an hour and a half, when the doorbell went. I was expecting a delivery of paper samples, so when I opened the door and saw Luke standing there, the surprise must have shown on my face.

'Sorry to turn up like this,' he said, with a small smile. 'I can come back if you're busy.'

'No, no, it's fine,' I replied, opening the door wider to let him in. 'I wondered if it was my delivery. Come in.' We went through to the kitchen, and I put the kettle on. 'Are you okay?'

He sighed deeply and shook his head.

'I'm not, no. I'm sorry for walking out yesterday, though – it was rude.'

'Thank you,' I said, acknowledging his apology. 'It must have been a huge shock.' I put some flapjacks on a plate. 'Do you want to come and sit in the garden? I promised the kittens some fresh air.'

We went outside and sat where we had before, each equipped with a cup of tea, a flapjack and a kitten.

'Have you thought about what you're going to do next? Did you go and see your parents?' I asked.

'No,' he replied, screwing up his face. 'I couldn't think what to say to them, and I was so angry that they had kept all this a secret for so long. It's better to cool off before I ask them anything.'

'I'm sure their reasons were good,' I said, hoping that this was the truth.

Luke shrugged.

'My father is good at getting what he wants, and he doesn't always worry about the cost to other people,' he said. 'I know I was angry with Diana yesterday, but I've been thinking about it and it's more likely that he didn't give her a choice. And if that's the case, how will I ever be able to forgive him?'

'But why would he have wanted her baby?' I asked, confused.

'My best guess is that he and Mum couldn't have children – or thought they couldn't,' he said quietly. 'He's hot on family and passing on the land and the title; if his unmarried sister had a baby boy, that would be better than nothing.'

'So, what about Sam?' I said.

He shrugged again.

'He came along years after me. Maybe they got lucky – or maybe he's got a birth family tucked away somewhere, too.'

I could hear the hurt in his voice, and I wasn't sure what to say. Luke carried on.

'I don't care about any of that – getting the land or the house or being Sir Luke,' he spat out. 'For God's sake, I'd rather have known my mother for longer than the couple of years before she died. And who's my father?'

He glared at me, and I winced.

'I'm sure your parents – Sir Henry and Lady Talbot, that is – will tell you if you speak to them.'

'Have you got anything left here – any more boxes to rummage through? You've seemed to hold all the answers up until now.'

His tone of voice was unusually harsh, and my stomach dropped. Much as I might have wanted to snap back at him and remind him that none of this was my fault, the years of my father's conditioning kicked in and I stared at the floor, speechless and scared.

'I'm sorry,' said Luke, his voice softer. 'Belle?'

I looked up.

'I'm sorry, I shouldn't have spoken to you like that.'

I swallowed and gave a little nod, then changed the subject.

'Do you have your birth certificate?'

'Yes,' he replied. 'I used it not long ago and I didn't think anything of it. Mum and Dad are listed as my parents and the house they lived in before moving here as my place of birth. Mum said that I came quickly, so a home birth was the only option.' He stared out to sea, and when he spoke again, there was no trace of anger left in his voice, just sadness and defeat. 'They've lied to me my entire life.'

'I'm so sorry,' I said. 'And I'm sorry that I was the one who brought it all up.'

He turned to me.

'Don't be. Diana wanted the truth to be known. You won't say anything to anyone yet, will you? I need some more time.'

I assured him that I would not and, soon after, he left, kissing me goodbye and leaving me wondering what was in store for us next.

I returned gratefully to my menus and my kittens, finding solace in their simplicity.

SEVENTEEN

It was later that day, when I was knee-deep in designing menus, instructing workmen, herding kittens and receiving, yet again, the vicar's gratitude for the money we raised at the barbecue via a phone call, that there was another knock at the door. Sure this time that it must be my paper samples, I went to open it.

'Mum! Oh, not you, vicar, no, sorry! My mum's arrived by surprise.'

This was finally sufficient to get him to hang up, and I chucked my phone on the hall table and hugged Mum. Her familiar, vanilla-scented embrace brought out a rush of love in me, and I didn't want to let her go.

'Are you going to let me inside?' she said, laughing. I laughed, too, and stood aside so she could pass.

'I'm so happy to see you!' I said. 'Did you send a message? Did I miss it?'

'No,' she said, spotting the kittens and scooping them up for a cuddle. 'It was a pretty spur of the moment thing. These two are completely adorable, by the way. I might get a cat.'

'I thought Dad was allergic?'

'He is,' she replied enigmatically, kissing the top of Bubble's head.

'So, how are you going to get a cat?' I asked, confused.

'Maybe we should sit down, darling,' said Mum. 'And I'll explain.'

For the second time that day, I found myself making tea and putting bakes out on a plate for a conversation I could not predict.

'So,' said Mum, taking a jam slice. 'The time has come to leave your father.'

My hand flew to my mouth and my eyes filled. For a moment, I was frozen, then I pushed back my chair, leapt up and threw my arms around her.

'Oh, Mum!' I managed to croak through my emotion. 'I'm so *glad*!'

'What a relief!' Her voice sounded shaky now, after her confident statement. 'I did wonder if you might be upset.'

I sat down again and shook my head soberly.

'No. Maybe I should be, but I've thought it for years, you know that.'

'Yes.' She reached across the table and grasped both my hands in hers. 'You have been such a support, my love. Perhaps I should have left sooner, and taken you with me. I will never know, and I have to live with that.'

'So, why now?' I asked. 'I did think you might leave when I moved in with Matt, but you didn't.'

She pressed her lips together.

'No. The truth is that – well, I wasn't that sure about Matt.'

'I thought you loved him!'

'Mmm. It was good to see you happy, but he never felt *solid* enough somehow.'

I pictured Luke, and how safe he made me feel.

'You were right. I was devastated, as you know, when he cancelled the wedding, but I do see now that we weren't right for each other. I'm even grateful to him, if you can believe it, for ending things. I would have been miserable married to him, with horrible Celia for a mother-in-law.'

'Do you remember that time we went for lunch?' she said. I

nodded. It had only been the once. 'She asked me not to wear pink to the wedding as it was "her" colour.'

I gasped, giggling.

'But the dress you went and got was pink!'

'Of course it was. I'd spent enough of my life being told what to do by your father; I wasn't going to let her join in. A shame she never got to see me in it.'

'Good for you,' I said, lifting my mug to clink it against hers. 'So, what gave you the final push?'

Mum bit into another jam slice.

'It was a few things. Your father's behaviour over the funeral was the start of the change in my thinking. God knows I've put up with enough over the years, but I managed to rationalise either his behaviour or my responses; this time the only reasons I could find were that he was a domineering bully, and I was scared of him. Those weren't good enough. I should have come to Diana's funeral, and I *wish* I had,' she said fiercely. 'I know I've not been a good role model to you, but *please*, Belle: having self-respect and an expectation of good treatment from others is everything. Or maybe seeing me put up with being rubbished for so many years has made you determined not to do the same?' she added hopefully.

My mind flitted over Matt and his patronising family and then, briefly, to Luke and my mute response to his unfair and accusatory words. I didn't want to blame Mum, but neither could I claim that I was some sort of confident dynamo. Yet.

'It's a work in progress,' I settled for saying. 'Like so much is in life.' I thought again about Luke, but this time about his own regret after he had spoken. 'Sometimes, maybe it's about recognising and hanging on to the good, and walking away from the bad, rather than fighting against it, trying to change it?'

'Wise words,' she said.

'I wish that I had been the one to walk away from Matt,' I said. 'Things weren't bad in the same way as they were with you and Dad, but I was play-acting a relationship and that was a drain on my self-respect, too – not able to be myself. I didn't think I'd ever be able to be with a man again, but...'

'Belle! Have you met someone?'

'I think so,' I said cautiously. 'It's early days. Don't worry,' I added, grinning. 'I'll keep you posted. Tell me what else helped you leave.'

She nodded, never one to pry.

'So, as I said, it was the funeral that let in the first chink of light. I suddenly started to see that leaving could be possible, and then it was as if the universe was conspiring to help. I picked up a magazine at the dentist which had an article on what you need to organise if you are leaving a partner quickly. I got talking to a woman in Sainsbury's who turned out to be a divorce lawyer.'

'How on earth did you find that out?'

'I dropped a pot of cream and it splashed everywhere, including on her shoes. She was incredibly nice about it, and I said something like: "Thank goodness it was you and not my husband". She said she was a divorce lawyer, and that people had split up over less and then I think she saw the look on my face, because she handed me her card and said she would help if I ever needed it. So, you see, once the idea of leaving had come into my head, there seemed to be support for the idea everywhere. I was glad that you were settled here,' she continued. 'And that, whether you stayed long term or not, Diana's inheritance meant that your future was secure. But the final straw came yesterday when you rang to tell me about Diana's baby. I don't know the details, of course, but I knew Diana for nearly forty years and there was always a sadness there. And now she's dead.'

The word sat heavily between us for a moment, like a dollop of gruel doled out by Mr Bumble.

'I couldn't, I *couldn't*, let that be my life. Otherwise, I, too, would die knowing that I had never pursued the life I wanted. I had already put certain things in motion. I've been building up a 'running away' fund for years and – I don't know if you know, but Diana bequeathed me some money as well.' I remembered the conditions that Mr Masterson said had been attached. 'Diana said I was only to receive it if and when I left your father.'

My eyebrows shot up into my hairline.

'Wow! That's pretty strong.'

'I agree. I was upset, at first, but I read the letter she had left me, and it helped to put things into perspective. Diana was a good friend; she only wanted the best for both of us.'

'I know,' I said. 'I wish I'd seen more of her.'

'So do I,' replied Mum. 'But the best thing we can do now is to honour her memory by making the right choices in our lives. So, when Dad left for work this morning, I packed up what I could into the car, and here I am. I want you to know, my darling, that I don't regret a second of my life so far because it has had you in it. You will always be the most important person and that's part of why all this is happening. It's time to show you what can be possible, with a little courage; although you are the one who has already shown me that.'

'I'm so proud of you,' I said. 'Where are you going to go? You could come and live here – there's plenty of room. I know Diana would have loved that, too.'

'Thank you. I knew you would offer, and part of me would like nothing more. But it's time for proper, brave change. I'd love to stay for a week or two, but then I am going to go and live in France again. I won't be far from St Malo and there's a ferry from Poole, so we can visit each other easily.'

'That's so exciting!' I said.

'I think so. I've already lined up viewings of some little houses and flats, and I've been exploring work opportunities in a casual way for a while. Thank goodness I kept my French going. Now, while I'm here, I want to be as much help as possible. How are things going with the tearoom's renovation? I've brought my sewing machine, so say if you need any curtains or anything running up.'

With a sense of contentment, which would have been complete if I still hadn't been so worried about Luke, I set about taking Mum on a tour of my new little world, with pride in what both of us were managing to achieve.

The days Mum and I spent together in Spindrift Bay couldn't have been happier. She was in many ways unchanged: still kind, funny and smart. But she now had a lightness to her that infected those she met with joy, and I loved watching her make friends with everyone I had got to know already in the village. She and Gloria bonded instantly and, by the time Mum left for France, had shared their life stories, their most closely guarded kitchen secrets and several bottles of wine.

'So, get yourself settled,' said Gloria, over the last lunch the three of us shared together, around a table in the back garden of the guest house. 'And I'll come over next month. Oh, I do envy you your new life abroad. Maybe it's time I went to live in Spain with Georgie.'

'Don't both disappear abroad,' I said, aghast.

'It's a hop, skip and a jump these days,' said Gloria, waving an airy hand at me. 'But far enough,' she then said, giving Mum's hand a reassuring pat. 'For it to be harder for certain people to turn up on your doorstep.'

She was, of course, referring to Dad, who had rung me the night Mum arrived, demanding to know where she was. It was the first time I had spoken to him since moving to Dorset. As advised by her, I said she wasn't with me but had told me she was going abroad for a while.

'Abroad?' he had spluttered, furious. 'Where?'

'I don't know. Sorry, Dad.'

'But we don't have passports.'

'She must have got one.'

'Well, how am I supposed to get her back?'

'You're not. I'm sorry, Dad, I don't think she wants to be found.'

He kept me on the phone for another twenty minutes, raging

then wheedling and finally losing his temper all together, telling me I was useless and cutting off the call.

'I'm so sorry to put you through that,' said Mum, giving me a big hug. 'I had to sit on my hands to stop myself snatching the phone away.'

I shook my head.

'It's okay. It needed to be done. Can you do everything else without contacting him again?'

'I think so,' she said. 'My lawyers will sort it all out.'

There was only one other thing that spoiled our time together, and that was the complete absence of Luke. I had ended up telling Mum about the kisses and how much I liked him, and I wanted her to meet him, casually, before she left. But messages I sent went undelivered, and when we strolled down to the village and bumped into Tessa, she said she hadn't seen him.

'I thought you might know where he is,' she went on. 'There's a locum at the surgery and no one seems to know what's going on. Even Mum can't find out, and she can usually get to the bottom of any village mystery.'

'I hope he's all right,' I said. I didn't want to divulge what we had found out about Diana, but I was worried. What if he had decided that the ghosts and secrets surrounding his family were too much to bear, and had gone away for good?

I waved Mum off on her adventure early one Saturday morning almost two weeks after she had turned up on my doorstep. She was driving to Poole, to catch the ferry, and then on to her new life. My feelings as I shut the door almost overwhelmed me as they clashed together. I was happy for Mum but missing her already. Part of me yearned to be doing the same as she was, until I reminded myself that I was only at the beginning of my own adventure, and that anything else now would be running away, not towards. I knew that keeping busy was the best way to fight off any feelings of gloom, so, after a quick breakfast, I headed down to the beach for the usual weekend clean-up. Help had picked up after the barbecue, which had awoken many people's community spirit and there were about ten people already there when I arrived. I felt a little thud of disappointment when none of them was Luke but dredged up a smile when Caleb came over.

'Morning, Belle!' he greeted me cheerily. 'Need a bag?'

'Yes, please,' I said, taking one. 'Did Luke leave you in charge of the clean-up?'

I tried to keep the hurt out of my voice but couldn't understand why he hadn't asked me. Was he that angry? I thought we had parted on good terms, but his silence was looking increasingly personal.

'Not exactly,' replied Caleb. 'We, er, realised that he had gone away, what with the locum at the surgery and everything, and we – Tessa and me, that is – didn't want this to stop. I knew he kept all the stuff in a cupboard at the surgery, so I stopped in and Addy let me take it. Didn't have any more information on Luke, though.'

He looked at me curiously, obviously suspecting that I knew more than he did. But what was I to say? I couldn't explain what we had discovered, and I didn't know myself where Luke had gone, why or for how long.

'Thanks,' I said blandly, knowing that he wouldn't press me for information. 'Great idea. I'd better get started, then.'

It was a ravishing morning, warm and bright with a soft breeze. As I walked up and down the beach collecting the bits and pieces that had been dropped or washed up, I wished my spirits would lift and I could enjoy the day properly, but worry, sadness and guilt lay about me like a thick blanket of fog, not allowing the sun's rays to penetrate. I was wrestling a particularly twisty piece of nylon rope into my bag when I heard a voice.

'Need a hand with that?'

I looked up to see Edward, Doris at his heels, nosing into the seaweed.

'Hello,' I said. 'Have you come to help with the clean-up?'

'Indeed, I have. It's been too long since I came to one, and it doesn't seem right to study the sea without seeing what she throws up onto the shore.' He caught hold of my tricky length of rope and wrangled it into the bag. 'I've spent all week cataloguing microplastics with my team. The more we reveal the secrets of what we're doing to the sea, the more I realise how desperately we need to publicise it and get support.'

I smiled as he went to collect a bag and grabber, thinking about his words. *Secrets in the sea as well as in the village.* I knew which felt simpler.

When the clean-up was over, Tessa tried to persuade me to join her and some of the others for a coffee at her house, but I declined.

'Thanks, but I'd better get home; there are some things I need to check over. Not long now until the tearooms open again, I hope, and then I'm intending for them to become a regular place for people to come to after working on the beach each Saturday.'

'All right,' she said, not fooled for a moment. 'But I'm around all weekend if you need to talk.'

'I know,' I said, giving her a hug. 'And thank you. I'm missing Mum.'

Back at home, I mooched around aimlessly for a while, doing small jobs and looking over what the workmen had done that week. It was true: it wouldn't be long before I could open up shop, but the thought failed to imbue me with the excitement that it normally did.

'This is no good,' I said to the kittens, as I dangled some wool for them. 'I'd better do something useful with the rest of the day or nothing's going to get any better. Maybe it's time to tackle that Dorset apple cake... What do you think?'

I took their excited scrambling after the wool as a "yes" and headed to the kitchen. I was already slightly more buoyant at having a task, even though it was one I had been putting off. I couldn't open a tearoom in Spindrift Bay without serving the classic cake of the county, but I also knew that any local who tried it would be more particular than any *Bake Off* judge.

An hour later, I took a delicious-smelling cake out of the oven. As it cooked, I had decided that it would be the perfect thing to take round to Edward, and had rung him to check that he was in.

'I'd be delighted to see you again so soon, Belle,' he had said. 'And I've got some cream from the farm that would go beautifully with that cake. Don't let Doris see it, though; she's partial to a bit of apple cake.'

So, I wrapped it in a tea towel and headed down to the village, still unsettled, but happy to be busy. Edward greeted me warmly, although he looked tired, and soon we were sitting in the front room with tea and a large slice each of the cake.

'Is it all right?' I asked. 'I'm nervous about it. Maybe I should live here for another twenty years before I'm qualified.'

'Done to perfection,' said Edward, with a chef's kiss on the end of his fingers. 'And I should know – I was weaned on Dorset apple cake and barely a week goes by when I don't have a piece. I had been missing Diana's, but you've made me very happy.'

'Thank you,' I said. 'It won't be long before I can open the tearooms again and I want everything to be perfect.'

'Things are rarely that,' said Edward. 'Other than Doris, of course.'

The dog looked up at the sound of her name and thumped her tail on the floor.

'Of course,' I said, smiling.

'But if you don't mind my saying,' he went on. 'Something else is worrying you.'

I nodded miserably.

'Is it to do with what you told me before – about Diana and the Talbots? I've noticed young Luke hasn't been around recently.'

A sob caught in my throat as I nodded again.

'Remember our circle of trust?' he continued gently. 'You, me and Doris. Would it help to share?'

'I don't know,' I said. 'Mum knows, and Luke, and things have only got worse. Well, better for Mum, but worse for Luke.'

Edward watched me sympathetically, without speaking, and I bent down to stroke Doris's head as I tried to gather my scattered thoughts. The urge to tell Edward threatened to overwhelm me and although I tried to stem the outpour, the words came tumbling out before I could stop them.

'We – Luke and I, that is – found some more stuff. We discovered the box that Diana mentioned when... when...' I paused. 'The box had photos and other things. Oh, Edward...' I looked up to see nothing but kind concern on his face. 'Luke is Diana's son.'

I don't know how I had expected him to react – maybe with interest, or questions or even advice – but I was not prepared for the way the blood drained completely from his face and his skin instantly took on a greenish, sickly pallor. For a moment, I thought he was angry with me, and I froze, but then his hand flew to his chest. He tried to speak, but couldn't get his words out. I flew over to his chair and knelt down next to him, taking his hand, which was cold and clammy.

'Edward, are you all right? Can I get you anything? A drink, any medication?'

He shook his head and started gasping for breath.

'Oh God, Edward. Try to breathe, try to breathe,' I gabbled, scrabbling at my pockets with trembling hands to find my phone. *Please don't die.* I managed to dial 999.

'I need an ambulance,' I gasped, barely noticing the tears pouring down my face. 'For my friend. I think he's having a heart attack.'

The calm voice of the operator helped me focus, and I was able to give him the address and explain the situation.

'He's pale and struggling to breathe. He had a shock, oh God, it's my fault. He says he doesn't need any medication. Yes, I can open the door when you get here. There's a dog, but she's friendly, I'll look after her.'

He kept me talking until I heard the sirens and ran to open the door to let the paramedics in. They got to work swiftly, putting on an oxygen mask and hooking Edward up to various machines. I put Doris on her lead and took her to the other side of the room, where we waited anxiously. After what felt like an eternity, they helped Edward into a wheelchair and one of the paramedics turned to me.

'Are you family? Would you like to come with him?'

'No, I'm a friend. I would come, but I think I should look after Doris. Is he going to be all right?'

'He's in good hands,' replied the paramedic, with a kind smile. 'He'll be comforted to know that his dog is being cared for. Give the hospital a call in the morning and they'll update you on how he's doing.'

I nodded silently as they took Edward away, then I returned to the silent sitting room and sank onto the sofa.

'Oh, Doris,' I said, leaning into the dog's comforting warmth. 'I'm so sorry.'

And I sobbed into her golden shoulder until I was too exhausted to cry anymore. I dragged myself around making sure that the house was secure and I had all of Doris's belongings. Pulling the door gently shut behind us, we started to trudge home.

EIGHTEEN

I awoke early the next morning after a fitful sleep. I hadn't wanted to disturb or worry Mum on her first night in France, and there was no one else I could turn to, as telling them Edward was in hospital would mean explaining the reason he had become so ill. Telling anyone else Diana and Luke's secret was not going to happen, even a trusted friend like Gloria. Instead, I picked at some dinner, then tossed and turned, eventually giving up and dragging myself out of bed before dawn broke and the sun's rays showed behind my curtains. Figuring that hospitals don't keep the same hours as the rest of us, I tapped in the phone number that was on the photocopied flyer the paramedic had given me. The information was titled "Friends and Family", but after the part I had played in Edward's collapse, I was unsure if I was eligible to call. I had expected to wait for my call to be answered, but the phone was picked up straight away.

'Hello, Charleston Ward.'

'Oh, hi. I'm ringing to check on a friend who was brought in last night – Edward Burns.'

'Ah yes. Here we are, yes. Mr Burns has made a full recovery; he can go home today.'

'He has?' Relief flooded my body. 'Is his heart okay?'

'I'm afraid I can't give out personal information over the phone.'

'Of course not. Shall I come and pick him up?'

There was some more tapping on a keyboard.

'Mr Burns will be taken home later today by hospital transport,' said the brisk voice. 'He's booked on the 2 p.m. bus.'

'I see. Could you give him a message?'

'Of course,' said the voice, softening a little.

'Thank you. Please tell him that Belle rang, and I'll come over later. Oh, and that Doris is fine.'

'Is that his dog?'

'Yes.'

'Good, he's been worried about her. I'll let him know.'

There was nothing for it now but to wait, and to keep busy. I managed to raise a wan smile. How much I had changed already since moving to Spindrift Bay. A mere few months ago, a setback would have seen me moping and navel-gazing for hours, but now I had learnt that the best thing to do was to keep moving.

An hour later, I was walking to the village with Doris, shopping list ready. Surely now the most helpful thing I could do for Edward was to make sure that Doris was happy and that he had enough to eat. In my naivety about village life, I had pictured myself stopping in and out of the shop and back home with little more than a cheery "hello!" to anyone I met. No such luck. When I went in, there was a little cluster of people around the counter, who turned as I came in.

'Belle!' said Gloria. 'Have you heard about Edward? Apparently, there was an ambulance at his place yesterday. No one knows anything about it. You've got Doris!'

I bit my lip.

'I was with him. I'm not sure exactly what happened; he had

difficulty breathing. I spoke to the hospital this morning and he's coming home today. I was doing some shopping to make him a few bits for the freezer.'

'Why didn't you tell us?' asked Gloria. 'Oh, poor Edward. I'll make him something, too.'

The other people agreed that they also wanted to help, and I took the opportunity to slip away from them and collect what I needed, hoping that Gloria wouldn't ask again why I hadn't said anything sooner. Luckily for me, they were now too busy drawing up a list of meals, so I paid and hurried back home to start cooking.

The one good thing about all of this, I reflected gloomily, as I put a pasta bake in the oven and started on some shortbread, was that I hadn't had the headspace to worry about Luke as well as Edward. My messages still hadn't been answered, and there wasn't anything else I could do. The kitchen was filled with the comforting smell of baking, and I was about to start mixing some icing for the shortbread, when there was a knock at the door. As I opened it, I had a tiny taste of what had made Edward so unwell yesterday. All the breath seemed to drain instantly from my body; my head spun and my legs were cold and weak. For there, standing at the door with a huge bunch of flowers and that familiar puppy-dog look on his face, was Matt.

'Belle,' he said, stepping forward and kissing my cheek. 'You look wonderful.'

Through the pounding of blood in my head and the spinning, panicky thoughts, one thing penetrated. That was a lie. I didn't look remotely wonderful after a terrible night's sleep and debilitating worry, standing there in a messy apron with my hair pulled hurriedly back and in my oldest clothes. Why was he lying? Again.

'What do you want?' I croaked, then cleared my throat and tried again, more strongly. 'What do you want?'

'To see you, of course,' he replied, looking confused. 'I've missed you.'

'You've got a funny way of showing it,' I snapped. 'You dumped me days before our wedding and left me to deal with the fallout. I lost my home and my job, and *you* got engaged to someone else on what should have been our honeymoon.'

Now, it was his turn to feel some shock.

'How did you know about that?'

'Oh, there's this little thing called social media? Makes it hard to keep big life events a secret.'

I bent down to pick up Bubble and Squeak, who were about to make a dash through the open door. Matt took his opportunity to step inside.

'Better shut this,' he said, closing the door. 'And these are for you.'

He held out the flowers, but I clung onto the kittens and didn't take them. Instead, I turned and walked back to the kitchen. I had no intention of making this easy for him.

'This is a great house,' he said, putting the flowers on the table and sitting down. 'I read about your inheritance.'

I waited for him to offer his condolences about Diana, but he said nothing more.

'Why are you here?' I asked.

He stood up and came over uncomfortably close to me. I took a step back.

'Belle, I made a terrible mistake. I have come to ask for your forgiveness. I want to try again.'

To my eternal gratitude, the oven timer went off.

'Excuse me, I need to get these out.'

I pushed past him, but he followed me, leaning over my shoulder.

'Those look delicious. I didn't know you could cook.'

I slid the shortbread onto a cooling rack without answering. Finally, he backed off, and sat down again, staring at his hands.

'You're cross with me,' he said in a small voice. 'And I don't blame you.'

'Actually,' I replied, stirring the icing with more vigour than was necessary, 'I'm not, not anymore. But I *am* busy.'

'Too busy even to offer me a cup of tea and a nibble?' he said pathetically. 'I've come a long way to see you, Belle.'

'I'm busy,' I repeated. 'The shortbread is for a friend and the kettle's there if you'd like a cuppa.'

'When did you get so *hard?*' he said, filling his voice with distress. 'I blame myself.'

'Good.'

'But I want to put things right – please let me.'

'There's no need.'

'Oh, but there is! I'm helpless without you and so are my parents. Not having you there has made us understand how much we value and – yes – *love* you, Belle.'

I nearly snorted with laughter at the thought that his mother, Celia, had the slightest bit of love for me. No, she had discovered that the business accounts weren't as easy as she had assumed and wanted her underpaid skivvy back. But, instead of barking all of this at him, I took some breaths and didn't reply.

'My engagement to Jessica was a mistake. I panicked, Belle, and I'm sorry.'

Finally, I turned to look at him. His handsome, sad face stirred nothing in me at all. I glanced around the room, at the evidence of what I had achieved and how much I had changed in the time since I had seen him last. I returned my gaze to him.

'No, Matt. It's too late. I've got a new life, and I'm happy. You should go.'

He pushed out his lips into a petulant pout; ah, this was the Matt I knew.

'Don't be so ridiculous. It's not been that long, and we were together for years. Come home. You can sell this place, and we can use the money to buy somewhere together.'

How had I ever loved this man, wanted to marry him?

'No,' I repeated, the anger rising within me. 'How dare you

turn up here, after everything you've done, and expect me to drop everything and run back to you? How *dare* you?'

'You've changed,' he said, a nasty edge to his voice.

'Yes, I have, thank God.'

He stood up.

'I'll go, then. You can keep the flowers,' he added magnanimously. 'I'll have the ring back, though.'

For a moment, I didn't know what he meant, then I understood. My heart thudded into my stomach.

'An engagement ring is a gift,' I said, keeping my voice steady.

'An expensive one,' he replied. 'I'll have it back, as you're refusing to see sense.'

I turned back to my icing, not wanting to meet his eye.

'You can't,' I said. 'I sold it.'

'You can't do that!' he gasped. 'I'll sue!'

I spun back to face him.

'Oh, do your worst. I was perfectly within my rights to sell it, and, frankly, it was the least you owed me after your family wilfully underpaid me for so long. It's gone, Matt, move on. If I can do it, you can.'

The look of incredulous horror on his face might have made me laugh, if I wasn't so deadly serious. I could almost feel Diana's presence in the room, silently supporting me in this show of strength and confidence that came as almost as much of a shock to me as to Matt.

'You'd better try to get Jessica's ring back off her,' I went on, slightly unnecessarily but nonetheless enjoyably. 'Recoup some of your losses. And then maybe have a think about how you treat people. I have to get on,' I continued, without giving him an opportunity to speak. 'So, unless you want to help me take these things to my friend, you'd better go.'

He didn't move so, picking up the kittens, I swept past him to the front door and held it open. He followed me, paused, opened his mouth to speak and closed it again. His demeanour as he left the house was deflated now, rather than angry, and I felt a pang of pity for him, taking a step forward to call him back. I hated leaving anything on a sour or unfinished note, and the urge to try to smooth things over, make sure Matt was okay and not cross with me, was overwhelming. But an image of three of the strong women in my life – Mum, Diana and Gloria – appeared in my head like a Greek chorus offering its guidance. *Sit with the discomfort* was the message. And then, more like a 1960s Liverpudlian rock band: *let it be*. I stepped back into the house and gently closed the door.

'Come on, you two,' I said to Bubble and Squeak. 'Edward will be home soon, so I need to get this shortbread iced.'

I would process that strange and unexpected interlude another time, when I had less important things to do.

Doris and I arrived at Edward's house at the same time as the hospital transport and I was glad to see him step down from the small bus without any help. He bent down to pat and fuss over his dog, who was delirious with joy to see him. He took her lead and smiled at me.

'Belle. Thank you for coming and for looking after Doris. Are you moving in?'

He nodded at the bags I was carrying, a twinkle in his eye. I had been terrified he would be either frail or angry with me for causing his collapse, or both, so my entire body sank in relief at his small joke.

'Not yet,' I said, smiling. 'This is Doris's belongings and some bits and pieces I thought you might like.'

'Come in,' he said, and I followed him into his little house.

Soon, we were in our usual chairs, with our usual tea and sweet treats. How wonderful it was for things to be *normal*.

'I'm sorry about yesterday,' said Edward. 'I must have given you a scare.'

'*You* don't have to be sorry!' I said. 'I'm the one who is sorry. I'm so sorry for upsetting you; I should learn to keep things to myself. It was selfish of me.'

I had already determined not to tell him about Matt's visit; I was saving that for Gloria and a bottle of wine.

'You mustn't blame yourself,' said Edward, his face troubled. 'You mustn't. I'm glad you told me. Glad that you could confide in me – and I don't want that to change, so don't go worrying about an old man's fit of the vapours, all right?'

I summoned up a weak smile.

'All right,' I said. 'But I do worry, even if you're not remotely old. Wasn't it your heart?'

'No,' he said. 'I'm embarrassed to say that it was nothing more than a panic attack. The doctors assure me that my heart is perfectly strong; it was my nerves that were at fault. So ridiculous, causing all that fuss.'

'It's not ridiculous at all,' I said. 'Panic attacks are frightening, especially the first time, when you don't know what's going on.'

'You've experienced them?'

'Yes. They're nothing to be ashamed of.'

He inclined his head.

'Very well. Thank you. I owe you an explanation, all the same. You see, when you said that Diana was Luke's mother...'

He trailed off, his voice wavering, and the realisation hit me full force.

'You're his father?'

'Yes. At least, I think so – I assume so. Diana and I were very much in love. We kept it under the radar, partly because of the social differences – even as recently as the eighties people cared about things like that much more than they do now. But also partly because Diana had been protected by her family because of her epilepsy. They treated her like a child, always supervising her and saying "no" to everything. You can imagine how well she took to that.'

I grinned, easily able to picture Diana chafing at the rules.

'Not at all well.'

'Exactly. The thought of her having a romantic relationship, marriage, and most of all a baby would have horrified her parents because of the perceived danger to her and maybe to the child, if they inherited her condition or she had seizures while looking after them. They were old-fashioned, I'm afraid, but their actions came from a place of love. So, we sneaked around, and we were in our own unrealistic bubble, but we were so happy. Then, one day, I received a note from Diana saying she couldn't see me anymore.'

Edward stood up and went to rummage in a small desk, eventually producing an envelope, which he handed to me. On the front his name was written in Diana's strong, distinctive handwriting.

'Please, read it,' he said.

I took out the single sheet of paper, soft at the folds as though it had been opened and read many times.

Dearest Edward,

I know you will find this hard. I do. It is not what I want, but it is for the best. We must stop seeing each other. Please forgive me, please be happy.

All my love,

Diana

'So you see,' he continued, 'I never knew she was pregnant. I tried to see her, to contact her, but it was impossible. Not long after, the family moved to Spindrift House. That might as well have been a fortress. Everyone knew that the new baronet and his family were there, but they were rarely seen, other than zipping by in a car, and initial excitement and curiosity soon died down. I picked up snippets of information and vaguely remember Luke being born, because there was a flurry of interest in the new heir to the baronetcy. I continued writing to Diana, but my letters were either returned or went unanswered. Then I received a note from her mother to say that Diana had moved abroad, and I should stop writing. That was the last I heard of her until she turned up in Spindrift Bay forty years later and took over the tearooms, asking me not to tell anyone who she was.'

'And then she met Luke.'

'That's right.'

His face clouded over with sorrow, and I waited quietly until he was ready to speak again.

'I knew Luke fairly well, because of Doris, and liked him. The way he has with animals – all that skill and patience. You can't fake that. I'm sure Diana sensed it, and it helped her befriend him. I can – *must* – feel nothing but happy that they got along so well and became so close before Diana died.' He paused and, again, I waited. 'Belle, can you forgive me if I tell you that I am so *angry* with Diana?'

As he spoke, his eyes became wet, and he drew the back of his hand across them roughly. 'Why didn't she tell us? I know it would have been difficult, but it would have brought joy, too. And now it's too late.'

'First of all,' I said, 'there's nothing to forgive. I'm angry with her, too, on behalf of all of you. But she must have been tortured by it all.'

Now, I started to cry, too, with ragged, deep gulps as I imagined how Diana must have suffered, particularly when she knew she was dying, and her secret might be lost forever.

'She must have been so scared,' I sobbed. 'But it's not too late for you and Luke.'

Edward handed me a box of tissues, and I pulled out several to mop my face and nose.

'I hope not,' he said sombrely.

'You *must* tell him!' I said. 'After all of this, it can't stay hidden.'

'I will,' said Edward. 'But Belle, you won't say anything, will you?'

'Of course not! I wouldn't dream of it – it's your secret to tell. But Luke deserves to know.'

'I know he does. I promise I'll tell him, and soon.'

'If he ever comes back,' I said, scrunching the tissues into a ball in my hand.

'He will,' said Edward. 'And all of this will be sorted out, hopefully without much more pain.'

I desperately hoped he was right. Either way, I would be there to help Luke learn – and cope with – the truth.

NINETEEN

The days passed, and still there was no word from Luke. Worry still squirmed in my stomach, but it had gradually been joined by anger – both towards him and turned towards myself.

'I'm a complete fool,' I said to Lottie, who had come to stay for a few days. Like the true friend she was, she had been helping me scrub out the tearoom kitchens, ready for the inspection booked in now that the workmen had nearly finished. Now, we were sitting in the garden as the sun lowered in the sky, sipping the hibiscus lemonade I had made. 'First I fell for Matt, who then completely disappeared on me—'

'Until he turned up here on your doorstep,' said Lottie, who had been stunned when I had told her the story.

'Well, quite. And then I fell for Luke – who also completely disappeared. Why can't I find a man who doesn't vanish? I must be a terrible judge of character.'

'No, you're not,' said Lottie loyally. 'Matt managed to pretend he was a good guy pretty convincingly – and maybe he was. He bought you that engagement ring, for one thing. That was the real deal.'

'I suppose so,' I said grudgingly. 'Matt's problem was his mother, more than anything.'

'And Luke sounded like he had potential,' she went on. 'Don't give up on him yet. He's had a shock; his whole identity has been turned upside down. I agree it's horrible of him to go AWOL, but isn't it worth waiting for an explanation before you write him off?'

I sipped my drink and pictured Luke's kind face, the care he had for his patients and their owners, his smile. Could I have got it so wrong?

'You've asked at the surgery?' said Lottie.

'Not exactly. Caleb said that Addy, the nurse, didn't know where Luke was.'

I knew I could have tried harder to find out, but I dreaded hearing that Luke had gone for good, furious with me as much as with Diana and his family, for the part I had played in unearthing the secret.

'Is there someone else we could go and ask?'

'There's Joe, on reception. I suppose he might know. But is there any point?'

'There's every point! Worst case scenario, he's gone away for ever, is selling up and you'll never see or hear from him again.'

'Ouch.'

'But at least you'd know, and you could move on.'

I sighed.

'You're right, I know you're right. Maybe that would be better. The worst thing is the *hope*. I can't seem to shake it, but it makes me feel sick. I did exactly the same with Matt, at first. For all that he left me in such a brutal way, so close to the wedding, with everything to sort out, I still felt a spark of hope, for weeks afterwards, that he would come and tell me it had all been a colossal mistake. How pathetic.'

Lottie was one of the few people I would confess something like this to, something that brought such a sense of shame. And it was shame that I was feeling again – that I still longed and hoped for Luke to come back and for everything to be all right when really, how could it?

'It's not pathetic,' she said, her voice full of compassion.

'Belle, you're one of the happiest, most open people I know. You expect the best from people and from situations, you trust that they are what they seem. Right now, you're seeing that as a weakness, but it's not, I promise you – it's one of your greatest strengths.'

I looked at her in surprise.

'It's okay, you can use some tough love, I know I'm naïve and should grow up.'

'Belle, please don't talk about yourself like that.' She looked upset now, and I sat up and took notice. 'Your hope, your belief in the fundamental goodness of people and that things will work out – it's got me through so much. Remember Kurt?'

How could I ever forget that nasty piece of work my sweet friend had once called her boyfriend?

'You never let me believe that I was broken. You understood how awful it was, and you didn't deny my feelings, but you insisted on keeping that flame of hope flickering, even when I was at my darkest. God knows what I would have done without you. You kept me out of the abyss, even when I had one foot over the edge, with your strength and your hope. And yes, you are strong,' she went on, seeing that I had opened my mouth to protest. 'Just because you feel stuff, and cry, and grit your teeth sometimes rather than creating a drama, doesn't mean you're weak: quite the opposite. How do you think your mum managed to stay with your dad all these years, and has only left now?'

'She stayed for me,' I said, another wave of shame and unworthiness washing through me. 'When I went, she went. She was the strong one.'

'But don't you see?' said Lottie, who knew my mum well. 'The way you are – it rubbed off on her, too. She could put up with the worst whilst believing in the hope of something better. I believe it was *that* that made leaving possible for her in the end. So many women stay, even when they promise themselves they won't. She knew *he* wouldn't change, but she was certain that the "something better" still existed for her.'

It was true that, over the years, I had tried to keep her buoyant, believing that she deserved, and could have, more.

'I'm so happy things are better for her now.'

'But you're not surprised, are you?' demanded Lottie. 'You always had that kernel of faith, like you did for me, that things would be better. Her leaving, my surviving Kurt – for you, these things were inevitable. So don't dismiss yourself as a pathetic Pollyanna. You've got grit.'

'But now that Diana's dead, how does it help anyone to have the truth dragged out?' I said angrily.

'Because Luke and Edward have a right to know,' said Lottie. 'There's still the opportunity for them to have a relationship as father and son. And, messy though it is, his younger brother should also know. It was what Diana wanted – you've honoured that, Belle. That means something. How would things look if you had found everything out, by chance because you were going through Diana's papers, and *not* told Luke? Or even if you had decided to ignore Diana's dying wishes and burn everything without looking through it? How would you be feeling about yourself?'

'Bad,' I said, finally raising a smile.

'Exactly. The relationship between you and Luke wouldn't be any better than it is now, because you're the one who would be absent – in spirit, if not in body. Now, shall we go and speak to this Joe, and see what else we can find out, or are you going to stay slumped against the wall you've hit?'

I pulled a face at her, already feeling better.

'Fine, let's go.'

The village was quiet as we walked through, but the early summer air was fresh, and my spirits lifted further. To my relief, there was no one other than Joe in the surgery waiting room, and he looked up and smiled as we came in.

'Morning, Belle.'

'Morning. This is my friend, Lottie. She's staying with me for a few days.'

Joe stood up to shake Lottie's hand.

'What can I do for you? Are the kittens okay?'

'Oh yes, they're fine. It was Luke I wanted to ask about. I'm worried – he's not been in touch at all since he went. Have you heard from him?'

He shook his head.

'Sorry, no. Before he went, I did wonder if he was okay – he started asking me about my family, how I'd feel if my parents had kept a big secret from me.' He laughed. 'I said that with six kids in the family, there was no chance of any secrets. The next thing I knew, he emailed to say that a locum was coming in and that he'd be back soon. The locum – guy called Pete – doesn't know how long he'll be here. That's it, I'm afraid. I can let you know if I hear from him?'

'Thank you,' I said, disappointed, and scribbled down my number.

'There you go,' said Lottie, once we were back on the street. 'He said he'd be back soon. That's the only fact we have, so stick with that.'

I gave her a wan smile.

'Now, it's my last night with you – didn't you say you had some friends coming over?'

I clapped my hand to my mouth.

'I'd completely forgotten! Yes, Tessa and Gloria are coming. Thank goodness you said – we'd better get some stuff while we're here!'

For a while, I managed to push my thoughts about Luke to the back of my mind as we bought food and drink and hurried home to start cooking. Lottie was right: the only fact we had was that Luke had told Joe he'd be back soon; anything else was imagination. I had to wait to find out how Luke was feeling, and if he would ever speak to me again.

TWENTY

After I had waved Lottie off, my mood started to dip. I had loved her being here with me. Our final evening, with Tessa and Gloria, had been full of deep conversations as well as laughter, and the atmosphere of support and solidarity had filled me with warmth and well-being. This morning, I was deflated and lonely, and my anger and fear at Luke's disappearance came back tenfold. There was even a change in the weather to match my mood; rather than another golden summer morning, it was grey and windy out. I remembered what Lottie had said to me the previous day, how I always had hope and how precious that was.

'Not feeling much of that this morning, boys,' I said to the kittens, who were busy stalking a small feather that had blown in. 'I'm wondering if my best hope is to sell this on and try again somewhere else.'

But even as I said it, the words sounded and felt meaningless and, to my surprise, it was this that showed me my little flame was still burning bravely on. I stood up.

'Of course I'm not going to do anything of the sort,' I said. 'Things will work out, one way or the other. Time to get busy.'

I dressed quickly, grabbed a litter picker and a bag and headed down to the beach. It wasn't a Saturday, so the organised group wasn't there and, because of the weather, neither was anyone else. The wind had whipped up the sea and a large amount of debris was scattered on the sand. I got to work and was soon so engrossed that I didn't notice the figure approaching, until it was a few feet away. My stomach rolled, but my heart sang.

'Luke?'

I pushed some stray hairs away from my face with my forearm, keeping on the heavy gloves and holding the picker and bag in front of me. I was so glad to see him that it was hard to summon up much anger, but, at the same time, I wasn't prepared to fling my arms around him. If these men would insist on reappearing, they should understand the damage they had done; I'd left Matt in no doubt about that, but I still wasn't sure how I wanted to handle things with Luke.

'Belle.' He took a step forward, then stopped awkwardly. 'I'm... You must be...' He shook his head and swallowed, looking past me out to sea. He had lost weight and looked grey, drawn and exhausted. My anger dissipated. I dropped the things I was holding and pulled off the gloves, then walked towards him, reaching out to touch his arm. He brought his gaze to me, and it was full of anguish.

'Come up,' I said simply, turning to collect my things. 'Come on.'

We walked to the house in silence and, apart from offering him tea or coffee, we didn't speak again until we were sitting at the large table.

'Belle, I'm so sorry for going away without telling you,' he said. 'I left my stupid phone at home, but I didn't realise until I got to the ferry terminal.'

'Ferry?' I asked. 'Where have you been?'

'France. I knew Diana lived there for a long time and – goodness knows why – I thought I might be able to find something out. I don't know why, or what I thought I would find. I wasn't thinking straight. I wanted to get away from here, that's the real reason, away from Mum and Dad.'

'Did you find out anything?'

'No, but I went to the village she had lived in and met people she knew. I saw her house. None of it served any purpose, but it did make me feel closer to her.'

'That sounds like a good purpose,' I said, and he raised a small smile.

'There's not much for me to cling to. It feels pathetic, telling you now, but it was good.' He dropped his gaze down to his lap for a moment, his fingers gripping his thick hair. 'I wish I had *known*,' he said, his voice muffled. 'Before it was too late.'

'Are you glad you know now?' I asked in a small voice.

He lifted his head.

'Sorry, what did you say?'

I cleared my throat.

'Are you glad you know now?'

He looked puzzled for a moment, before his face cleared.

'Yes! Oh Belle, I'm *so* glad. It's not easy, but I'd much rather know. You haven't been worried, have you?'

'Very. I would understand if you hated me, for being the one to dig it all up.'

He jumped up, showing some of his old vigour, and came around the table to kneel beside me, taking both my hands in his.

'I could never hate you, and certainly not for this. You found it out for all the right reasons, because Diana wanted the truth known, even if she had been unable to share it. I'm grateful, Belle, not angry.'

Now, I couldn't stop the tears from falling, tears of relief, releasing all the worry and pain that had inhabited my body for the past week.

'Sorry,' I sobbed, standing up to get a box of tissues and leaning on the counter as I mopped at my face. 'I've been so worried. I thought everything was my fault and I'd have to leave Spindrift Bay, and when Edward collapsed...'

'Edward collapsed?' said Luke. 'My God, is he all right? What happened?'

Uh oh. I mustn't tell him that Edward is his father. I made a promise.

I sat down again as Luke returned to his chair.

'Edward knew – well, believed – that Diana was your aunt,' I began carefully.

'Yes,' he said. 'You told me at the beach barbecue.'

'We were talking about her, and he had a panic attack. Neither of us knew what it was; I thought it was a heart attack and he probably did, too. Anyway, I called an ambulance, and he was in hospital overnight. He's okay now, and back home.'

'I'll go and see him,' said Luke. 'Poor guy – he misses her a lot.'

'I'm sure he'd love to see you,' I said. 'I had Doris here for the night; she was so good with the kittens, let them climb all over her and pounce on her tail when she wagged it.'

'I'll go over and see him later,' he said. 'Thank goodness he's all right.'

'I know. And half the village has lavished him with meals, so he'll be all right for a while to come.'

Luke laughed, and it was so good to see his face lighten, before his expression dropped again and a frown creased his brow.

'But what's all this about you leaving the bay?'

For a moment, I was puzzled, then remembered that I had poured this out a few moments previously. I put a hand to my head and groaned as my cheeks reddened.

'Sorry, I shouldn't have said that. I didn't mean it. That is, I was so worried that—that I'd ruined everything, that for a moment I thought my fresh start had gone stale, and I should try again somewhere else.'

'I see,' said Luke, grinning. 'A dramatic exit. Where were you going to go?'

I shrugged, mirroring his grin.

'Good question. Possibly to France, to be with my mum, or maybe – I don't know. Guatemala?'

His hand crept across the table a little closer to mine.

'I'd be sorry if you did that – although I hear that Guatemalan coffee is delicious. You could send me some.'

'Ha ha,' I replied, turning my hand to hook his fingers as they touched mine. 'Maybe you should go instead. You could become a specialist quetzal vet.'

His fingers were stroking my wrist, now, and the worry in my stomach had become a flurry of excited butterflies.

'I've got another idea,' he said. 'How about we both stay here doing exactly what we're doing, but...' He cleared his throat. 'Maybe a little more of some of it?'

He wrapped his fingers round my wrist and tugged gently. I stood up and he pulled me onto his lap, one arm slipping round my waist and the other hand coming softly to the back of my neck, little pressure needed for me to move my mouth to his and kiss him, with all the pent-up tension and fear of the last week leaving my body in a glorious explosion of joy and relief. I had been untethered when he had gone away, but now, kissing him at my kitchen table, wearing my old beach cleaning clothes and with a flurry of summer rain pattering against the window, I was safe again. I was home.

An hour later, and it was the bedroom window being streaked by the wind-blown rain. I snuggled close into Luke as we lay under the duvet, a smile on my face that wouldn't be suppressed. We were both sleepy, but suddenly he jumped.

'Was that you?'

'Was what me?'

'On my toes.'

He lifted himself onto an elbow and I gazed lazily down the bed, then we both laughed. There was Bubble, clinging with all his might to Luke's foot under the duvet. He wiggled it, and the kitten grasped on even more tightly, and let out a little growl.

'Hey, guy, I'll need that back,' said Luke, but Bubble was impervious. He would make a prize of that foot if it was the last thing he did. Luke slowly drew his leg toward him, until he could detach the determined kitten, who took it in good part and changed tack to scaling the pillows for his favourite challenge of trying to get to the top of the wooden bedstead. A tiny mew came from the floor beside me. I peered over.

'Aw, Squeak, are you feeling left out?'

I scooped up the little scrap, who immediately cuddled into my neck and started purring loudly. I looked at Luke, who was smiling at me.

'Not such a bad life, is it?' he said.

'Not a bit.'

'I don't want to ruin the atmosphere,' he went on. 'But there is something I'd like to ask you about.'

'Mmhmm,' I said, a little shot of dread darting through me. Had I trusted him too quickly? Should I have made as short work of him as I did of Matt?

'When I'm ready to talk to my parents, will you come with me?'

'I *can*,' I said. 'That is, of course I will, if you want me to. But won't they mind? It's a family secret that's been kept for so long – won't they want to speak to you privately?'

'Probably,' he said, his voice hardening. 'But in my opinion, they've forfeited the right to have a say in that. It—it would mean a lot to me to have your support.'

'Then I'll be there,' I said. 'Let me know when you're ready.'

He felt for my hand which wasn't stroking Squeak and squeezed it. Our fingers twined together.

'Thank you. And I'm sorry again for going away and being stupid enough to leave my phone behind. Although, in a way, it was a good thing I had. It gave me the space I needed to sort through everything that has been thrown up. It's weird to find out that your parents aren't your parents, even though they have been good parents to me.'

'Are you very angry with them?' I asked.

He sighed.

'I don't know. That may sound ridiculous, but it's the truth. I know I'm hurt, and offended to have had the wool pulled over my eyes my entire life, and I'm devastated that I never got to know Diana as her son...' He broke off and took a few deep breaths. 'And I have no idea who my father is. It's shaken me, Belle, made me wonder who *I* am. My God, Belle, what if—what if Diana was raped? What if she couldn't bear the sight of me and begged them to take me as their own?'

I felt desperate to tell him what I knew, to comfort him at least with the fact that his father would have wanted him. But I kept Edward's secret.

'I know,' I replied quietly. 'You need answers.'

'I don't know how to feel until I've got some – whether to be angry with them or grateful.'

'Yes. I'm sure they had good reasons for what they did.'

'I bloody well hope so. If it turns out simply that Dad was so desperate for an heir that he forced his young sister to give me up...'

His voice cracked and I pushed Squeak out of the way so that I could wrap my arms around him.

'Wait and see,' I said, wishing I had something more profound to offer.

'It's all I can do,' he said. 'And I want you to know how special you are to me, Belle. Nothing can change that. I missed you so much when I was away.'

'I missed you, too,' I said, realising now that the torrent of feelings I had been wrestling with in his absence all boiled down to that one simple fact. 'But we can start from today, with no secrets between us.'

Other than the fact that I know who your father is.

As he started to kiss me again, I hoped with all my heart that I wasn't doing the wrong thing by leaving that secret for someone else to tell.

TWENTY-ONE

The next morning, Luke left early to go to the surgery and ask the locum to stay on a little longer. I drifted around the house, hazy with happiness, texting Lottie and Mum, nibbling at bits of food and flicking through recipe books to try and decide if there was anything else I wanted to put on the menu of The Coastal Kettle. I already had a long list of bakes, sandwiches and drinks that I was confident would be popular, but the final idea I wanted to try out was something I had seen once at a wedding: gourmet marshmallows. I wouldn't be able to arrange an open fire for people to toast them on, as they had done there, but they might be a hit if people wanted a small, sweet treat that was lighter than cake or cookies. I also wondered if there might be any mileage in offering them in boxes, for people to take to beach barbecues. The wedding caterers had made at least ten different flavours, ranging from blackcurrant to chocolate orange and even whisky, but I was considering staying within brand and trying to concoct marshmallows in flavours such as Earl Grey tea, strawberry jam and cream, and sea buckthorn, or even gorse. I started looking up recipes, quickly realising that the ingredients and equipment I needed would require a trip to a large supermarket, rather than just opening my kitchen cupboards. Relieved, as I was too lazy and content to embark on a big experimental cooking project, I satisfied myself with making a shopping list and had another cup of tea.

Ten or fifteen minutes later, there was a knock at the door – not the front door, for once, but the door that led from the tearoom kitchen into the house. I opened it, to find the builder in charge of the extra works on the tearoom.

'Hi, Dominic, everything okay?'

'More than: we've finished!'

He grinned, a gold tooth glinting as he did so. Dominic would have made an excellent pirate, with his shaggy dark hair, dense stubble and wicked laugh, but it was my good fortune that he had chosen the building trade, rather than sailing the seven seas, as he had been doing such a good job for me.

'Have you? I wasn't expecting you to say those words for another week or so!'

'Do you want to come and see?'

'Yes! Let me put some shoes on.'

Three minutes later, I was being taken on a guided tour of a transformed *Coastal Kettle*.

'Most of your problems were due to the brickwork,' explained Dominic. 'The pointing mix that had been used wasn't strong enough and a lot of it had blown away; that's what was causing your damp problems. We've redone it all with more cement, so you shouldn't have any more trouble.'

'That's a relief. The kitchen looks so much smarter.'

I gazed round at the freshly plastered, painted and tiled walls.

'A lot better,' agreed Dominic. 'And it's all proper grade materials, antibacterial paint and so on. But come through to the front.'

Pleased with what had been done, I followed him, not expecting to be wowed. After all, Tessa and I had already done a lot of work in there and I didn't think that the work Dominic and his team were doing would have elevated it much more. I was wrong.

'Oh, it looks gorgeous!' I said, gazing around in delight. 'I can't believe how much difference it's made!'

He smiled broadly, the gold tooth winking in the sunlight that flooded in through the windows.

'Good, isn't it? Your paint job wasn't bad, but we went over it again. It's the wood that's been the game changer.'

He was right. I ran my hand along the counter, which had been filled, sanded and polished until it shone; the window frames had undergone the same treatment and looked like they belonged in a chic London cake shop rather than a seaside tearoom. They had replaced the cracked menu boards with smooth new ones, all ready for me to chalk up the day's offerings, and the glass in the cabinets gleamed.

'Did you change all of this?' I asked, unable to resist running my hand along its curved, gleaming lengths.

'Only that middle part,' said Dominic, with a nod towards it. 'It had a nasty crack we couldn't sort. The rest only needed some small fixes – and we redid the adhesive. What do you think of the floor?'

I looked down at the glowing quarry tiles beneath my feet then back, in wonderment, to Dominic's proud face.

'I barely recognise them. They *are* the same ones?'

'Very much so. They've been deep cleaned with a rotary floor scrubber, then we fixed the cracks up, replaced a couple of broken ones before sealing and waxing the lot. They've come up well, haven't they?'

'You've done an incredible job,' I said, beaming. 'And you've even hung my curtains!'

'We like to finish a job properly. I expect we'll all be back in from time to time for a cuppa.'

'You'd be welcome,' I said, meaning it. I had never worked with contractors like them before, and I would gladly stand them a whole pot of tea, never mind just a cup, whenever they wanted it.

As soon as they had gone, I called Tessa to tell her the good news. It was my luck that she wasn't far away, with Noah, and ten minutes later was standing in the tearooms, gazing around with as much pleasure as I had.

'You must be thrilled,' she said. 'They've done a fantastic job. How soon can we open?'

'Hopefully in a few weeks,' I said. 'It's got to make it through a few inspections, but once those are out of the way, we'll be in business!'

A shiver went through me at the thought of it; the dream was almost a reality.

'Let me know as soon as you do,' said Tessa. 'I've loved my time with Noah, but it'll be good to get back to work. And Belle?'

'Yes?'

'I hope you don't mind me saying, but you're looking even happier than these tearooms warrant. Anything to tell me?'

I couldn't help myself from smiling at her.

'That obvious?'

'I'm afraid so. Something to do with a certain veterinarian of the village?'

'Well, he's back and things have—' I cleared my throat, a little shy. 'Well, things have moved on between us.'

She gave me a big hug.

'That's brilliant! I thought you two would be great together and I was so worried when he suddenly vanished like that. Is every-thing okay?'

'It's all right,' I said. 'Or, at least, I think it will be. I'm sorry, I can't tell you anything now – it's not mine to tell.'

'Of course not,' she said. How lucky I was to have found a friend who didn't push or pry. 'I'm thrilled that love is in the air!'

Luke came back around lunchtime and, after proudly showing him the finished tearooms, I took out a stack of papers.

'I kept looking through those boxes,' I said. 'I've not found anything more about you – yet – but you might like to see these. They're photos and a few letters that Diana saved. I've only had a quick look at them, but maybe you'd like to learn more about her. I can put them away again if you'd rather.'

'No,' said Luke, placing a hand on top of the small pile. 'Thank you, I'd like to see them.'

He pulled out a photo at random, studied it for a moment or two, then smiled.

'Look,' he said, and I moved to sit next to him. He turned the picture over. 'This was 1992, so several years after she moved to France. It's good to see her looking so happy.'

The photo showed Diana sitting at a table in a pretty square with three friends, all laughing as they squinted against the sun. Diana was holding a coffee and wearing a long skirt with a stylish white shirt.

'She looks amazing!' I said. 'And I remember that woman sitting next to her. Genevieve – although Diana called her Ginette. I met her once or twice when Mum and I visited. They were good friends; Diana worked in her family's bakery and café.'

'I met her!' exclaimed Luke, studying the photo more closely. 'Yes, it's definitely her, now I look. She said she was a great friend of Diana's, and was devastated when I told her what had happened.'

'Did you tell her who you were?'

'Not exactly. It felt too raw. But I asked her if Diana had ever had children and she said no, but she had often wondered why not. Apparently, her own children called her *Tante*, and they were close. Lucky them.'

His voice hardened on the last words, and I chose my own carefully.

'It sounds as if Diana missed you. I'm sure that being like an aunt to Ginette's children was only a poor substitution for being with you.'

'Maybe that's how my mother and father felt about me, especially when Sam came along. After all, I'm their nephew, not their son.'

I bit my lip. Had I said the wrong thing again?

'How do you feel about them – now that you know?'

'Confused,' he replied. 'Of course, I still think of them as Mum and Dad, and of Sam as my brother, but now I *know* that's not true, and I can't put the two things together and have them make sense. I know that most people would tell me that they're the ones who brought me up, so they're my parents – and they were great, I've got no complaints. But blood is so important to my father.'

'You are a blood relative, though,' I said. 'Surely you would have inherited, anyway, if they hadn't gone on to have Sam?'

'Probably,' he said. 'But I know my father. He's a good man, but the difference between people seeing his son inherit rather than his – I assume – illegitimate nephew would have been important to him.'

'Would you have been able to inherit if you were illegitimate?'

'Yes, the law changed a while back. But Dad would have most cared about how it looked to outsiders. And I need to know what happened, why I ended up with them, who wanted or didn't want me.'

'It's not a good feeling,' I said, knowing that I was going to tell him something that produced a twist of shame every time I thought of it, that I had never told anyone, even though I knew that the shame shouldn't be mine. 'My father didn't want me.'

He looked up at me sharply, frowning. I carried on.

'He told me fairly regularly.' I emitted a dry laugh, but there was nothing funny about this. 'He blamed my mother for getting pregnant and not telling him in time for her to have a termination.'

'Belle, that's awful.'

I shrugged.

'Yes. And he never stopped resenting me, just for existing. But I knew that my mother loved me very, very much, and wanted me. She told me once, after my father had told me in detail how he had tried to wangle a late-term abortion, that she had known about the pregnancy from early on, and had loved and wanted me so much that she had taken huge risks to conceal it from him until it was too late for him to do anything about it. And she never made me feel anything *but* loved; she was fierce about it. And that gave me some protection from *him*.'

Luke looked horrified, as well he might.

'Why did she stay with him?'

'It's more complicated than I understand, but she thought it was the best thing. She's left him now – gone to France, in fact. Diana would be pleased.'

'I agree,' said Luke. He took my hand, squeezing it.

'So, I'm not the best person to talk to about what family means,' I said. 'I met Matt young, and I was impressed by his parents. They're closeknit and his mother – Celia – was protective. I believed, as Matt's girlfriend and then his fiancée, that I could become part of that, but what I didn't realise was that there was no chink for an outsider to slip through, ever. So they never accepted me as part of their family; I was an outsider. And when Matt broke off the engagement – I suspect because Celia told him to – the drawbridge was raised and there was no feeling at all for me.'

'I'm so sorry,' said Luke, sounding distressed. 'I had no idea.'

'*I'm* sorry,' I said, with a weak smile. 'I didn't mean to hijack the conversation.'

'You haven't,' he said. 'You have the right to tell your story. Belle, I want us to know each other – know *about* each other. I know I'm in the middle of all this stuff, but if it brings things up for you, then I'm glad to hear about them.'

'Thank you. There was plenty of good, too. I felt connected to Diana, same as Mum did, and coming to Spindrift Bay has been like coming home, even though I don't have any family here.'

'Except for Bubble and Squeak,' said Luke, grinning.

'Well, of course,' I replied. 'And they have no trouble at all behaving like they own the place!'

'God knows what will happen with the estate now,' said Luke, his face serious again. 'I can't inherit it, not that I ever wanted to.' He stopped suddenly, then shrugged. 'Although it feels weird to know now that it was never mine for the taking, that I have no right to it.'

'Do you think you were mentally prepared to take it on when your dad died, even though you don't want to?'

'Probably. I guess that's another adjustment I'll need to make, although I'm sure it's not what I wanted. I suppose it makes sense now why Dad suddenly stopped trying to teach me how to manage it when Sam came along, and I was allowed to go off and train to be a vet. He had his real son at last, and as soon as he was old enough, Dad started all that with him. Sam took to it like a duck to water, of course. Maybe there is something to be said for blood. I wonder if my real father – my birth father – is a vet, or works with animals or something. Do you think my parents know who he is?'

I was cold with stress, the urge to blurt out what I knew battling with the promise I had made to Edward.

'I don't know,' I managed to say. 'But you need to talk to them soon; there are too many unanswered questions, and we can't keep filling in the blanks with guesses.'

'I know,' he said quietly. 'But Belle, I'm so frightened of what I might find out.'

TWENTY-TWO

We sat in silence for a moment. I could understand his fear. Why had the baronet and his wife taken him on as a baby? And why had the truth about his birth been concealed, to the point of falsifying his birth certificate? Had Diana not wanted him? Or had she been persuaded – or even forced – to give him up? And what would happen now – to the family, to the title and the land, to the story that had been so carefully constructed?

'I know you're frightened,' I said softly. 'But you have to confront it all. I know it's not fair that you're the one to do it, when none of this is your doing. I'm there for you, I'll be with you for all of it, if you want me to be.'

He looked at me, his eyes shadowed with worry and uncertainty.

'I know you are, and that means everything. I've been so adrift since I found out; I barely knew what I was doing when I went to France. I was beside myself with grief and confused with guilt that I was mourning my mother when the only mother I've ever known was healthy and well at Spindrift House. But through all of that, I've thought of you, and that kept me safe. It was like there was a rope, keeping me tethered however much I believed myself to be battered and flung around. Even as I felt the connection to my parents and home fraying, and knew that I couldn't reach Diana now, however much I wanted to, you were like an island, Belle, a safe place with a little light on, that I could come back to. I could hardly bear it that I couldn't contact you, that I was stupid enough to have left my phone behind. All I could do was hope that I was right, that, that...'

He broke off, his voice so thick with emotion now that he could barely get the words out. Tears were flowing freely down my face and I stood up to wrap my arms around him, stroking and kissing his hair, shushing him with comforting murmurs, even as I needed the comfort myself. He took a shaky breath.

'All I could hope was that I was right,' he repeated. 'Right to dare to believe that *you* might be my family, that I've found that with you. No blood, no secrets, no lies.'

I nodded vigorously, barely able to speak.

'Yes,' I managed. 'I hope so, too.'

We stayed like that for a while, until we were interrupted by a plaintive 'mew'. Luke pulled me onto his lap, reaching down as he did so to pick up both kittens.

'Funny old family we make,' he said.

I giggled.

'At least there's no question of who's in charge: it's these two.'

We played with them for a while, laughing as they rolled over and over to catch a feathery mouse on the end of a stick, until they tired and wandered off to find a patch of sunlight to snooze in.

'I will go and see my parents,' said Luke. 'But first of all, I'd like to go and visit Diana's grave tomorrow.'

'Would you like me to come with you?'

'I'd love that.'

The next day, we woke early and collected some flowers from the garden, flowers that only grew there because of Diana, into a colourful bunch, then set off for the church. The vicar was there, oiling the hinges of the huge wooden doors. Scaffolding was up all around the building.

'Good morning!' he called when he saw us, and we went over. 'I have to do this job all the time,' he said, holding up the oil can. 'Or every time someone comes in late to a service the heads of the entire congregation swivel round to see who's caused the squeaking. I'm glad to see you both, though, very glad. The money you raised from your barbecue is already being put to good use.' He waved a hand at the scaffolding. 'The roof is getting the attention it needed and I'm so grateful. Everyone seems happier, too. It did them good to contribute together to the cause.'

'That's wonderful,' said Luke. 'We'll have to plan something else.'

'Make sure you let me know,' said the vicar. 'I'll help in any way I can.' His eyes dropped to the flowers Luke was holding. 'Ah, come to visit someone?'

'Diana,' I said.

'Good, good. Well, I won't hold you up – you know where to go.'

We said goodbye as he resumed his job and walked through the graveyard to where Diana was buried, the plot still looking new beside the others, some of which were several hundred years old, their headstones cracked and sunken. We crouched down and Luke lay the flowers on top of the mound.

'We should have brought a vase,' he said. 'They won't last long.'

'It doesn't matter,' I replied. 'They look beautiful.'

'Would it be weird to talk to her?' he went on.

'Not at all. Isn't that what we're here for? Do you want me to leave you alone?'

He shook his head.

'No, it's fine. She'll probably want to hear from you, too.'

'Hi, Diana,' I said out loud, guessing that Luke would appreciate me getting things started. 'I hope you like these flowers – they're from your garden. We do *miss* you.'

'We do,' said Luke quietly. For a moment, there was silence

before he spoke again, his voice stronger this time. 'Diana, what you said to Tessa when... when...' He swallowed and I took his hand and squeezed it.

'It's okay,' I murmured. 'Go on.'

'At the end,' he said. 'When you told Tessa that you wanted "him" to know. Well, I think I'm that him and you wanted me to know that... that...' He stopped again, looked up to the sky and exhaled sharply, then turned to me with a faltering smile. 'This is hard.'

'I know,' I said, turning to the grave. 'Diana, it's difficult for us, talking to you like this. Sorry if we're struggling.'

A little robin came hopping across the grass and paused next to the flowers we had laid, putting its head on one side. Luke started speaking again.

'Yes,' he said, with a dry little laugh. 'It is difficult. But there are things I want to say. Need to say. I think that you wanted me to know that I'm your son.' He stopped again, and the word hung in the air. 'That I'm your son, you were – are – my mother. Belle found it all out. I'm glad she did. But there are a lot of questions, still. I'm going to make sure I know everything; I guess that's what you wanted, too. I'll find out why you left, why Mum and Dad took me – maybe even who my father is. I hope you wanted me to know all that, Diana.'

He stopped again, and I spoke.

'We *wish* you had told us – Luke – sooner. More than anything, we wish you were still here.'

I brushed a tear from my cheek.

'That's right,' said Luke. 'But I'm so happy that I got to know you, that we became friends. I remember the first time I met you. You'd only been in Spindrift Bay for a day or two, and there had been chatter about who had taken over the tearooms, but you hadn't been spotted in the village yet. I was locking up for the day when you came knocking at the surgery window, holding something wrapped in a tea towel. It turned out you'd found a baby fox. Poor thing, its back leg was almost off and you had blood all over your top. You said – do you remember? – "I know this little girl doesn't have much chance, but do what you can, will you?" And then you stayed while I operated. It was only later, when we'd done all we could that you asked my name. I assumed that your reaction – I thought you were going to faint, you went so pale – was some sort of delayed shock over the fox cub. I offered you some sweet tea, but you suggested whisky, so we both had one, and we were friends from then on. I have plenty of happy memories of you; that's more, I guess, than a lot of people have. And I hope you've found peace. You mustn't worry about me, or about Belle. We're looking after each other now.'

The tightness in my throat made it impossible to speak.

'We'll come to visit,' continued Luke. 'We both owe you so much, and we miss you.'

His body relaxed next to me, and I knew he had said what he needed to say, and was ready to leave. But I wasn't. My throat released, and the words came out in a rush.

'Diana, I need to thank you for everything you've done for me and for Mum. You've changed our lives. Maybe you already know, but Mum has left Dad and it's thanks to you. Thanks to the fresh start and security you gave me and the money and confidence you gave her.' I paused to catch my breath. 'I know...' My voice cracked and I tried again. 'I know that you understand that no matter how long something takes to come right, when it does, the years that have gone before, they fall away, they don't matter. Mum is so *happy* now, and so am I. I *wish* you were here to share it with us.'

The momentousness of Diana's gifts and the full understanding that she had gone became crystal clear in a way that they hadn't before, as if some soft-focus protective shield had been pulled away and I was facing the raw, painful, uncompromising truth for the first time. My legs were weak and Luke caught me as I stumbled, holding me close to him, muttering soothing words I could barely hear as I sobbed and keened for the loss of this special woman. After a while I started to calm down, responding to Luke's soothing hand as he stroked my back.

'Sorry,' I mumbled into his shoulder. 'We came here for you. I don't know what happened.'

'Don't be sorry,' he said. 'If anything, I *like* seeing how much you loved her, that my mother was a woman who inspired that in others.'

I sniffled and pulled away to look up at him.

'She did. Mum loved her so much, too.'

'I'd like to meet your mother,' said Luke.

'You will,' I replied, wiping at my face with the cuff of my shirt, as I saw the vicar beetling over, looking concerned. 'Sorry, Fergus,' I said. 'It suddenly sort of hit me, about Diana. I miss her.'

My eyes started to moisten again, but he didn't flinch. I suppose vicars get used to it.

'No apologies needed, my dear,' he said. 'I wondered if you needed any solace but' – he smiled indulgently – 'Luke is more than capable of providing that. Ah! I believe this is someone else come to honour Diana. A much-loved woman indeed. She was kind to me and Gillian. Kind, and non-judgemental.'

I didn't have time to ponder what he meant by this cryptic comment, as Edward approached, Doris trotting sedately beside him. He was carrying a similar bunch of cottage garden flowers to the one that we had laid. He held it up in greeting.

'I see we had the same idea,' he said. 'Diana's favourites. She helped me with my little garden, so they seemed a fitting tribute.'

'I will leave you together,' said Fergus. 'But you know where I am if you need me, any time.'

Edward put down the bag he was carrying and, kneeling beside it, began to take things out.

'I did have an idea to help them last a little longer,' he said. 'I wonder if you would like your flowers to share it?' He held up a large glass jar and a slender trowel. 'I thought I could put this in the ground, and I have some water, too.'

'Let me do that,' said Luke, and we both knelt down as well, which earned me a friendly lick from Doris. Luke took the trowel and dug a small hole, then pushed the jar in firmly. Edward took out the Thermos flask I had seen before.

'Don't worry,' he said, smiling gently. 'Not tea this time.'

Instead, he poured water into the jar and put in both posies of flowers, taking a moment to arrange them.

'They look so pretty,' I said, hoping I wasn't going to start crying again.

'Thank you for bringing them,' said Luke to Edward, suddenly going stone still next to me. 'I know you cared for Diana a lot.' He paused, looking confused. Was he about to tell Edward what he already knew, that Diana was his mother? I held my breath, but he didn't speak again.

'I did,' said Edward simply. 'I knew her for a very, very long time and I loved her for all of it. I miss her dreadfully. I understand from Belle that you believe Diana was family? I had also wondered over the years if she was, perhaps, your aunt, but we lost touch for many years. Once we were reconciled, she didn't wish to speak of the past.'

Luke was looking pale, but when he spoke, his voice was strong.

'She was my mother,' he said. 'I – Belle and I, that is – only found out recently. Nobody else knows yet, or knows that I know, not even my parents.'

'I won't tell anyone,' replied Edward. I could sense the effort he was making to keep his voice steady.

'Thank you,' said Luke. 'I wanted you to know. You loved her.'

'Yes,' replied Edward. 'Always. Thank you for confiding in me. I hope you find all the answers you must be seeking.'

He started to push himself to his feet and I jumped up to help him. He handed me Doris's lead, but otherwise brushed me away.

'You're so kind, Belle, but I have to keep doing these things, or I won't be able to. There, I'm up.'

I handed him back the lead, and he bent to pick up his bag. I could see Luke looking at him questioningly, but he held out his hand for the man to shake.

'See you again soon, I hope.'

'That you will,' replied Edward. 'Doris and I aren't far. I'd always be glad of your company. Goodbye for now.'

As he walked slowly away, Luke looked as if he were going to say something, then changed his mind with a little shake of the head.

'Are you ready to go?' I asked, and he smiled.

'Yes. Feel like a detour over the cliffs? I could do with blowing the cobwebs away.'

'Good idea,' I said, and we set off out of the churchyard and away from the village.

'It was perfect to come up here,' I said ten minutes later, as we walked along a chalky path on the top of the cliff, surrounded by gorse bushes smothered in bright yellow flowers. The wind was brisk and refreshing after my emotional outburst.

'I love this view of the village,' said Luke, pausing as we reached the crest of the hill. Below us, we could see the entirety of Spindrift Bay: the almost circular cove that curled deep into the land; the pretty houses and shops that made up the village and high street, with my house and the tearoom set aside, a little way up the side of the hill as the path wound down towards the beach. If I looked further back, to the right, I could make out parts of the road that led to Spindrift House and see the tips of some of its chimneys.

Maybe he had followed my gaze or maybe we were on the same wavelength, because Luke said, 'I'm ready to speak to my parents.'

I pulled my gaze away from the view and back to him.

'Would you still like me to come with you?'

'Would you?'

'Of course.'

He took my hand and we carried on walking, my eyes drifting back to the glimpses of the manor house. *What secrets are hidden within your walls? And is finding out the right thing to do?*

TWENTY-THREE

The next morning, we both woke early. I could only imagine how Luke felt, but I had a heavy ball of dread in my stomach. I was worried for him, that what he found out today would add to his pain rather than alleviate it. I was also anxious for his parents. I knew Luke was angry and confused and, even without knowing exactly what happened or why they had made the decisions they did all those years ago, I couldn't help feeling that they should at least have told the truth. Did they really think that such a huge secret would stay hidden forever? We dealt with the kittens and had breakfast in near silence, until Luke suddenly reached across the table and grabbed my hand.

'It'll be okay,' he said.

Who was he trying to convince?

'I hope so,' I said. 'I hope they give you the answers.'

'They have to,' he replied. 'I won't leave until they do. Have you got the birth certificate and other things?'

I rose and picked up a large white envelope that was lying near the toaster.

'Here it all is.'

'Thanks.'

He opened the envelope and slid out its meagre contents,

pieces of paper and photographs – and the hospital bracelets – that looked so mundane, but which held such life-changing information. He studied each for a moment before pushing them back inside.

'Shall we go?'

When we pulled up in front of the house, it was still early and there was no one about. Without hesitating, Luke marched straight up to the front door and knocked. A few moments later, it was opened by his father, who looked from Luke to me and back again, then frowned.

'Good morning. This is an early call. Why didn't you let yourself in?'

'It didn't feel right,' said Luke stiffly.

'Oh. Er, well, come in then, do. Both of you.'

I followed Luke inside and tried not to seem too gauche as I looked around the magnificent hallway. The floorboards glowed with centuries of expert care, and a couple of rugs lent some cosiness to the space. To my right, there was a wide staircase, carpeted in deep royal blue, and ahead there were three doors, all closed.

Sir Henry paused, looking confused. I could guess that this was an unusual feeling for him; last time we had met, he had been the one in control.

'Would you like to come through? Your mother's in the drawing room. Or have you come for something else? More barbecues, perhaps?'

He smiled weakly and I felt a pang of compassion for him.

'I need to speak to both of you,' said Luke firmly, walking past his father to open one of the doors. Sir Henry took a step back and indicated that I should follow Luke. He entered the room behind me and shut the door softly.

'Luke!' said Lady Talbot, looking up from the broadsheet newspaper she was reading. 'This is a pleasant surprise. And Belle, isn't it?'

I was astonished that she knew my name. I suppose impeccable manners are a hallmark of the aristocracy and they make it their business to know who's who.

'Yes,' I said, trying to sound neutral. 'Lovely to meet you.'

'Likewise. Sit down, both of you. Would you like tea?'

I glanced at Luke as we sat on an antique-looking sofa immaculately upholstered in cream scattered with tiny blue flowers.

'No thanks. We've – well, I've – come here today because there's something I need to ask you both. Will you sit down, Dad?'

Sir Henry had been standing to one side, his hands clasped behind his back. Now, he frowned slightly as he sat down near his wife in a chair covered with the same fabric as our sofa.

'Thanks,' said Luke. 'The thing is – oh, I might as well come out and say it. I know about Diana.'

I looked closely at his parents to see what their reaction would be. His mother lost all her composure, briefly. Her hand flew to her chest, all the blood drained from her face, and she looked at Luke in horror, then immediately turned her eyes to her husband. Sir Henry behaved differently. He became stiller, if anything, his face failing to betray any reaction. His wife went to speak, and he reached across to lay a silencing hand on her knee.

'What is it you think you know about Diana?' he asked, his voice chillingly calm. If it had been me he was speaking to, I would have quailed and fumbled for an answer, as I had so many times with my own father, but Luke spoke strongly.

'Not *think* I know, *do* know,' he said, his voice almost matching Sir Henry's for icy calm. 'I know that Diana Dalton was, in fact, Diana Talbot – your sister and my mother.'

'Henry...' croaked Lady Talbot, all her composure now gone. 'Henry...'

'Let me deal with this,' he said to his wife, in a tone that was firm but not unkind.

Maybe I should go and sit next to her and try to offer her some comfort. I wholly supported Luke, but it upset me to see her so devastated. I couldn't decide quickly enough either whether she would welcome the comfort of a complete stranger, or if Luke would see me as disloyal in some way if I went over, before his father had started speaking again.

'Why do you believe this?' He glanced at me, and I forced myself to maintain eye contact until he looked away. I had done nothing wrong, and I didn't want him to think I was scared of him. Even though I was, a little. 'Does your friend here have something to do with it?'

Luke took out the white envelope.

'Belle found some information when she was sorting through Diana's effects. Then together we found some other stuff.'

He leant forward and tipped out the contents of the envelope onto the small, polished wooden table in the middle of the seating area.

'This is Diana's birth certificate,' he said, tapping it. 'And these' – his voice cracked slightly, but he carried on – 'these are the hospital wristbands from when she had me. And some photos.'

He leant forward, breathing heavily, and I put my hand on his back.

'He *knows*,' burst out Lady Talbot, standing up and bending to put her arms around Luke. For a moment, he let her, then he, too, stood up and faced her.

'I'm so sorry,' she said, beginning to cry. 'I love you so much, my darling. I-I wanted you to know. But you have always been my beloved boy, nothing can ever change that.'

'But I'm not, am I?' said Luke, his voice bleak. 'I was Diana's darling boy. Or was I? Didn't she want me?'

He spat out the last words more violently, perhaps, than he had meant to, and Sir Henry jumped up and went over.

'Please don't speak to your mother like that. None of this is her fault.' He put a hand on his wife's shoulder and spoke more gently than I would have believed him able to. 'Let's sit down, Gwendoline. Maybe it's time this all came out.'

She returned to the sofa she had been sitting on before, and he turned to Luke.

'Please, sit down and we'll explain. Please.'

Luke sat down, wordlessly, next to me and Sir Henry went to sit with his wife. He took her hand.

'I'm sorry that you found out this way,' he said. 'We created this... secret... years ago, when you were born. It seemed like an excellent solution at the time, for all involved. Your mother and I couldn't have children, or at least we didn't think we could. We wanted a baby very much, both of us. I know you believe that I only care about what is inherited, but that's not the case, although it is partly true. I wanted a family as much as Gwen did. But it wasn't to be, the doctors had assured us of that. We had started discussing adoption when my sister, Diana, came to me and admitted that she was pregnant. I, of course, said we must tell our parents. They were angry but also worried. Diana was insisting that she was going to keep the baby, but my father was insistent – *insistent* – that she wouldn't be able to care for it – for you.'

'Because she was so young?' asked Luke.

'Partly. But also...' The baronet paused and took a deep breath. 'I'm sorry. This is painful for me.' He shook his head, staring across the room. In the time that we had been there – only about fifteen minutes, although it felt longer – he had gone from a confident aristocrat to a gaunt, bereaved brother and father. How much had keeping the secret weighed on him and his wife over the years? Lady Talbot took his hand and squeezed it.

'Shall I take the story up from here?' she asked in a quiet but strong voice.

He shook his head, dragged his eyes back to Luke and continued speaking. 'When Diana died, it was because of an epileptic fit.'

Luke and I nodded.

'Yes,' he said. 'It caused her to fall down the stairs.'

'That's right. Well, you see, when she was younger, the epilepsy was much more severe. It was mostly controlled with strong drugs, but, even then, she still occasionally had fits. She didn't know it, nobody had spoken to her about it because she was still so young and, of course, not married, but the doctors had said that it might be unwise for her ever to have children. They were worried about the medications she was taking and the risks of birth complications. My father – who was not, I'm afraid, a kind man – also insisted that, coupled with her young age, the risk of fits meant that she would be unsafe to look after a baby. I believe that his main concern was the shame and stigma of illegitimacy, but he gave us all – Diana included – compelling reason to believe that she was incapable of looking after you.'

He stopped talking and Lady Talbot, with a concerned glance at her husband, suddenly spoke.

'You must understand that your father and I acted with sincerity, with love. Your grandfather was a forceful man and made a good case. Even Diana was persuaded by him into believing it was all for the best.'

'It was he who said you should take me?' asked Luke, his voice almost a whisper.

'Yes,' said Sir Henry. 'He was obsessed with the family line continuing, had been' – he glanced across at his wife – 'cruel to us about our inability to conceive. We were broken by him. I know that might be hard to believe, but we were young and vulnerable, desperately sad not to have a family. Our future was tied up in my inheritance, whether we liked it or not; I couldn't assert my independence and do as I chose. You may think this in bad taste, but when Diana left to live in France, a part of me was envious of her. She lost everything, but she gained her freedom.'

'Did it make up for having to give up her baby?' asked Luke, bitterness in his voice.

'No,' said his father candidly. 'Of course not. I'm trying to show how things were. And we – your mother and I – were so thrilled with you and so relieved that, seemingly, our problems had been solved, that we maybe wanted to believe that Diana was somehow emancipated. The truth, of course, is that she never stopped grieving your loss, and I accept responsibility for the part I played in that.'

His face had now taken on a tinge of grey and I was appallingly sorry for him. For everyone. I could only pray that opening up this old wound would lead to healing, rather than causing an incurable rift.

'Diana was your sister,' said Luke. 'Wasn't her blood good enough running through my veins for the inheritance?'

Sir Henry shook his head.

'As Diana's illegitimate son you couldn't have inherited. It looked like the house would go to the son of a distant cousin, eventually, someone we barely knew. Of course, had Diana married it would have changed things, but she wouldn't tell us who the father was. She assured us that the relationship had been consensual, and we assumed that he was already married.'

'I wondered...' The words spilled out of Lady Talbot's mouth and seemed almost as much of a surprise to her as to us as she snapped her lips together.

'Wondered what?' demanded Luke.

Lady Talbot glanced at her husband, but his face revealed nothing. She continued.

'It's probably nothing, but I can't imagine Diana with a married man. It doesn't seem very... *her*. Even at twenty-two she had such integrity. It was one of the things that made it possible for her to give you up; she believed she was doing the best she could for you.'

'So, why wouldn't she simply have married my father and made me legitimate?'

'I don't know. I can only guess that maybe she didn't want to feel she was forcing him into marriage – or maybe something happened between them? Perhaps he knew she was pregnant and didn't want to be involved. We can only guess.'

'There was someone – a man – who enquired after her repeatedly when we moved to Spindrift House,' said Sir Henry. 'I don't know if he was a boyfriend, though. Diana made it clear she didn't want to see him.'

'Do you remember his name?' asked Luke.

Sir Henry shook his head, and his brow creased.

'I'm sorry, it was such a long time ago.'

'Could it have been Edward?'

'I don't remember, I'm sorry.'

I wasn't surprised that Luke had pieced that part of the puzzle together for himself. I only hoped that the two men spoke soon, so that I wouldn't have to keep the secret any longer. Desperate though I was to blurt out what I knew and tidy some of this mess up, I knew it wasn't my place to divulge Luke's paternity.

'What about my birth certificate?' asked Luke suddenly. 'You're named as my parents on it, but Diana had me in hospital, so it's not as if you were pretending Mum was pregnant and there was some weird secret swap.'

Sir Henry shrugged, looking uncomfortable.

'Your birth certificate is illegal,' he said simply.

'*What?* But how?'

'Money, power, influence, it wasn't difficult, particularly back then when computer records were much patchier and most things were still being done by hand, or much more slowly than they are now. Diana had to have you in hospital, because of the risks associated with her epilepsy, but once we knew you were both fine, she moved into a private nursing home for her recovery. The staff there didn't ask questions and one of the doctors was a friend.' He shrugged again, the easy acceptance of his own ability to have things the way he wanted them. 'It wasn't hard for him to tweak some records, and there's very little needed when you register a birth. Your mother and I took you home, and soon after that my father died and we moved here, which gave us the opportunity for a fresh start. It was only a month or so later that Diana went to France.'

'And you could play happy families now everyone was out of the way.'

Luke's voice shook with anger, and I put my hand on his knee. He took it in his but was not calmed.

'You falsified a document, paid people and dispatched a twenty-two-year-old girl who not only suffered a potentially dangerous condition but had been *persuaded*' – his voice dripped with sarcasm – 'to give up her baby, to go and live abroad. Then presumably you touted me around proudly as the heir you finally had in your possession. My God, poor Diana. You must have been quaking in your boots when she turned up in Spindrift Bay again. And what the hell did you think when Sam came along? A convenient spare, or did you kick yourselves for taking in your teenage sister's bastard, now you had a real son of your own?'

'Luke, stop!' His mother's voice rose in a shriek, which seemed to be half-anger and half-grief. All eyes darted towards her. She was deathly white and her hand clutched and clawed at the arm of the sofa. 'It wasn't *like* that! How can you say those things? We did what we thought was best, all of us.' She started sobbing and her husband patted her knee ineffectually, either too shocked himself to do more or too hidebound by the class conventions he had been steeped in his entire life. I couldn't bear it any longer. I jumped up, grabbed my bag and went to kneel beside her, scrabbling through my things for a packet of tissues. I pulled one out and handed it to her then, hardly feeling the courage it must have taken me, tersely asked Sir Henry to move up so that I could sit beside the weeping woman and link my arm through hers, finding another tissue and gently wiping her face as I muttered meaningless words of comfort. She leant into me and her sobs quietened. Only then did I dare glance across at Luke, who looked so distressed that I nearly yoyoed back over to him.

'I'm sorry,' he said, his voice thick with emotion. 'I'm trying to understand.'

'I know,' said his mother. 'It's so hard to explain, so awful. There's no getting away from that. But what I'm so desperate for you to understand is that everything we did came from a place of love. My father-in-law was a different matter and yes, he did have a lot of influence over how things unfolded, but we loved you and we loved Diana. If you take nothing else from today, please take that.' She turned her huge, wet, imploring eyes to me. 'You will make him see that, won't you, Belle? You do believe me?'

I nodded, uncomfortable even as I agreed with her.

'Of course I do.'

Sir Henry took up the reins of the conversation.

'When we discovered that we were expecting Sam, we were completely shocked. Delighted, of course, but shocked. We had been told when we were younger that we had no hopes of conceiving so, given the years that had passed, we had stopped thinking about it. At first, neither of us made the connection that Sam was the "rightful heir", and when we did – well, it simply didn't matter. My father had died by then, and his obsession with the bloodlines died with him. We always thought of Sam as our *second* son, loved and wanted every bit as much as our first had been.'

I saw Luke's face soften as he gave a little nod.

'Thank you.'

'It's how it was. Even if it hadn't been, what choice would we have had? There was so much water under the bridge, so many lies, so much pain, not to mention your illegal birth certificate. If anything, all that was a relief: we had no choice but to carry on, which was all we wanted to do, anyway.'

'You were a perfect big brother,' said Lady Talbot, the smile that appeared wiping away the tragedy on her face. 'Always so sweet and kind with Sam, from when he was tiny. But you were kind to everyone – people and animals.'

'You let me train as a vet,' said Luke. 'That should have been unheard of if I was expected to take over the estate one day.'

'It was obvious you had a natural gift,' said his mother. 'I was in favour of it...'

She stopped abruptly, glancing at her husband.

'I wasn't,' he said frankly. 'I'm not going to lie, because there have been enough lies. I wasn't in favour, because I wanted you to work with me here, with a view to taking over one day. But as Sam grew up and showed such interest in it all, it seemed serendipitous to steer him towards the estate and support you in your chosen career.' He shrugged. 'It felt like, this way, everybody could win.'

'And blood could do its thing,' said Luke wryly.

'Maybe,' said Sir Henry. 'But Sam would never receive the title – that was yours.'

I caught the flicker of Luke's eyebrows at the mention of it. *How tempted was he to tell them that he wasn't interested in their precious title, either? Or did it mean more to him than he was letting on, to me or to himself?*

'Shouldn't we all have a cup of tea?' said Lady Talbot. 'Or maybe something stronger? I could do with something myself.'

'Mum! It's only just gone 9 a.m.!'

The atmosphere momentarily lightened as everyone laughed weakly.

'Has it? Oh dear, it feels like it should be much later than that. I suppose it *is* kind of early for pre-lunch drinks. But do let's have some coffee.'

She started to stand up and I also rose; a break from the intensity might be no bad thing.

'Can I help?'

'No, no, please sit down,' she said. 'I won't be long.'

The next few minutes were interminable. I went back to sit with Luke, while his father stood looking out of the window.

'Are you all right?' I murmured.

He squeezed my hand.

'Yup. Thank you for being here. Thanks for going over to Mum.'

'Of course.'

We fell silent. I tried to relax, but the loud ticking of the ornate clock on the mantelpiece, and Sir Henry's brooding presence, were never going to let that happen. Thankfully, Lady Talbot wasn't long, and the quiet was soon broken with polite conversation about milk and sugar as everyone was given coffee. It was served in exquisitely delicate porcelain cups, balanced on fragile saucers. I could have done with a huge, comforting mugful, so I hoped it was strong. After we had all taken a few sips, Luke spoke.

'So, why did Diana come back to Spindrift Bay after all those years?'

'She had been away long enough,' said Sir Henry, who was sitting down next to his wife again. 'She wrote to me before she came – not asking my permission, exactly, but to test the water.'

'And what did you say?' asked Luke. I could hear that the edge was back in his voice, although he tried to sound casual.

'We said that we would dearly love to see her return,' said Lady Talbot, and Sir Henry nodded.

'We had visited her a few times over the years, but not often,' he continued. 'She said that she didn't want to upset the apple cart and had no intention of telling you or anyone else who she was, but that she would like to see you, of course. She had her own money, but we helped her with the practicalities of buying the house and the tearooms. It was good to see her home, and happy. It gave her enormous joy to get to know you. If she hadn't... If she hadn't died so suddenly, we may have worked towards sharing the truth, eventually.'

'And when she did die, were you relieved when you believed the secret had died with her?'

Sir Henry put his hand to his throat and loosened his tie.

'You still think me heartless, don't you? I was devastated by my sister's death, a death that came far too soon. And I was distraught that you and she would never be reunited as mother and son.' His voice thickened and he cleared his throat before trying to speak again. 'I don't know...'

The words petered out and this time it was his wife's turn to come to his rescue.

'Her death was an appalling shock. All we knew was that we had to take some time before making any decisions, rather than acting rashly in our grief. When you came to get the barbecues, Henry realised that you knew something.'

'I wish someone had *told* me!' Luke burst out. 'I could have known her as my mother, and she could have put her arms around me as her son, but we were denied that, and now it's too late.'

The words hung in the air between us all.

'Yes,' said Sir Henry, his voice now a croak. 'It's too late and I can't change that. I'm so sorry, so sorry. I don't know how we move forward now.'

'Neither do I,' said Luke sadly. 'I don't even know if we can.'

Silence fell and I looked around at the broken family. Lady Talbot was hollow-eyed and pale, Sir Henry's jaw and shoulders rigid with tension. And Luke's look of bleak despair broke my heart. What had I done?

TWENTY-FOUR

We left Spindrift House shortly after; there was nothing more to say, for now. Luke and I walked in silence back down to the village, until we came to the place where the roads diverged.

'Are you going to go to the surgery?' I asked.

'No,' replied Luke. 'The locum's there and he's keeping me updated, so things are under control. What I feel like doing is something physical... Maybe I'll go and do a beach clean. It's a shame the renovations are finished on the tearooms; I could have happily spent the day chipping off old plaster or something.'

'If you're serious, I might have just the job,' I said. 'I've been thinking of overhauling some of the rooms to use as holidays lets; it's a big job, and I'm not planning on getting the lets up and running any time soon, but we could make a start on it.'

'Perfect,' said Luke, and took the turning up towards my house.

I got the feeling that he wanted to forget all about the conversation with his parents, for now, so when we got home, we spent a little time with Bubble and Squeak, then went into the room where Diana had been keeping the boxes and a few pieces of furniture.

'She obviously never used this room,' I said. 'And didn't even have it redecorated when she moved in.'

'No,' said Luke, running his hand down the dated embossed

wallpaper. 'Let's hope this eighties relic isn't covering up any horrors. People often use it to hide crumbling plaster.'

'With any luck, the people who lived here chose it because they loved it,' I said. 'And I'm hoping that the thing they *did* hide was a fireplace – you can see where it should be. There's a chance they boarded over it, rather than ripping the whole thing out.'

'Do you want to save the carpet?' asked Luke. 'It's reasonably inoffensive.'

'Maybe,' I said. 'Let's start by taking out what we can and see where that leaves us.'

We hauled out the crates that I had sorted through; four could now be disposed of, as the contents were old papers of no interest. I had gathered any personal items into one crate, and there were still three to go through.

'I was going to put this away upstairs,' I said, indicating the organised paperwork. 'But I wonder if you would like it. There are letters and photos, a couple of diaries.'

'Yes, I would, thank you.'

We put it to one side, then put the three unopened crates in the kitchen, to go through later.

'I'm going to keep the furniture,' I said. 'Unless you want to take it? It does feel kind of *odd*, that all this belongs to me now, when rightfully it's your inheritance from your mum.' The words, which had been knocking around my brain for a while now, worrying me, poured out in a rush. 'The house, the tearooms – they're yours, really.'

Although I felt this strongly, I was also desperately worried. What if Luke agreed, and challenged Diana's will? I wouldn't keep her inheritance from him, but I would be back to square one: homeless, jobless and alone.

A hand on my shoulder jerked me out of my catastrophising.

'Belle. Belle!'

'Sorry.'

'I'm not going to take anything. Diana wrote the will she wanted to write, for her own good reasons. She loved you and your mother and wanted you to have this and be happy. God knows I've got enough complications with the other inheritance, which isn't mine. I'd be perfectly happy with neither. I'm lucky enough that I have my business and my own home; I'd much rather things were shared out fairly and that you and Sam benefit. And besides...' He gave me a wicked grin that made my stomach do exciting flipflops. 'I'm hoping you'll let me spend plenty of time up here.'

I put my head on one side and frowned.

'Let you into my queendom?' I said teasingly. 'I'll have to check with the kittens, but I suppose it might be possible.'

'They'll be no obstacle,' said Luke. 'Far too easy to bribe. As long as I have a pocketful of treats, I'm sorted. Now, this furniture. Do you want it to stay in this room?'

'For now,' I said, warm with love and relief as I looked at this kind, honourable man. 'This might be some sort of sitting room for people staying here, rather than a bedroom, but I'll have to look at the financials properly before I decide.'

'Okay, so let's put it all in the middle of the room and cover it up, then we can get to work on that wallpaper.'

An hour and a half later, my arms were aching and I was covered in dust, but we had six large binbags full of stiff, painted textured wallpaper and the softer lining paper from underneath. It had come off easily with the steamer I had brought with me from mine and Matt's house, and the plaster behind was sound.

'Shall we have some lunch before we tackle the fireplace?' I said. 'I'm done for the morning.'

Luke agreed and so, after washing ourselves off as best we could, we sat down to a simple lunch of items I was planning on making up the ploughman's lunches from, that Luke had tried previously. When we had finished, and I was making coffee, my sore arms burnt, and I was exhausted.

'I'm not sure I can face attacking that fireplace now,' I said.

'Would you mind? We could open up these last few boxes instead – unless you're not in the mood.'

'I wasn't earlier,' replied Luke. 'But I'm feeling much better for ripping off all that horrible wallpaper and stuffing it into bags. We're going to need some more tools to tackle the fireplace, anyway. Let's do the boxes.'

The next two we opened were, like so many of the others, full of out-of-date accounts and other paperwork, mostly French, that could all go straight to the recycling. I didn't want to uncover any more family secrets, but I had been hoping that we might find some other things that Luke could keep; things that revealed more about his mother and maybe let him feel a little closer to her. My disappointment was assuaged by the contents of the third box. It was obvious from the moment that we pried off the lid that this contained a different sort of life admin.

'Look,' I said, my voice hushed.

I lifted up a small, white blanket that lay folded at the top of the box. Under that, there was a single piece of shiny A5 paper.

'It's one of the flyers for the surgery,' said Luke, taking it. 'From when I first opened it. Look – here are the details about the ten per cent welcome offer. Why has Diana got this? And how? I opened the surgery several years before she came to Spindrift Bay.'

Next came a shoebox, which I took out and handed straight to Luke. He took off the lid to reveal a mass of photos, which he picked up and spread on the table. They were all of him, from baby photos through the toddler and child years, adolescence and graduation. A couple showed him as an adult; in one he was standing outside the surgery, next to the 'sold' sign. Tears came to my eyes. I swallowed hard, and tried to brush them away quickly; my emotions weren't the important thing right now, however much I was moved by this evidence of Diana's love for the son she had given up.

'She's got everything,' said Luke, picking up the photos one by one. He raised his eyes to meet mine. 'But I don't understand *how*.'

I took one of the photos and turned it over. Written on the back it said: *Luke at three months old.* I picked another at random and this said: *Luke winning the Science Prize (14 years old).*

'It's all in Diana's writing,' I said. 'So that doesn't get us anywhere. Shall we see what else is in here?'

Luke nodded, so I took out the next item, a soft, plastic envelope file, and handed it to him. He pulled off the elastic and took out a sheaf of papers and newspaper clippings which, again, he laid out on the table.

'Someone must have been sending her these,' he said. 'It's everything I've ever done.' He pointed to a few A4 sheets held together with a paperclip. 'Those are photocopies of my GSCE results and these' – he pulled out a similar pack from underneath – 'are my A levels.'

I took the certificate duplicates from him and grinned.

'A clean sweep of top grades; clever boy. I bet Diana was proud of you. She set a lot of store by education.'

'Did she?' asked Luke, his face eager. 'It wasn't something we ever discussed.'

'She thought it was hugely important,' I replied. 'I struggled when I was sixteen or seventeen and was about to chuck it all in. My father shouted at me and told me I was stupid for considering it, but so stupid that maybe I shouldn't bother with continuing my education.'

'I'm sorry,' said Luke. 'That must have been hard to hear.'

I shrugged.

'It's funny. In one way I can throw off all his hurtful words; I *know* they say more about him than they do about me. But they still have the power to make me feel ashamed, even now. And that makes me angry, that I'm still allowing him to get to me.' I took a deep breath. 'Anyway. Mum didn't say much, especially in front of him, but I know she was worried about my mental health and wanted me to do whatever it took to be happy. I was on the verge of running off, to get away from the pressure and the worry, so I rang Diana, hoping I could go and stay with her in France for a while. She said she would always be glad to have me, but that she thought it would be – and I remember her words exactly – *a grave mistake* to ditch my education. Diana always spoke to me like an equal, and this time wasn't any different. She didn't deem me too young to decide, or too silly or worthless or fragile. She said that she believed me to be intelligent and capable and emphasised that education gives you power, and choices. She suggested that focusing on my studies might help my mental health, whereas having less to occupy my brain would give it more space to ruminate and catastrophise. She acknowledged that I could return to education later, but that it was much easier to get it over and done with now.' I smiled at Luke, who was listening intently. 'She emphasised that two years was *nothing, Belle, a blink of an eye*, even though it was a lifetime from my perspective.'

'So, you stayed at school?'

'I did, and I did well, and after that I did an English degree. I should have done accounting then, of course, but that's another story. Staying in education did everything Diana knew it should. I had more confidence, more experience and my mental health improved. I ended up temping in offices while I was deciding what my next move should be, and that's how I met Matt. He was happy with me staying in my lane as a general office manager, minimising the impact of the work I did on the accounts. If I suggested doing an accountancy qualification at night school, he all but patted me on the head and gave me some filing.'

'I'm glad it didn't work out,' said Luke simply, reaching out his hand to me.

'So am I,' I said. 'Very. Now, shall we see what else is in here?'

At the bottom of the crate was a large box file. Luke opened it to find that it contained dozens of envelopes, addressed to Diana at French addresses.

'This is my mother's handwriting,' he said. 'She must have been writing to Diana.'

He picked one up and pulled out the letter.

'Dear Diana,' he read. 'I hope this finds you well. Luke continues to do well at school and came top of his class in reading

for the third time in a row. We took him to the zoo to celebrate –
here is a photograph of him with the giraffes, which were his
favourite.'

He broke off and sorted through the photos until he found the
right one. Turning it over, we saw that Diana had written the date
that corresponded with the letter and the words: *Luke at the zoo
with his favourite animals.* He put the letter back in the envelope
and chose another. This was from several years later and detailed
his sixteenth birthday. Again, there was a photo that had been sent
with the letter.

'Mum wrote to her for my entire life,' said Luke. 'I wonder if
Dad knew. And I was so hard on her today; I made her cry.' His
face grew pale. 'When for all these years she was generous enough,
kind enough, *honest* enough to share all of this with Diana.'

He suddenly started sorting through the envelopes, checking
the dates on the postmarks until he found what he was looking for.
This time when he pulled out the letter, a photograph also fell out,
of a baby.

'Dear Diana,' he read out. 'I wanted to share with you the news
that I have safely delivered a baby boy – your nephew. His name is
Sam, and I have enclosed a photograph. Luke is the kindest big
brother, gentle with him and sensitive to his needs, so much more
than you might expect a teenager to be. Until now, I have only
been able to imagine what it must have been like for you to leave
your baby with us. It is only now that I have given birth myself that
I can truly have any understanding of the colossal pain it must have
caused you. I hope my letters over the years, along with the knowledge that Luke is dearly and thoroughly loved by us both, have
offered you some consolation. I had wondered if you might meet
someone and become a mother again. Maybe that is a path you will
still choose; you have many years in which to do so.

'I should stop writing for today. The birth left me tired and in
some pain, and my emotions are not what they usually are. Maybe
you would say that they are usually too tightly controlled? Well,
that is not true at the moment, but I still do not want to spill them

too loosely onto the page and, in the process, affect you. With all my love, Gwen.'

'What a miserable situation,' I said. 'I'm sure your grandfather believed he was doing the right thing, but he caused a lot of pain.'

'I never met him,' said Luke. 'And I'm glad I didn't. It was good of Mum to write to Diana, but I still wish they had been honest about it all. I wonder, truly, if they would ever have told me, after Diana died, if you hadn't found what you did.'

I didn't reply. My guess was that they would have kept a grateful silence, seeing no need to rake up the past. Should I have done the same thing?

Luke stayed with me for the next few days, and we worked from morning until evening on the downstairs room and one of the bedrooms, which had also remained untouched. In that short space of time, we slipped into a comfortable routine: after breakfast in the garden, enjoying the first rays of sunshine and the fresh scent of the dewy grass, chatting about this and that and playing with the kittens, we got to work. Wallpaper was stripped, paintwork sanded and carpets ripped up. We made a couple of outings – to the dump and the local DIY emporium – before returning home, putting on a local radio station and working to the endless cheesy tunes and snippets of community news. At lunchtime, I would put together something simple but filling, often trying out ideas for the tearooms, and then we would get back to work. We stopped each day around six, when we would open a couple of beers or a bottle of wine and return to the garden for a lazy, easy evening. We spoke little of Luke's family, of the sad and secretive past, instead talking about our renovations, our ideas for the future and sharing our likes and dislikes, getting to know each other better. When it was time to turn in, we spent magical nights together, half-awake and half-asleep as we turned to each other repeatedly, finding the love, comfort and security that we both so craved.

. . .

It was a Thursday afternoon when a knock came at the door.

'Are you expecting anything?' asked Luke, looking up from the wainscoting he was painting.

'No,' I said. 'The brushes I ordered came earlier. I'll go and see who it is.'

Wiping my hands, sticky with wallpaper paste, on my old jeans, I opened the door to find Edward there, with Doris.

'Hello!' I said. 'How nice to see you, do come in. I'm afraid you find us all at sixes and sevens with some redecorating.'

He looked worried.

'I don't want to disturb you. Maybe I should come back another time?'

'Not at all; it's a good time for us to take a break, anyway. Luke!' I called. 'Come and get a cup of tea. Edward and Doris are here.'

We went into the kitchen, followed shortly by Luke, and soon we were sitting at the table with mugs and a plate of spiced buns. Doris was lying on the floor, patiently allowing Bubble and Squeak to scramble over her, as they so loved to do. Edward was picking at his bun, rather than eating it with the delight he normally showed.

'Is everything okay?' I asked him.

He looked up, his eyes troubled.

'This visit is overdue,' he said, a tremor in his voice. 'You see...'

He broke off and his eyes darted between me and Luke, who suddenly bent down and picked up Squeak, muttering nonsense words of affection to him. After a moment, he looked up, directly at Edward.

'Have you come to tell me that you're my father?' he asked gently.

'I'm so sorry, I should have come sooner. I-I wasn't sure *what* to say. I don't even know for sure that it's true, but I think it must be. Diana and I were deeply in love, and I trusted her.'

'What happened?' asked Luke.

He explained to him, as he had to me, the passionate love affair between the two of them, the note Diana had written him, his attempts to contact her; his desperate, broken heart.

'When she returned to Spindrift Bay, after all those years,' he continued, 'I approached her with caution. She had pushed me away so completely that I didn't know how pleased she would be to find me still there. But she was happy. She asked me to keep her connection with the baronet secret, and I readily agreed. I didn't ask any questions; I was so happy to have her back in my life.'

'And she never told you she had a baby – your baby?'

'Never. I would have so loved a son.'

Doris shook off Bubble, who was gnawing at her ear, and came trotting over to her master, laying her beautiful golden head on his knee. He stroked her for a moment, gathering himself.

'I wonder...' I said, and both men looked at me. 'I do wonder if the "he" who Diana said should know about the box was you, Edward. Or maybe it was both of you. I'm sure she wanted you to know.'

'Well, I'm glad I do,' said Luke firmly. 'I'm angry with my parents, and disappointed in them, but they've been good to me. The way Mum stayed in touch with Diana... She sent her photos of my entire life, Edward. I'll show them to you... if you'd like?'

'I'd like that a lot,' said the older man, his voice full of warmth. 'We have some catching up to do.'

I watched them as Luke shared the photos and letters, hesitantly at first, but gradually responding to Edward's enthusiasm as he told stories of his own schooldays and even shyly pointed out some family resemblances he spotted in the old pictures of Luke. I could see it, too, looking at them with their heads together. I collected up both kittens and cuddled them as I finished my tea, thinking back to how devastated I had been when Matt cancelled the wedding, how I thought my life was over; yet here was Edward, who must be well into his sixties, beaming as though his own life had just begun. I smiled myself as I watched them; I, too, knew the joy that a painful ending followed by a hopeful new beginning could bring.

TWENTY-FIVE

Two days later, we had done more hard work on the two rooms, which were now stripped and sanded, filled and lined, ready for me to make some decisions on the wallpaper, paint, floor coverings and furnishings I would like.

'It seems bad, after all our hard work, not to crack on immediately,' I said, sipping my herbal tea and gazing out to sea, where the sun was beginning to head towards the horizon and give us another glorious sunset. 'But I need to start making some money, rather than drawing on my reserves.'

'Good idea,' said Luke. 'You'll have enough on your hands once the tearooms open again, without worrying about guests. At least the rooms are ready to decorate now.'

'Thanks to you,' I said. 'I'd never have got all that done on my own, and it would have been expensive to get someone in.'

'I enjoyed it,' said Luke. 'I find that sort of thing satisfying, anyway, but it gave me the headspace I needed, so it's you I should be thanking. It was a week of therapy!'

'Just call me Dr Walker!' I quipped. 'Hey, maybe that's a good idea – I could advertise it: *Therapy by the sea. Come and stay. Work for your board and lodging and feel better in the process.* I'd have the whole place redone by Christmas!'

'You joke,' said Luke. 'But hard work like that is good for the soul. I can usually immerse myself in my patients, but I was too distracted, and you can't take chances when you're operating or making treatment decisions.'

'Are you ready to go back yet?' I asked.

'Trying to get rid of me now the graft's done?' he said, with a grin.

'If you want to stay, you're welcome,' I said, painting on the most serious face I could. 'But I'll have to teach you to bake, next.'

'If I wasn't ready before, that kind of tough love has pushed me over! Seriously, though, I am ready – to go back to work and to speak to my parents again. Now I've had a chance to let everything percolate, I'm calmer. My grandfather was obviously a man with a lot of power and control, and they were all in his thrall to some degree, not only Diana. And I suppose, on the surface, it was a good solution; but it was only when Mum had Sam that she realised what it might mean to be parted from your baby. I feel sorry for all of them. They should have told me, but I can see why they didn't.'

'Too complicated?'

'Exactly. They'd broken the law and so had the doctor who helped them. Once the dust had settled, they can't have seen much point in suddenly breaking out the truth, and I guess that became the norm after so many years had passed.'

'So you've forgiven them?'

He shrugged.

'It's hard to take the position of being wronged, and the one to dole out forgiveness, when they were trying to do the right thing. I'd say that, more than forgiving, I feel understanding.'

As he gazed out to sea, I reflected for the millionth time how fortunate I was to be with such a thoughtful, compassionate man and sent up the same silent prayer I did every day: *thank you that Matt left me.*

'Will you come with me again?' asked Luke, taking my hand.

'Of course I will.'

· · ·

The next morning, a little later in the day than our previous visit, and by arrangement with his parents, Luke and I went to Spindrift House. As we pulled up, the front door opened and they both emerged. His father's face was unreadable, but Lady Talbot smiled, although her nerves were obvious in the way she twisted the string of pearls around her neck, and her eyes darted from Luke to me to her husband. His parents didn't move from the threshold so, after an awkward moment while we hovered on the gravel drive, Luke strode forward and hugged his mother, then shook his father's hand. The faces of both relaxed into genuine smiles. Sir Henry gave me a half-wave, half-salute in greeting, and Lady Talbot stepped forward past him, her arms slightly raised.

'Belle,' she said warmly. 'How lovely to see you again.'

I stepped forward and she gave me a brief hug and a gentle kiss on the cheek, tucking her arm through mine to lead me back to the room we had sat in before, the men following us. I was startled to see Sam there, standing by the window in a pose so similar to his father's that his parentage, at least, could be in no doubt. But the friendly smile he gave as we entered was his own. He stepped forward to shake Luke's hand, then draw him into a hug.

'Mum and Dad have told me everything,' he said. 'I want you to know before anything else is said that nothing has changed for me.'

'But all this is yours,' said Luke, with a sweep of his hand. 'Surely...'

'It doesn't *matter*,' interrupted Sam, emotion making his voice shake. 'You're my big brother. Nothing has changed for me.'

Lady Talbot withdrew her arm from mine and indicated the sofa.

'Please, take a seat, Belle.' She turned to her younger son and took his hand. 'Sam, come and sit down, too. We so appreciate your understanding. Come on.'

He allowed his mother to lead him to a sofa, where she sat by him. Luke came to sit next to me, and his father took an armchair.

'I'm sorry I haven't been in touch,' started Luke. 'I needed a few days.'

'Of course,' said his father. 'We're just happy to see you – both – here now.'

It was a relief to see how their attitude had changed. It seemed like they had done some thinking.

'Thank you,' said Luke. 'We don't need to rehash everything, but I want to tell you that I'm beginning to understand. I wish you had told me, but I also understand why you didn't. Mum, we saw the letters, and I wanted to thank you for those. She kept them all. That was a kind thing you did.'

'Letters?' said Sir Henry, frowning.

'Yes,' said Lady Talbot, her voice calm but strong. 'I wrote to Diana many times over the years, sent her photographs of Luke, told her what he was doing. She didn't write back, but on the few occasions we saw her, she mentioned them, hoped I would keep writing, even if she couldn't bring herself to reply. She said she treasured them.'

'But that was incredibly dangerous,' spluttered Sir Henry. 'To put it all in writing.'

'She was his mother,' said Lady Talbot simply. 'It was the right thing to do.'

I suspected that there would be another conversation about this, between the two of them, but Luke now continued speaking. I doubt he wanted the conversation derailed.

'There is also,' he said, 'the question of who my father is.' He turned to Sir Henry with a rueful smile. 'My blood father, that is. I'm pretty confident that it is Edward Burns.'

'You mentioned an Edward last time you were here,' said Lady Talbot. 'Is he the man who kept trying to get hold of Diana?'

'Yes,' replied Luke. 'You said you didn't know he was the father.'

'We didn't,' she said. 'He never mentioned anything about her pregnancy and only said he was a friend. Diana said he was a friend she'd fallen out with, and that she didn't want to see him.' She shrugged. 'We were happy not to ask any more questions. You've—you've spoken with him?'

'Yes. I've known him for years. He and Diana had been in love, but he had no idea she was pregnant when she left. I'm not sure he ever got over the heartbreak, but he was glad to know who we are to each other.'

'We will reach out to him,' said Sir Henry suddenly. I was almost as surprised by hearing him use such a modern expression as I was by the suggestion itself. 'When you think the time is right. We can't undo the wrong that has been done, but perhaps there is some path forward.'

'Thank you,' said Luke. 'I know it's not easy but thank you.'

His voice cracked and I rubbed his back gently. Abruptly, he stood up, went over to where his father was sitting and held out his hand.

'Thank you,' he said again.

Ignoring the hand, Sir Henry rose as well and the two men embraced. I'm sure I wasn't the only one in the room discreetly dabbing away a tear.

A few moments later, Luke returned to sit next to me, his face showing less strain now.

'Anyway,' he said. 'I have come to a decision.'

Every face in the room, including mine, turned to him. *What decision?*

'You're right when you say that some of the wrongs in all of this can't be righted, but there is one that can. I've been looking into what can be done legally, without revealing that the law was broken when I was born and the birth registered. I want us to break the entail on the estate so that Sam inherits, not me.'

Luke's parents and brother looked at each other, frowning. Sam went to speak, but Luke turned to me before he had a chance.

'The entail is a legal thing that means an inheritance must go to a certain person – usually the next male heir.' He turned back to his family. 'It's simple to change; you and I need to sign something, Dad.'

'Well, I don't know about all this,' spluttered his father. 'It seems a dramatic step. I know the truth is all out in the open now, but you are our *son*, Luke, our eldest son. The inheritance is yours.'

He looked so distressed that, for a terrible moment, I thought he was going to cry. Then Lady Talbot, whose face was ashen, spoke up.

'I agree with your father. This isn't what any of us want.'

'It's all *wrong*,' exploded Sam, his own tears flowing unchecked. 'I said before that nothing has changed, and I meant it.' He scrubbed angrily at his wet face. 'You're my big brother; I don't want that to change.'

'And it won't, it hasn't,' said Luke, who was also looking pale. *Had he expected a different reaction to his idea?* 'But by rights the estate is yours, and anyway, you'd be much, much better than me at running it. You're far more interested in it than I ever was, and you even studied rural estate management at university. You're already doing it with Dad; you're the natural successor. And Mum, Dad – you have to admit that this is what you want. Otherwise, you'd never have let me go off and train to be a vet, set up my practice, buy a place to live. Over the years I've worried all the time about what would happen when I had to give up the life I love to come back to Spindrift House. This would eliminate all that. It makes sense. Sam, admit you love it here.'

'I do. You all know that. I had hoped that you would allow me to help you run it, when the time came.'

'But you would already be an expert, and I'd be dreaming about stitching up cats and putting puppies in plaster!'

Everyone laughed, and the atmosphere lightened.

'It would be daft. We'd all be much happier to know that, when the time comes, which we hope isn't for decades yet, that every-thing was in place. If I need to resort to emotional blackmail, I'll ask you all to give me peace of mind and agree.'

'When you put it like that,' said Sam, 'it doesn't seem right to stand in your way. But I will want my big brother around for advice and friendship. You have to promise that.'

'It goes without saying,' said Luke, smiling. He turned to Sir Henry. 'Dad? Will you agree? I know it wasn't the plan, my grandfather's plan, all those years ago, but things changed. It would be a way to bring some peace and fairness to all this.'

'I understand. I will discuss it with your mother, and you must accept that you will still receive a significant inheritance, but, in principle, I agree.'

'Thank you, again,' said Luke. 'I doubt many people would be thrilled to learn they *weren't* going to inherit a huge estate, but I feel like celebrating!'

'Probably too early for champagne,' said Lady Talbot, 'but maybe we could all do with a coffee?'

'I'll come and help you, my dear,' said her husband, and they left the room.

While they were gone, Luke and Sam talked excitedly about the new futures ahead of them. I sat quietly, lost in thoughts about my own family. So much water had gone under the bridge in both cases, but the Talbots had found their way to a harmonious solution, which had barely seemed possible with so much pain and dishonesty woven into their story. Would it ever be possible for my father and me to reconcile in any way? It wasn't what I wanted at the moment, and I couldn't imagine a time when I could forgive and forget sufficiently to ever speak to him again. But that didn't make me happy. What I would have loved was a healthy, equal relationship with him. Would he ever change enough to make that possible? I couldn't help hoping so and that, if I left the door open a tiny bit, the possibility would always be there.

Luke's parents came back in with a large wooden tray, and we all jumped up to help them set out cups and saucers, small plates and a platter laden with shortbread and small cakes.

'Shop-bought, I'm afraid,' said Lady Talbot, with a twinkle in her eye. 'Maybe you will bring some of your own delicious bakes again next time, Belle?'

I beamed with pleasure. The suggestion that I would be welcomed back made my heart sing.

'I'd be delighted to.'

Once we were all settled down, Luke spoke.

'I'm sorry to be serious yet again, but I want to make sure that *everything* is right. There's still the matter of the title. It's not rightfully mine. And besides.' He smiled drily. 'I've earned a few letters after my name, so I don't feel any need for inherited ones before it.'

'You never were one for any sort of pomp,' said his father. 'And I'm forced to agree that somehow "Sir Luke" will never be you, whereas Luke Talbot MRCVS suits you well.' He paused, and a smile touched his lips. 'You're so like Diana in that way. She was the most fantastic free spirit; no wonder our father was terrified of her.'

'My grandfather, terrified of his vulnerable young daughter?' asked Luke, scepticism lacing his voice.

'Oh yes – that's what caused him to be so draconian with her when he saw his opportunity,' said Sir Henry. 'He knew that, given the tiniest chink of a chance, she would have kept you and been proud to be your mother. She didn't give a hoot for convention or what people might say. The rest of us were only too hidebound by it all.'

'I do respect all these old institutions,' continued Luke. 'But to allow myself to become the baronet one day feels dishonest – and as if I'm cheating Sam out of it. I haven't found out if it's possible to transfer the title as well as the physical inheritance. I thought you might know.'

Sir Henry shook his head.

'It can't be changed,' he said. 'A hereditary title isn't like property; you can't transfer it or leave it in a will. It is what it is. The only way to change that would be to make everything public, making your mother and I – not to mention the doctor who helped with the records at the time, if he's still alive – liable to whatever penalties the law considered right. And you, of course, would have to be legally deprived of your legitimacy.'

'Look, I don't mind at all,' said Sam, rolling his eyes dramatically. Laughter rippled around the room at the welcome moment of levity. 'I've made that pretty clear already. And I *still* don't mind. It would be nuts to go through all that for the sake of a title which doesn't come with anything else.'

'What do you mean?' I asked.

'He's right,' said Sir Henry. 'A baronet isn't a member of the peerage, so there are no other ramifications, such as a seat in the House of Lords. It's a title that is passed down from father to eldest son, a memory of a favour conferred by a monarch, usually a few hundred years ago. You're not depriving your brother of anything, Luke. You are part of this family, in more ways than one. You deserve something, even if it is more or less meaningless. I'd like you to inherit the title, and for your son, if you have one, to take it after you.' He paused, then said, 'Please.'

'Of course. Thank you.'

'Is there anything else?' said Lady Talbot brightly. 'Anyone?' We all looked around at each other, smiling slightly and shaking our heads. 'Marvellous!' she said, with a little clap of her hands. 'In that case, I'm sure you'll all agree that, as it is *finally* past midday and everything is decided, a little drop of something might be in order.'

'Why not?' said Sir Henry, and soon we were all equipped with a beautiful crystal flute of champagne.

'What should we drink to?' asked Sam.

'I think,' said his father, 'we should raise a glass to family – in all its forms.'

TWENTY-SIX

We ended up staying at Spindrift House for lunch. A few weeks ago, I never could have imagined such a friendly and convivial time spent with Luke's family, but the emergence of the truth seemed to have brought them relief. It wasn't that unusual, I mused, as we waved them goodbye; keeping such a big secret must take its toll over the years. Having had a couple of glasses of champagne, Luke suggested leaving his car there and taking a long walk home over the cliffs.

'I'd like that,' I said, stretching my arms sleepily. 'I'm not used to champagne at lunchtime – or at any time – and I'll probably curl up and nod off right here if I don't get some fresh air.'

We strode out towards the coast and soon we were taking in the view of the calm blue sea before us, seagulls swooping and screeching in the sky. If we turned around, Spindrift House had disappeared behind the trees, but fields lay like patchwork, in dozens of different shades of green, roads snaking between them with occasional cars passing along, their windows flashing in the sun. To our left, the coast swept along for miles, towns and villages just visible and, to our right, lay Spindrift Bay, the houses and shops nestled snugly in the deep curve the land made. I could see my house and the tearooms up on their little perch. The thought of the cosy living room, the large kitchen and the kittens gave me an unexpected thrill. *Home.*

'I love seeing it all laid out like this from up here,' said Luke. 'It's so comforting to know I'll be going back there, that it welcomes me. It's a wonderful home.'

'I was thinking the same thing,' I said. 'It's funny, but I have such a strong pull towards it. I never felt like that about where I lived with my parents, or with Matt.'

'It's because it's yours,' said Luke, pulling me gently to face him, taking both my hands in his. 'You've made your own life here and what went before has melted away. Your mum's happy in her own new home and Matt...'

I had told him about Matt's unexpected visit.

'Matt will be fine,' I said, raising an eyebrow. 'He – or his mother – will find some poor girl who suits them both, God help her.'

We both laughed. I bore no ill will towards Matt – how could I, when he had made it possible for me to find such happiness? – but I also couldn't bring myself to care about him anymore.

'And what about you?' I said. 'Have you worked out where and what your home and family are? Or is that a work in progress?'

He screwed his face up.

'Everything's still shaking down,' he said. 'I still want to know more about Diana, try to get to know her as my mother a little better. And I'm looking forward to spending time with Edward. Mum and Dad feel different now; not because I know they're not my birth parents, but because they've changed, too. Even as a little boy I never saw them as relaxed as they were today – and they love you! I can't believe Dad was offering to take you out in his vintage Aston Martin.' He made a mock-offended face. 'That thing goes on the road about once a decade, and the rest of the time he restricts himself to polishing it lovingly. He'll be handing you the keys next!'

'Your parents are great,' I said truthfully. 'And so is Sam. He was as upset by the thought of depriving *you* of anything as you were the other way around.'

'He's amazing, and he'll be brilliant at running the estate. I hope you don't mind the fact that you won't be living in the big house, but tourists will love Lady Talbot running The Coastal Kettle, if you fancy using the title.'

I stared at him, my brain scrambling for something to say. *Are you proposing?* felt too blunt to say out loud, and I couldn't come up with a light-hearted quip, as *are you proposing?* was the only thought in my head. He stared back at me, as the implications of what he had said sank in.

'Oh gosh,' he stammered. 'I'm sorry, that wasn't very elegant. The thing is, since I first met you, the idea of us being together forever has taken up residency in my head and it feels so natural to me that I guess it popped out. Literally popping the question, although I haven't even asked you yet. Sorry, I'm babbling now.'

'It's all good, don't stop!'

'I'd been thinking about how to do it properly, with a gorgeous ring and some idyllic setting, not on a windy hill with no ring and no rehearsal.'

'Luke,' I said. 'This *is* idyllic. I wouldn't want it any other way. I don't need doves and champagne and a rehearsed speech, and I *definitely* couldn't care less about a big ring. But if you *do* want to ask me, the one thing I really want to do is say yes.'

He squeezed my hands and pulled me closer to him.

'Belle, I know it's only been a few months, but I love you. Families are crazy, but I can't wait for us to be our own little version of crazy. Will you marry me?'

Quick it might have been, but when it's right, it's right. My experience with Matt, however painful it had been, had taught me that. There had been so many little niggles with him, so much capitulation on my part, reasoned away as 'compromise'. With Luke, I could be myself, and love him for who he was, too.

'Yes,' I said, a huge smile spreading across my face. 'Yes, of course I will!'

And we kissed until even the seagulls had started to leave for the day; then, hand in hand, we walked home.

EPILOGUE

A FEW WEEKS LATER

The day was already heating up when I went downstairs to put on the kettle and open the door for the kittens, who were allowed into the garden now. As I put teabags into mugs, Luke came up behind me and wrapped his arms around me.

'Good morning. Ready for the grand opening?'

For the tearooms were finally ready, licences obtained and menu decided. It was late in the holiday season, but there were still plenty of tourists around who would be grateful of a drink and a slice of cake, and I was overflowing with ideas for expanding the business in other directions so that it brought in a good income all year. One of the bedrooms for paying guests had been finished – Sam had helped Luke and me with the decorating, and it had turned out to be a great way to get to know my new brother-in-law-to-be. I was going to wait to get the tearooms up and running before turning my attentions to the B&B business, but the room was already hosting a guest: Mum.

'I think so. I'm so excited – I hope lots of people come.'

'They will,' he said reassuringly. 'We've advertised widely enough and the whole village will be there. They all want to see it do well.'

'Morning, you two,' came Mum's voice behind us. 'Is that a boiling kettle I can hear?'

'It is,' I said, going over to give her a hug. The years had fallen away from her since she left Dad, and her new life in France clearly suited her. 'And I'll get some breakfast going, too. Oh, there's the post, I'll grab that first.'

I picked up a couple of letters from the mat, admiring the sparkle of my engagement ring as I did so. It was an art deco emerald and diamond ring that Lady Talbot – or Gwen, as I now called her – had insisted I should have.

'It's a family ring of the Talbots,' she said. 'And would have gone to Diana, anyway, so it's only right that her son should have it for you.'

I was so joyful to be engaged to Luke that I wouldn't have cared if he'd given me a ring made of tin, but at the same time I couldn't help admiring the beautiful piece of jewellery a hundred times a day.

I opened the top letter, addressed to me, assuming that it would be some business to do with the tearooms, but as I walked back into the kitchen, my face must have shown my shock.

'Are you all right?' asked Luke, coming over. 'What is it?'

'It's from Dad,' I said. 'Well, from his lawyer. He—he's writing to say that Dad has disinherited me.'

'*What?*' said Mum, standing up and taking the letter to read herself. 'Oh, Belle, how could he? It's one thing to change his will, another to send *this*.' She threw the letter on the table in disgust. 'To drive his message home. It's spiteful and completely unnecessary.'

For a moment, I was numb, unable to speak. I walked over to the kettle and continued making the tea, then pulled out some bread and started cutting it. Seeing Luke's family manage to navigate their way through such pain had given me hope that, one day, Dad and I might be able to do the same, to find a new, adult relationship where the past was remembered, and regretted, but not a determiner of the future.

This letter made it clear that it was never going to be that way. As I put the bread in the toaster and went through all the motions of making breakfast, watched silently and respectfully by Mum and Luke, the initial shock began to lift and, in its place, rose relief. I turned to them.

'It's like Matt,' I said. 'I should write back and thank him. He's relieved me of the burden of himself.'

I took the letter from the table and tore it into tiny pieces, which I scattered over the delighted kittens, who immediately began to chase and pat them.

'That's it, boys,' I said. 'Someone should get some pleasure from it.'

'Are you all right?' asked Mum. 'We could fight this, you know?'

'I don't want to,' I said. 'Luke's not the only one who doesn't want an inheritance.' We all laughed, and my heart lightened further. 'I want to think about today, to new beginnings.' I handed everyone a mug of tea. 'We can all drink to those.'

After breakfast, things got busy quickly. Once Tessa arrived, the next person to come was Lottie, who had been staying at Gloria's guest house with her new boyfriend, Daniel. Apparently, she had explained apologetically on the phone a couple of weeks ago, he "didn't feel comfortable" staying with me, and would prefer to be more anonymous to his host. I grinned to myself. *Good luck with Gloria. She'll get the skinny on him in no time.* But I didn't say anything to Lottie, just thanked her for coming to support me, and crossed my fingers that Daniel was no worse than a bit shy. Either way, he had decided to come to the opening at the official time, rather than a couple of hours earlier to help. But we didn't need him. Between the rest of us we soon had The Coastal Kettle looking inviting and alive, with bunting dancing in the breeze outside and piles of cakes and shortbread and scones and pastries ready to be eaten. I had finally decided on the tea I would be offering, and was interested to see if anyone would be daring enough to try sea buckthorn over English Breakfast and if I would see my gamble pay off. Caleb had provided several of his delicious loaves of sourdough, should anyone want sandwiches, but we were keeping the rest of the menu until the first official day of service, tomorrow.

I needn't have worried about people coming. A steady stream made their way up to the tearooms, from familiar village faces to strangers. I was taken aback when Gloria arrived, as stunning and colourful as ever, with a man who was wearing a comically obvious wig and false moustache. I went over to greet her and find out who her odd companion was.

'Meet Gregor!' she said loudly, then leant in to whisper: 'It's Georgie! He said he couldn't bear being apart from me a minute longer, so came over on a passport he picked up God knows where and is in disguise! Isn't it terrific?'

Before I had a chance to reply, he had seized my hand and was pumping it enthusiastically, thanking me for being such a good friend to his beloved Gloria. Laughing, I said how pleased I was to meet him, and directed them both towards the cakes.

A slight ripple, led by Beverly, went around the assembled company when Gwen, Henry and Sam arrived. They, of course, made no fanfare, and the interested chatter soon died down as they took plates and cups of tea like everyone else. Soon, Sir Henry and Lady Talbot were talking to Edward, who they had been getting to know, and Sam had gone to help Lottie, who had been doing more than her fair share in keeping clean plates and cups ready.

An hour and a half into the opening, there was a lull as everyone there had everything they needed. I stood by the side, looking at what I had created with the help of my friends and family. Mum came and stood next to me.

'Next time I come over, I expect it will be for wedding stuff,' she said. 'I might be allowed to do more than I was last time.'

I hugged her.

'Definitely. No Celia or Dad getting in our way, although the wedding will be much less grand than the one Matt and his parents wanted – or didn't want, as it happened.'

'Do it your own way,' she said. 'The pair of you are so happy that it will be beautiful, no matter what.'

'I hope so. Luke's decided that he's going to have three best men, because he can't choose between them, so Henry, Edward and Sam are going to share the job.'

'What about you?' asked Mum. 'Bridesmaids?'

'Maybe Lottie,' I said. 'Although she might prefer to be a guest. But Mum, I did want to ask you – will you walk me down the aisle?'

'I'd be honoured,' she said, drawing me to her for a hug. 'I'm sorry you don't have your father to give you away, though.'

I shook my head.

'It's okay. I'm not asking you to give me away, either, just be there with me. I've already given myself to Luke, heart and soul.'

'Diana would have approved,' said Mum, her eyes becoming misty. 'That seems like a fitting legacy to someone else who was very much her own woman.'

At that moment, Tessa caught my eye and beckoned me over to sort something out. I squeezed Mum's hand, kissed her and went back to work, sending up thanks that despite the lies and secrets, the pain and the losses, life had put me exactly where I was meant to be.

A LETTER FROM HANNAH'S EDITOR

Hannah Langdon sadly passed away before this book was published – a huge tragedy and shock. She was talented, funny, hard-working and wise and will be hugely missed by everyone who knew her.

If you enjoyed *The Tea Room Inheritance*, I encourage you to seek out Hannah's other books, which are just as wonderful. Here is a list of them below:

Christmas with the Lords
Christmas with the Knights
Christmas with the Princes

Escape to the Country Kitchen
Escape to the Country Garden

You can also leave a review to help other readers discover Hannah's writing.

Hannah loved being an author and was thrilled by the reviews and messages her readers left her. Thank you for all your support for her books over the years.

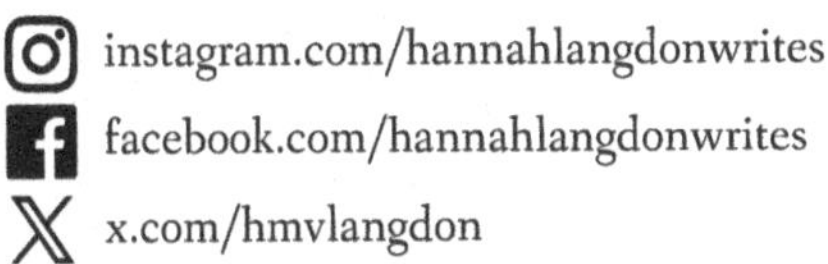

instagram.com/hannahlangdonwrites
facebook.com/hannahlangdonwrites
x.com/hmvlangdon